To Live Again

Unoma Nwankwor

A KEVSTELGROUP BOOK
PUBLISHED BY KEVSTEL PUBLICATIONS

KevStel Group LLC
Lawrenceville GA 30046
Copyright © 2018 by Unoma Nwankwor
All Rights Reserved. No part of this book may be reproduced in any form or by any means without proper consent of the Publisher, excepting brief quotes used in reviews.

This is a work of fiction. Any reference or similarities to actual events, real people, living or dead or to real locales are intended to give the novel a sense of reality. Any similarities to other names, characters, place and incident are entirely fictional.

ISBN: 1986272079
ISBN-13: 978-1986272070
First printing March 2018
Printed in the United States of America
www.kevstelgroup.com

Praise for Unoma Nwankwor

"Unoma really is the best kept secret in Christian romance. I love how she weaves in African culture into her stories. Love The Final Ultimatum, love it, love it." **Pat Simmons, award-winning author of Carmen Sister series**

"I loved this story from beginning to end. He Changed My Name has a double meaning and I loved them both."~ **Barbara Joe, author of Forgive Us This Day**

In He Changed My Name, Unoma takes readers on a page-turning, beautiful journey of second chances. This is one of her best. ~ **Vivian Kay, author of Secret Places**

Unoma delivers a satisfying "truth is stranger than fiction" tale every time with her plot twists, plus some godly interventions. Romance isn't a fairy-tale in Unoma's **Anchored by Love**. It's real! **~Pat Simmons, award-winning author of Carmen Sister series**

Unoma has woven a compelling story of regret, forgiveness, love and God's amazing grace in this beautifully written novel. Poignant. Engaging, a great read -that cleverly demonstrates how God is able to use the most horrific situations and turn them around for his grace. Five stars! **~Abimbola Dare, Author of The Small Print and When Broken Chords Sing**

This sexy romance weaves forgiveness and love into a warm blanket rich with comfort. Nwankwor writes a well written story with several universal themes of family, forgiveness and love ~ **Readers Paradise on A Scoop Of Love.**

"Unoma sets up each scene in **When You Let Go** with an emotional punch that will keep your heart racing to the finish line. Warning: You will lose sleep trying to get there!" ~**Pat Simmons, award-winning author of The Guilty series.**

"**When You Let Go** is a true testament of the power of God within ourselves and our marriage. Although, we are tested every day, it is up to us to lean on our faith to get through those difficult times and offer forgiveness to those who may have hurt us in the process. Amara and Ejike's faith was tested throughout this novel but once they learned to put God at the forefront of their household, they were able to weather the storm." ~ **Diva's Literary World**

"I love how Unoma Nwankwor weaves the distinctive, spicy flavor of West Africa into her novels. I feel right at home with the food, pidgin English, quirky expressions, and cultural norms. I'm also enjoying watching her grow as an author. **~Sherri L. Lewis, Bestselling Author and Missionary**

Nwankwor adds more depth with the cultural nuances that could be a roadblock or a gateway to understanding. She expertly intertwines all of these elements, including faith lessons, to make a tightly woven story for a reader's enjoyment.~ **USA Today Review of An Unexpected Blessing.**

"In **An Unexpected Blessing**, Unoma Nwankwor has penned a sweet romance with an important message about love and acceptance. She's definitely a writer to watch." ~**Rhonda McKnight, Black Expressions Bestselling Author of What Kind of Fool and An Inconvenient Friend.**

"What woman hasn't felt the pangs of unfulfilled desire? In **An Unexpected Blessing**, Unoma Nwankwor weaves deception, cultures and the intrigue of love for a romantic journey that spans two continents and challenges the cornerstone of faith."~ **Valerie J. Lewis Coleman, best-selling author of The Forbidden Secrets of the Goody Box TheGoodyBoxBook.com**

"I read **An Unexpected Blessing** and I must admit I loved it very, very much. I look forward to reading your next novel."~ **Diane Ndaba, reviewer Africa Book Club**

"Unoma's writing reads effortlessly. There is the perfect infusion of faith and international flavor. Readers are quickly swept up on a romantic literary adventure. **The Christmas Ultimatum** is a great read for anytime of the year"~ **Norma Jarrett Essence Best Selling author of Sunday Bruch**

"I loved it. **The Christmas Ultimatum** is my first read from Unoma and it won't be my last. I enjoyed the international favor she gave to the story. There is nothing sexier than a Christian man who goes after who and what he wants. Kudos!" ~ **Pat Simmons Award winning author of the Guilty Series**

Dedication

To my husband Kevin, and my kids—Fumnanya & Ugo.
Their support is immeasurable.

Acknowledgments

To my Lord and Savior Jesus Christ. I thank you for paying the ultimate price that I may have life and for your grace which I do not deserve. Thank You for the gift of writing and I humbly pray I continue to be a vessel in this journey.

To my family, my husband Kevin who is my number one fan, cheering me along every step of the way. I love you and thank you. To my kids Fumnanya and Ugo, my gang, my pookies, my munchkins they keep me sane when insanity sometimes abound. I love you both more than words can express. I pray for God's continued protection over you.

To my parents and mother in-law, *Daalu*. Thank you for your constant prayers and speaking words of life, courage and hope upon me.

To my readers, author friends and sistah writers thank you, thank you. Sometimes support doesn't always come from the people or places you expect but trust in God and He will send the right people to you.

Note from the Author

It's number 10!!!

Wow! I'm so thankful for the support my readers have shown. Your words of encouragement have kept me pushing on.

So here we are again, my next set of books is a two-book series titled **Invisible Shackles.** The series will tell the story of two sisters: Itohan and Isoken(Keni) Adolo. Each book is a complete stand-alone story. The Adolo sisters deal with emotional baggage that threaten to destroy them and the happiness they desperately desire but are afraid to have.

Being in a prison isn't always about the physical location of a 5 by 7 cell. Often as humans, we are also shackled by invisible chains that hinder our progress.

To Live Again is the first book and you get to meet Osaro (pronounced O- sah-ro), Itohan (pronounced E-toe-han) and their pack of family and friends.

Youcan always reach me through www.unomanwankwor.com

Unoma

1

Benin City, Nigeria.

"Yes, to the dress!!" Twenty-five-year-old, Itohan Adolo, flung her hands up and twirled around, holding the perfect dress against her body.

A crease settled on her forehead when she noticed Ajoke Lade, her best friend, and her sister, Isoken, were no longer behind her. Itohan's eyes roamed the medium-sized store for her girls. Granted, this was the tenth bridal shop they'd followed her to in the last two weeks, but still— it was her wedding. She looked in the full-length mirror and noticed the attendant in her peripheral vision. The look she wore was a mix of admiration and relief. Itohan knew she'd been worrisome, but they sold the dress she wanted to someone else last week. So, helping her find the perfect one was only right.

The door chimed and in walked Ajoke and Isoken.

"Where did you girls go?" Itohan frowned.

"My dear, hunger wanted to kill me. We've been here for almost five hours." Isoken, who insisted that she only be called Keni, grumbled. With only eighteen months separating them, the sisters were truly best friends. Keni popped a groundnut in her mouth and bit into her *bole*, a roasted plantain delicacy. Seeing her sister holding up the incredible gown, she nodded her approval. Returning to her seat, Keni lifted her hands to the heavens and gave a dramatic sigh. "*Osanobua,* God, we thank you, Sir. This girl has finally found a dress."

"Keni, leave her alone. You know it's hard to make these decisions," Ajoke said. "Itoh, go put it on. Let's see."

Itohan handed the dress to the attendant and walked over to where Keni was sitting. She grabbed some groundnuts from her pack. "You didn't get any for me?"

Keni looked over at Ajoke and laughed. "Sis, I love you, but no. You've been crazy, talking about your nonexistent weight. If you throw away my hard-earned money in the form of my snacks, how you did Joks last week, we'd be fighting."

"You like causing trouble. Why are you bringing that up again?" Itohan remembered her irrational behavior when Ajoke bought her some meat pie last week. She threw it in the trash, accusing her friend of trying to get her to put on weight before her big day.

"Itoh, leave these groundnuts. Go and try on the dress so we can get it and leave," Ajoke said.

Itohan headed back to the dressing rooms.

"I'm happy she found her dress. *E remain small* I would've suggested she tie wrapper," Keni whispered to Ajoke.

"I heard that," Itohan hollered.

"Good, now put on the dress, let's go. And you better like it after you put it on." Keni rolled her eyes and Ajoke chuckled.

Minutes later, Itohan reemerged. She walked up to the mirror. Her girls approached and stood by her side. Tears welled up in her eyes. She was marrying the love of her life, finally.

"You look beautiful." Ajoke was the first to speak.

"You look stunning. Let's make sure Aidenoje doesn't faint when he sees you," Keni chimed in.

Itohan nodded, too afraid to speak. Her throat closed with overwhelming emotion. She thought about her fiancé, Aidenoje Iyere. They had been through so much before her father finally gave them permission to marry. Her father always said there was something about Aidenoje that didn't sit well with him, but she saw nothing. He was the sweetest, most caring, loving man she had ever dated. Not to forget how fine he was. Most of all, she loved him and he loved her.

Her royal bloodline and the fact that her family was wealthy made her father suspicious of everyone. He labeled Aidenoje as a gold digger. A little under two years ago, Aidenoje proposed to her and she accepted – an engagement her father refused to acknowledge until just seven months ago. After much pleading and convincing, her father finally gave her man the consent to come with his family to start the traditional rights. A month later, they had an elaborate traditional wedding. One her parents thought was benefitting of the firstborn child. The event was talked about for weeks after it was over.

An hour later, the three women were walking out of the store. The gown was being adjusted to fit and Itohan would be able to pick it up in a couple of days. The ladies sat in the back of her dad's car, being chauffeured through the streets of Benin City, Nigeria, discussing the church wedding, which was eight weeks away.

Minutes later, the car pulled up to the Adolo family home. Itohan, Keni and Zogie, her brother, all lived in the lavish compound.

"What's your man doing here? I thought he wouldn't be back until tomorrow," Ajoke asked, inclining her head to Aidenoje who was leaning on one of the cars in the compound.

"Me too. I'm happy he's back *sha*." Itohan opened the door. She couldn't hide her smile as Aidenoje walked up to them.

Electricity shot up her body as his hands connected with the small of her back and he kissed her cheek.

"Ladies…" He acknowledged her girls with a head nod.

"Welcome back. How was Lagos?" Keni asked.

"It was great." He turned to Itohan, "Honey, I need to talk to you."

"Sis, we'll be inside." Keni pulled Ajoke with her.

Itohan nodded. It was early afternoon, and the heat of the mid July day stung. Aidenoje suggested they head toward the pool on the other side of the house. He held her hand and with each step they took in silence, Itohan's heartbeat accelerated. She sat on a lounge chair and he sat beside her.

"What's…" her words trailed off at his huge grin and the piece of paper he was waving.

"Honey, it came. It finally came."

"What's that?" She frowned.

Aidenoje handed her the paper. With each line she read, her heart plummeted. She finished reading and handed it back to him slowly. A beat of silence passed.

"Itohan, say something. Why are you quiet?" Anxiety laced his tone.

She contemplated for a few moments. *Was he serious right now? What was she to say?*

Granted, they'd thought this was the route to take when they graduated college a while ago, but it didn't work. While she was okay to travel to America – being a citizen – he wasn't. And the schools he'd applied to then for a master's denied him. She wasn't travelling without him, so that was that. How was she to know that while they were currently planning their life here, he was still applying to schools in America?

"I don't know what to say. That letter says you're admitted into Bowie State University and the school year starts in two months." She paused as her eyes welled up. "What about our plans? We're to be married. We've paid for an apartment in Lagos. My job? Everything…"

"Honey, America is the land of milk and honey. Once I get there, I'll send for you. Six months tops. We're already married traditionally, so the other part can wait."

Itohan ran her hand through her hair. "But I just bought my dress. We've paid some vendors—"

"The wedding is two months out. Surely we can get a refund on that stuff." Aidenoje grabbed her hands. "Honey, I heard things are really good in America. I'll send for you in no time. We'll do the court wedding there, too and have the wedding you want later," he pleaded.

Itohan wrapped her arms around her body. *So many plans. Everything was going down the drain.*

"Look at me. Don't you trust me?"

Itohan trained her misty eyes on his face. She chided herself for her doubts. She loved this man and he loved her. "I do."

"Then believe when I say, I'll send for you after some months.

Don't move to Lagos, stay here, closer to family."

"How will you pay for tuition?" She hoped he wasn't hiding money from her. As far as she knew, all they had was for their wedding and living expenses. They wanted to do this free of her parents' contribution.

Aidenoje scratched his nose. Itohan frowned. He always did that when he knew she wouldn't like what he had to say.

"I...I... need to borrow our... funds," he stuttered.

"What?!"

"Honey. Hear me out…"

Seven Years Later

2

"Itoh, stop being a Debbie Downer." Ajoke nudged Itohan's shoulder.

"Debbie is even better. She's graduated to *Kelechi Kill Joy*," Keni said.

Itohan tuned out her sister and friend on either side of her and took her Piña Colada from the sexy bartender. She walked back to her spot on the beach and as expected, they followed. Girls or not, Itohan wasn't getting in the water. No matter how fine the instructor was, and she had told them that before.

Ajoke was now a registered nurse in the United States based in Atlanta, Georgia. She was married with a beautiful son. She was the more reserved of the trio. At five feet, seven inches, her milk chocolate skin was nicknamed "ever glow" because it was always glowing. She kept her thick, black hair in micro braids.

Keni was now based in Lagos, Nigeria and was an air hostess for KLM. Keni was the one that always got them the hook up for cheaper tickets for their annual summer getaway. This time, Keni also got to pick their location and the island of Nosy Be won. The East African Island off the coast of Madagascar was the busiest and biggest tourist attraction in the country.

Keni shared the same deep chocolate skin tone as Itohan. They both stood at five feet eight inches. The Adolo sisters were nicknamed, "African Butter" because of their beauty. In their younger years, they also wore their jet-black hair the same—big curls. Some years ago, however, Keni had dyed hers blonde. Keni was outspoken and she and Ajoke almost always had polar opinions. So Itohan balanced out the trio.

It was late July and they had only two more days left on their trip. Itohan desperately wanted to enjoy it in peace. She'd compromised enough; on this, she wouldn't. Her sarong lifted with the wind, exposing her skin. With her free hand, she secured her hat and made her way to the cabana they'd rented for the day. Itohan set her drink down and relaxed on the beach lounger.

"Call me what you like. When we agreed to come here and you girls were talking about water, I told you then, I'm not getting in."

Her Kindle was charged, and she was ready to look out into the open seas, enjoy the sun and read about women who were destined to find love. That ship had since sailed for her, so she was going to live vicariously through the women in the pages of her romance novel.

"Why is your life like this *sef*?" Keni asked with her hands firmly on her hips.

"My life is just fine." Itohan sipped on her drink, making a slurping sound to get on their nerves. They were getting on hers, so why not?

Ajoke sat opposite her on the beach bed. Itohan rolled her eyes and exhaled. She waited on the speech she now knew from memory.

"Itoh, this isn't living o. All you do is carry your camera about and teach those kids. You can't stop living because of one bad experience," Ajoke said. Her tone was soft.

Itohan knew she meant well, but she was tired of hearing it. She put her drink down and took off her oversized hat and sunshades, so she could look her in the eye. She ignored Keni who stood tapping her feet in the corner. Hopefully, after this, they'd leave her alone.

"I love both of you so much, but I'm sick and tired of you girls thinking that because I'm not living life like you want me to, that I'm not living," Itohan said.

Keni opened her mouth to say something, but Itohan raised her hand to silence her. "I'm a long way from where I was when…" her voice became shaky and she paused. She had vowed that she'd shed her last tear when she got on a plane and relocated to America three years ago. Her hurt and anger, however, weren't so easy to let go.

She cleared her throat. "I'm doing good. I don't want to go in the water. Let me be great, please. Stop worrying about me. Now go and enjoy your jet ski while you still have the waves and the sun. Let me stay here and look pretty, then laugh when you fall in the water."

Keni sat next to her. She took her right hand while Ajoke took the left one.

"We're sorry and you're right. You don't talk about what happened and we're scared that your silence is unhealthy. It's been so long, so we tend to try to force you into things to open you up. We'll try to back off," Keni said.

"I know you girls care, but I'm fine," Itohan reassured them.

They hugged and Itohan giggled as her girls took off their sarongs and tossed them on her before running to the other side of the beach. Itohan stretched her neck and saw the instructor. He was easy on the eyes. Very easy, but her heart wasn't set up like that anymore.

Itohan put her shades back on and relaxed. She looked out into the seas and marveled at the work of God. Her relationship with Him had dwindled considerably, but that didn't mean she'd ever deny His magnificence. In creation, He told the seas just how far they should go. He told the sun just how far away from the earth to stand. The stars stayed in place at His command. So why couldn't He have given her a sign that Aidenoje would turn out to be the biggest mistake of her life?

The shame and humiliation he put her through four years ago made her beloved Benin City unbearable to live in. The talk of him demanding her family return the dowry he'd paid followed her everywhere. After all they went through, the battle she had with her parents, the big fanfare of a traditional marriage, his assurance that he would send for her. How he could do her like that, continued to haunt her.

Her fingers stroked the straw of her drink and her chest tightened as her mind drifted to that day. After a full day of teaching six-year-olds, all she'd needed was her bed. That need quickly faded when she entered her father's compound and saw cars she knew didn't belong to her dad. Her steps quickened when she thought Aidenoje had finally arrived from America. The six months he promised her had turned into three years. She'd offered to join him on her own since she was a citizen, but he refused, saying he wasn't ready. He accused her of trying to wear the pants in the marriage. She trusted him, so she'd stayed put.

That day, she walked in and her heart dropped to the pit of her stomach when she looked at the faces of his uncles. The look of pity they'd given her would be etched in her memory forever. Itohan initially thought something had happened to Aidenoje. However, nothing prepared her for what they told her dad.

"Our son, Aidenoje, in America, sent us to collect back the dowry we paid on your daughter's head," one of his uncles said.

Her ears started ringing. Certainly, they were playing tricks on her. She couldn't have heard correctly.

"He says he's no longer interested in the marriage," another of his uncles said.

Itohan heard nothing else, as she had passed out after that. When she came to, her father wouldn't speak to her. She'd brought shame to the family because he warned her about Aidenoje's character. For three years, Aidenoje had strung her along. If he'd broken things off after six months, she would've been okay. Hurt, but okay. Instead, he kept her thinking he was preparing for her. How could he traditionally divorce her before they even got to the church altar?

All attempts to reach Aidenoje after that were futile. He never had a social media presence and all his numbers no longer worked. The months that followed were pure agony. The whispers got louder, the pitiful stares got bolder, and she couldn't take it. She fled to Lagos to stay with her sister, but her tragic love story followed. About a year later, her parents approached her about relocating to Florida in the US. She was thankful for the escape.

She was determined to make a living on her own. She'd caused her parents enough shame. The sad part, however, was that she knew it was more about her leaving to save their reputation in the society than her happiness. It'd been seven years since she'd seen Aidenoje, but as far as she was concerned, their relationship was over only four years ago.

Itohan shook her head to dismiss the memory. She was on

vacation and reminiscing about the past wasn't the move. Itohan now lived in St. Petersburg, Florida and had another chance to start over in life. It wasn't supposed to be this way. She was thirty-two and often wondered what her life would've been like. She should've had kids by now.

Thinking of kids, she wondered if she would get to substitute this upcoming school year. Itohan was able to live her passion through her photography business, Han's Shots, but she still loved to teach. Her parents, especially her father, never understood why she pursued a double degree in Education and Child Psychology. They wanted her to be a lawyer, but she stood her ground.

After a couple of certifications when she got to the United States, she qualified to teach in the state of Florida. It was a little harder getting into the public school system, so she settled for the private sector. She worked as a photographer full time, but when she got a call from Cultivating Excellence Christian Preparatory, she was excited and grateful for the opportunity to mold young minds.

Suddenly, the hair on the back of her neck stood and she could feel a piercing stare. She turned to her left and her heart stopped. The Bible did say God rested on the seventh day. However, He must've created the man she was looking at on the seventh day, after He'd gotten enough rest. The man's chest was bare, showing the taut ripples that adorned it. His beach shorts hung low on his hips and his chocolate skin shone against the kiss of the sun. He had on reflectors and wore his hair in what looked like braids on top of his head.

He's probably a hoodlum. He gave her a head nod in acknowledgement. The gesture quickly knocked her sense back into her. *Men are the enemy.* She responded with a hesitant wave and roll of her eyes. For a fleeting minute, she thought that was rude, but he was in the next cabana, so probably couldn't see her. None of that species could be trusted. Well, except her father and brother. The mystery man would remain one of her romance novel fantasy heroes.

Itohan faced forward and took in a deep breath, allowing the fresh ocean air to invade her nostrils. She could still feel the man's gaze, but ignored him. Letting out a long breath, she glanced up at the clear blue sky and resolved to stay in the present.

She took out her Nikon 3400D camera, positioned herself and

focused the lens to get a clearer view of the horizon. She clicked the camera at different angles. Looking back through her shots through the fixed screen, she beamed in satisfaction. The right amount of sunlight gave the pictures depth and warmth; much like her heart once upon a time. Now it had turned cold and allergic to the emotion called love. In its place was the need for payback. Aidenoje owed her.

She looked up to the skies, "If You do nothing else, pay him back. I've been waiting …please."

Leaning back, she put her headphones on and let the lyrics of "Me, Myself & I" by Beyoncé take her away.

3

Osaro Ikimi pulled into the Avon Park neighborhood he'd called home for most of his youth. As he put his car in park, he heard the siren of a police car race by. It was a sound he was very familiar with growing up in the Floridian city. Using his key fob, he activated the locks of his 2016 Dodge Durango. He gave a head nod to the group of teenagers sitting on the corner.

"Aye, look out for my baby, a'ight," he said.

"Sure thing, Ro," one of the teenagers responded.

He jogged up to the front porch of his auntie's house. He was already late for Sunday dinner. He could do nothing about the traffic on FL-64E, so was braced for the tongue-lashing he was about to receive. He normally wouldn't have taken that route, but he had to pick up something from a client.

On the porch, he turned around and let his eyes roam the neighborhood. This was where he grew up, so he knew all too well that anything could pop off at any moment. It wasn't a terrible area, but it wasn't an extremely good one either. He'd tried to get his Auntie to move many times, but she absolutely refused to leave the house where she and her late husband raised him and his siblings. According to her, if she was ever going to leave, it would be back home to Nigeria. He inhaled and exhaled, then rang the doorbell.

"You love getting Auntie worked up, don't you?" His brother, Ehi, chuckled once he opened the door.

They dapped each other and Osaro pulled off his shoes. "She'll be all right. At least I'm here more Sundays than you. I'm surprised you're here today, Mr. Policeman."

The brothers strolled through the homey, three-bedroom house toward the dining area. The memories here were bittersweet for Osaro. Elizabeth Phillips, better known as Auntie Lizzy, sat at the head of the table with a half-eaten plate of moi-moi, Jollof rice, fried plantains and goat meat in front of her. Since they were kids, his auntie went all out for Sunday dinner.

"Osaro, when did I tell you to be here?" his auntie ripped into him.

He hid his smile as he knew the sight of it would aggravate her more. This woman was his whole heart, but he knew not to mess with her. He remembered once when he was eleven, he'd let her height deceive him into thinking she was a pushover. At thirty-three, he still got flashbacks when he saw a spatula. Auntie Lizzy put in work on his behind like it was her full-time job. He never made the mistake again.

"My one and only, *no vex*. I had to make a stop, since I'm going to chill with you today." Osaro walked over and kissed her on her cheek.

At sixty-two, her caramel skin was free of blemish or the wrinkles of a woman her age. When she lifted her hand, he ducked because she thought her playful hits didn't hurt, but they did. Ehi resumed his position on her left and Osaro took his place on her right.

"I thought computer people are smart. Didn't I ask you a question?" Auntie Lizzy asked.

Ehi stuffed his mouth with fried plantain and chuckled. Osaro gave him an evil stare. He'd always been an instigator.

"*Ah*, Auntie, mercy *na*." Osaro looked at the clock that hung above the picture of her late husband, Dwayne. Osaro noted he was only thirty minutes late. Using African time, he was punctual. In fact, he was early, but he wouldn't dare tell her that. Her American husband made her too American.

"Okay, one-thirty. I'm sorry, Ma." Osaro gave in.

"Hmm."

After washing his hands, Osaro grabbed the wrapped pounded yam and scooped some Owoh soup into his bowl. He wasn't in the mood for rice. Besides, he could cook that for himself, but he only got to eat *poundo* when he visited. He blessed the food and dug in.

"Where's my Baby Cakes?" Osaro asked.

"She ate already and became sleepy, so she's taking a nap," Auntie Lizzy responded.

His six-year-old niece, Eseosa was his heartbeat. He used his free hand to touch the locket on the gold thin necklace he never took off. It contained a picture of his late sister, Ivie. He'd failed her and would never forgive himself for it. Eseosa, her daughter, was his second chance and he wouldn't misuse it. He was her legal guardian, but because of his schedule, she lived with Auntie Lizzy. His auntie had finally retired and would be moving back to Nigeria at the end of the year, so Eseosa would be living with him full time. He'd had a year to prepare for it.

"Ro, you ready for this, man?" Ehi asked. "By the way, how was your trip?"

"My trip was good. You know that was my last time flying that far for a client. If they weren't one of my biggest clients, I wouldn't have done it," Osaro answered as he contemplated the first question.

"Yes, my son, you know that what you're doing isn't going to be easy," Auntie Lizzy added before he could get his response out.

Nodding, he swallowed the food in his mouth. He understood their concern, but this was something he wanted to, had to and would do.

"Auntie, I'm fine. Once you made up your mind about *Naija*, I started putting things into place to be more stable here in Florida. All summer, Eseosa has been with me. I've hired a nanny to help me. We're good," Osaro reassured them.

His auntie and brother nodded. He knew they still had some reservations because his job as a web designer and developer sometimes carried him all over the country. But he was determined to do this. The first step was to move out of his apartment and buy a house. He then worked on securing more contract jobs with companies around and within Florida. Finally, he put in a bid for the contract of a lifetime for his company, RoMac Technologies LLC – a multi-year, million-dollar contract with an international conglomerate. He had a good feeling about his bid and was more than ready to be the steady parent his niece needed him to be.

"Did you get to meet her teacher?" Auntie Lizzy asked.

"We went for orientation and dropped off all her supplies, but the teacher wasn't there. We met an assistant." He paused. "I was pissed."

Osaro remembered his irritation when he was told the regular teacher couldn't make it for orientation. He had a very important meeting scheduled on the first day of school. His plan had been to spend enough time with the teacher during orientation so that on the first day, he could be in and out. Now with her being absent, he wouldn't get that chance to get to know her and her style or expectations.

What kind of teacher would she be if she didn't deem it fit to make herself available for something as important as orientation? Not only would his niece be going to a new class, but also a new school. He knew the importance of working with the teacher to make sure she was properly adjusted.

"Well, you don't know why she wasn't there. Osaro, I'm warning you, don't go there fussing with my baby's teacher." She shook her head at him and made her way to the kitchen.

Ehi grunted.

"You got something to say, Lil bro?" Osaro smirked.

"Everything can't always go your way, man. Chill out."

Osaro waved him off. His family accused him of being a control freak. He wondered when it was a crime to want everything to go accordingly. After the mistakes of his youth and his sister's death, he was taking no chances.

"Where is Robin?" Osaro asked.

Robin was his brother's wife of one year. They all grew up together and Ehi had loved her since forever, but he'd been in denial and told everyone they were just friends. Ehi finally stopped the, "she's my friend" song and manned up when she graduated nursing school and was about to accept a job out of state.

"She's working, but should be here a little later."

Osaro nodded and the brothers conversed. They were close, but their bond became tighter with the absence of their sister. Osaro worried about his brother being a member of the Police Department. However, that was what he had dreamed about doing ever since he was a kid. Who was he to use his inhibitions to stop Ehi from doing what he loved? His job was to pray for God's protection on him. He was already short a sibling, so he trusted God not to let anything happen to the only one he had left.

They finished eating and the brothers cleaned up the kitchen and dining area while their auntie relaxed in the living room. Once they were done, Ehi went to keep her company while Osaro made his way up the stairs to his niece's room. He gently pushed the door that was slightly ajar and leaned against the doorframe. His niece was still asleep. He noticed her hair was freshly braided in preparation for school. He stepped into the room that was formerly his sister's and sat on the floor with his back against the bed. Leaning his head back, Osaro closed his eyes and recalled the circumstances that led to him and his siblings moving to the US from Nigeria.

Their parents had died in a house fire when he was nine. He was the oldest, followed by his sister, then brother, with two years between each of them. They had no living grandparents and their mother was an only child. The only family they had was Auntie Lizzy, their father's only sister, who lived in Florida. She visited home once a year, so she wasn't a stranger to them. Despite wanting children, she and her husband Dwayne never could have any of their own. They filed for him and his siblings and some months after their parent's death, they were in America.

His aunt and her husband weren't rich, but he and his siblings never lacked anything. The one thing his aunt and uncle harped on was that they made good grades and not get caught up in their environment. Living in Avon Park, their auntie was afraid they would be caught up with the wrong crowd.

Everything was fine, until Uncle Dwayne became sick in Osaro's junior year of high school. He had to cut back on his job as a truck driver. Osaro saw how his auntie struggled to keep up with everything. It was up to him to step up. She would disown him if he turned to the streets, so he decided to use basketball to get them a better life. He was already the star basketballer for his high school and was being scouted.

Between school, basketball, his after-school job and helping his siblings, he was so busy. With his hectic schedule came fatigue. His auntie and uncle asked him to slow down, but they'd done so much for he and his siblings that he couldn't let them down. He promised them he would slow down after he secured his college basketball scholarship.

As the big game approached where he knew college coaches would be watching, he panicked. His fear pushed him to make a decision he'd forever regret. The other kids did it and nothing happened. He never expected that the first and only day he tried a performance enhancement drug was the day they'd perform a random drug test. That day changed the trajectory of not only his life, but also his siblings'.

After he was suspended from school for taking steroids, and despite his pleas that it was a one-time mistake, Auntie Lizzy insisted he go to a three-month rehab program. The next thing he knew, he was on a plane back to Nigeria.

"As long as I'm alive, you will not make a mockery of your father's name," she'd fussed. *"Since you want to be a nuisance, I'll send you back home, so you see how hard your mates have it. You're here taking drugs because you can't handle pressure. Oya, go home so you can see what real pressure is."*

Osaro had to repeat his junior year and completed his high school education staying with his auntie's best friend. When it was time for college and the Nigerian lecturers went on one of their extended strikes for the second time asking for a salary increase, Auntie Lizzy had had it. No matter how angry she was, his education came first. She brought him back to the US. By then, professional basketball was no longer an option for him.

Sorrow threatened to engulf him but was halted by the feel of a small hand creeping through his locs.

Osaro turned and looked into the face of his niece who was a carbon copy of his sister. "Hey Baby Cakes, you had a good nap?"

She nodded and wiped her eyes. "Uncle Ro, I want some juice."

"What's the magic word?"

"Please…"

Osaro stood and lifted her from the bed. She wiggled in his arms and he set her down. She liked to remind him she wasn't a baby. He took her hand and escorted her out of the room.

"Did you enjoy your weekend with Nana Lizzy?"

"Yes."

"You ready to come home and start school?"

"Yes. I can't wait to meet my new teacher," she said.

Me too.

Once they entered the living room, Osaro let go of her hand and she ran to Ehi. He went to the kitchen to get her juice. He opened the fridge and whispered a prayer to the One who he accepted as his personal Savior about a year and a half ago.

"Lord, I know that by my strength I can't do this, but in my weakness, Your strength is made perfect. Help me make my sister proud."

4

"Zogie, get off my phone. I need to get to school." Itohan spoke into her headset as she brought down the visor to check her appearance again. She was stuck at the train track and was irritated at the number of cars the train had. It seemed endless. She smacked her lips to even out her burgundy lipstick and ran her pinkie finger over her arched eyebrows. Her jet-black, oversized curls fell on her shoulder and partially covered her hoop earrings. She fluffed her bangs and was grateful her hair was still intact despite the harsh humidity of the early August day. Florida weather was so unpredictable, but when the sun decided to come out, it took no prisoners. She knew that by midterm, she'd be back to her usual ponytail, but it was the first day of school and she didn't want parents to think she didn't care.

"Sis, when I stop calling you, you'll complain. I call you and you're just mean," Zogie said.

Itohan put up the visor as the cars began to move. She wasn't prepared to be a substitute on the first day of school, but here she was. The regular teacher, who decided she could work until her due date, unexpectedly went into labor last weekend and the school called her last minute.

"I'm sorry, my love, but this is a really bad time."

Zogie worked as a Petroleum Engineer in the oil sector. Her siblings were the only family members she spoke to regularly. Her father always had disappointment in his tone from her "disgrace of the family name." Her mother was constantly harassing her about finding a husband and settling down. Both topics, she was so over, therefore, she kept her communication with them to a minimum. She had since told her mom to look to her other children for grandkids. She was nowhere ready to trust her heart to someone again.

"I was just checking on you since another summer holiday has passed and you didn't come home," he said. "Only Keni gets to see you."

Itohan heard the sadness in his tone, but she wasn't ready to return to Benin now, even if it was just for a visit.

"We Facetime and Skype *abi*? But I'll come soon, I promise. Have you decided if you're doing your master's there or over here?"

She and her siblings were born in Houston where her parents went to school in the early eighties. On their graduation, they moved the family back to Nigeria. During that time, there was a huge push by the Nigerian government to make sure their students abroad came back home to build the country with what they'd learned from the West.

Part of the reason her parents were so disappointed with her after the Aidenoje fiasco, was that they'd planned for her and her siblings to return to the US to go to college. However, when Itohan met Aidenoje she refused to leave him, so she stayed in Nigeria. Keni and Zogie followed in her footsteps.

"Not yet. I miss you, Sis. I'd come over to visit, but my job keeps me out on the rig most times." He sighed. "You can't run from home forever. By the way, I saw Aidenoje's father driving a new car some weeks ago. I'm sure that punk bought it for him."

Her interest was piqued. Did Aidenoje visit? For a while, she pretended she didn't care to keep herself sane. As time passed, her need for closure grew, but the lack of it had her wanting revenge.

"Did you see him?"

Her brother grunted. She bet, in that moment, he regretted mentioning Aidenoje's name.

"Now you know if I did, I would've beaten the living daylights out of him on principle alone," Zogie huffed.

She remained silent.

"All I know is that he must be doing good working in Maryland there."

"He works in Maryland? Do you know the name of the company?"

"No. I don't know where he works. I mentioned Maryland

because that's where he schooled. It's not important and I shouldn't have brought him up. Forget him, Sis. Remember God will repay him."

Itohan rolled her eyes as though her brother could see her. She'd been waiting for God's vengeance for years and He hadn't come through. As she drove through downtown St. Petersburg where her school was located, he caught her up on the latest happenings back home since Keni never seemed to know what was going on. During the conversation, he continued to slip in pleas for her to consider coming to visit for Christmas. The only way he'd get off the phone was if she said she'd think about it. She did, and he hung up.

As she pulled into the parking lot of Cultivating Excellence Christian Preparatory, her phone buzzed. She grinned at her sister's WhatsApp message wishing her a good day with a poem.

Today is the first day of school

I know those kids can be a tool

Whatever you do, always look cute

Open your heart and you may meet your boo

I love you sis…Keni

Itohan shook her head in amusement. The girl had no sense. While she and Ajoke made their way back to the States, Keni went back to Lagos. She missed her sister, but since she was always popping up in America, Itohan was sure she'd see her soon.

Itohan responded and turned the phone off. She knew that next it would be Ajoke with her affirmation quote of the day and Bible verse. She loved them, but they were exhausting. Somewhere along the line, they both started thinking she was their child.

Itohan got out of her silver Camry and opened the back door. She smoothed down her polka-dotted skirt, which she matched with a yellow blouse, a navy, three-quarter cardigan and a belt around her waist. She took out her black leather satchel and lunch and closed the door.

It was seven thirty a.m.; enough time for her to set up and make sure her class was all set for her students when the first bell rang in fifteen minutes. As she made her way down the hall, she returned the warm smiles of the other teachers. She loved this place. Setting her things down on her teacher table, Itohan looked around at what would be her second-grade classroom for at least the next twelve weeks.

***

"Welcome to the second grade. Find your name on your seats and put your supplies on the floor beside you," Itohan said, beaming at each child that entered her class.

As expected, parents and guardians had been in and out all morning, taking pictures and asking questions. She glanced at her watch, and looked around the room. The second bell would soon ring, and she was missing three students. She looked at the young, excited faces of the six and seven-year-olds she would get to know this year. She shared their excitement about what the school year had in store.

A few minutes later, Itohan stood in the front of the class. The class was diverse, and she liked that.

"Class, welcome again to a new school year; I'm your teacher, Ms. Adolo, while Mrs. Herington is out spending time with her baby." She paused but no one said anything. "I want you to, in order, bring your supplies and place them in the bins up here at the front. Keep your notebooks with you and put them into the slot in your desk," she instructed.

The class became rowdy again as the kids did what she instructed them to do. She was so lost in the enthusiasm that she didn't see the school administrator standing at her door trying to gain her attention. She acknowledged her and walked over. She stopped in her tracks as her body temperature increased. It was him. There right outside the door stood the hoodlum. She panicked. *He might not remember me.*

He looked good when she saw him the first time but now, she had no words. At least none she could say out loud. He looked like he could be on the cover of one of those romance novels she read. Dressed in a pinstripe, fitted suit, he looked taller than before, well over six feet. His hair wasn't in plaits, it was locked. She never cared for locs, but these looked so neat, she could almost see his ultra-clean scalp She wasn't sure of their length because they were in a single plait at his back.

He smirked at her and Itohan quickly switched her eyes to Monica, one of the school's administrators. They'd been on him too long, anyway.

"Ms. Adolo, this is Mr. Ikimi, Eseosa's Uncle. They're new to the school, so I decided to walk them back. I'll leave you two to it," Monica said, turning to leave.

"Thank you, Ms. Richards," Mr. Ikimi said. Neither his tone nor face held any expression.

Itohan smiled at the little girl, who she looked petrified. When she looked at his face again, there was a glare on it. She didn't know if he had a problem with her, but she ignored him. Itohan moved closer to Eseosa and bent to the little girl's height.

"Eseosa, that's a beautiful name. I'm Ms. Adolo. I'll be your teacher this year." Itohan extended her hand to the little girl.

As the little girl contemplated whether she could trust her, Itohan felt her body ignite with fire beneath the intense stare of her uncle. The little girl took her hand and Itohan straightened to her full height. Itohan observed his stiff and perusing gaze and confirmed there was something which displeased him. She had a class of curious kids to get back to and needed to hurry it along. She looked at Eseosa.

"Your supplies are already on your seat." Itohan pointed to the seat in the front. "Do what the other kids are doing. Take out your notebooks and keep them at your desk and put everything else in the bins up front according to the labels."

"Hey Baby Cakes, give me a hug," her uncle said. Eseosa complied. "Have a good day and I'll be waiting for you when you get out, okay?"

The little girl nodded and went to the join the class. Itohan noticed her uncle's eyes followed her every move.

Itohan cleared her throat. "Do you have any questions, Mr. Ikimi?"

He put his hands in his pockets. "I do, but I couldn't ask them because you were lying on the beach instead of being here for orientation."

"Excuse me?"

So, he did remember her. She was two seconds away from snapping at him. She was stunned by his audacity and offended.

"My niece is going through a lot of changes and I want to make sure she has as much stability as possible."

He was obviously implying she didn't take her job seriously. She contemplated setting him straight but decided not to bother. Ajoke was always preaching this "pay evil with good" thing.

She plastered on a smile and responded. "Circumstances beyond my control kept me away. Eseosa is in good hands. Her success this year will be a joint effort between school and home."

He studied her for a few seconds as though weighing the sincerity of her words. He nodded. "Have a good day, Ms. Adolo."

"You do the same." She turned back to her class and beckoned to Eseosa to come to the front. She introduced her to the class. She asked the class to do name tents and write on the familiarity chart she had made. The chart sped up the process of them getting to know each other.

As the class worked, Itohan's thoughts went back to Mr. Ikimi. *There goes a ruined romance novel fantasy. He just had to go and open his mouth.*

5

With his favorite dark roast in one hand and his phone in the other, Osaro walked into the offices of RoMac Technologies LLC. The medium-sized space was in downtown St. Petersburg. It consisted of a reception area, two offices, a conference room, a breakroom and restroom. He intentionally set out to have Eseosa's school, his office, and new home within a thirty-mile radius of each other. Previously, he would work from home or on the go. Leasing this office was another step in planting his jet-setting roots.

"Ehi, she's doing good. I just dropped her off. I'll have her Facetime you when we get home."

Osaro smiled at Mrs. Jones, his receptionist, as he made his way to his office. Nancy Jones was a middle-aged woman who was a godsend. She was hired only to answer the phones, but seeing his need for help in other areas, she also served as his assistant. In his opinion, she had gone over and beyond even that, as she was also responsible for decorating the office. She picked out the furniture and gave the space a minimalist techy look he liked.

"Okay, I'll let you get to your nerdy stuff then," Ehi joked.

"Yeah, you do that. And don't get caught eating donuts while the bad guys get away." Osaro chuckled when his brother hung up on him for that remark.

He set his coffee down on his desk, put his computer bag to the side and unbuttoned his jacket. He normally went for a business casual look, but because he had an out-of-office meeting later today, he decided to dress it up a bit. While his different monitors powered on, he rounded his desk, picked up his coffee and walked over to his oversized windows.

The streets were already buzzing with activity. The office was between Beach Drive and the Sundial in the St. Pete Shopping

District. It was a busy district with shops and restaurants. The view from his twentieth-floor office was a huge plus. He could see Tampa Bay, the Pier and marina. With coding and designing, there were times when he needed a break to observe nature.

"Isn't it too early to be daydreaming?" Malcolm "Mac" Bryson, one of his closest friends and business partner, asked.

Osaro turned around and smirked at him. "You back? How was it?"

"Yeah, I got in last night. You were right. Cyber security is where it's at. Expanding our business model to include it was a great idea." Malcolm pulled out one of the chairs in front of Osaro's desk. "Like a one-stop shop; web design, development and then security, can't get any better than that."

Osaro nodded. "You know people are getting lazier and need everything at their fingertips. No one wants to go around shopping for a web developer, then a designer then a separate entity to offer security." He walked over to his desk, pulled out his own chair and sat.

Osaro was introduced to Malcolm by his boy, Tekena Tamuno, when they were in high school. Back then, they were called "Triple Threat" because they dominated the areas of sports they chose to indulge in. Osaro selected basketball, while Malcolm excelled in football and Tekena ran track. Tekena, or Tex's, love for speed and cars made him indulge in the illegal sport of drag racing then. They all went on to attend HBCU's but because of his setback, both of his friends graduated college a year ahead of him.

Tekena was now a professional racecar driver and lived between New York and Lagos. Malcolm retired from professional football early after an injury in his second year. Upon his own graduation from Morehouse College, Osaro tested the waters by getting a regular job as a web code analyst. Within a year, however, he knew that being an employee wasn't for him. He quit and spent years as a freelancer, slowly building his clientele. Some years ago, he approached Malcolm about joining him in a joint venture and five years ago, RoMac Technologies LLC was born.

Osaro was the face of the business, and was well versed in designing and developing sites for their customers. He had a group of off-shore workers who he hired as consultants for heavy jobs. Client sourcing and finances were Malcolm's thing. Two years ago, Osaro became interested in cyber security. He took several courses and certifications, then officially added it to their business model along with Web Mastering for VIP clients.

Malcolm stood and pushed the chair back in. "Aye man, don't forget to send me that proposal for South Tran Corp so I can put the numbers in it and we can send it out."

"Got it. Imma get it to you before lunch because I have that presentation with Maxim, that new client we got two months ago."

"Wow man, you're done with their stuff already?" Malcolm asked, leaning against the doorframe.

"Yeah, they didn't need much, and I was able to get it done real quick. All I gotta do now is go to their office and demo it for them. They launch next week." Osaro sat behind his desk and moved his mouse to exit the screensaver.

"Good look, man." Malcolm left him to his thoughts.

Osaro quickly checked his emails and his heart skipped a beat when he saw an email from Eseosa's school. Clicking on it, he relaxed and smiled when he saw it was a picture of his niece during what he assumed was carpet time. There was a message from her teacher.

Hello Mr. Ikimi,

I thought this would ease your mind.

Have a good day.

Ms. Adolo.

His mind drifted to the chocolate-skinned beauty he saw earlier. He was completely blown away when he realized she was the rude hottie from Madagascar. He covered up his surprise better than she did.

He was in Nosy Be Island for C-Gar, one of his first clients. He had never met them in person, just over conference calls and Skype sessions, but they wanted his presence this time. After the meeting, he decided to take in the beach.

When he first saw her, she caused his insides to tangle. Her rudeness, however, quickly brought him to his senses and he never gave her another glance. Osaro wasn't opposed to love or relationships, but he wasn't searching either. Especially since he split with Cassie a year ago. He shook his head at that memory. Women weren't the way for him right now. Too many distractions came with them.

When Ms. Adolo was in his presence, he couldn't do anything to stop the scent of her perfume from driving him crazy. When he walked into her class with his niece, he took the time to observe her. She was probably a size ten, enough to put his arm around. The skirt she wore stopped at her knee and hugged her curves in all the right places, while the belt she wore accentuated her small waist.

He had every intention of doing exactly what his brother and auntie warned—not give her a hard time. But he had to do something to halt the impact she was having on him. The fact that she was his niece's teacher sent his unease through the roof. She was off limits. He couldn't afford anything to go wrong and his niece be mistreated by a scorned woman. He quickly typed a response of gratitude to the teacher and opened his Power Point presentation.

Several minutes later, he'd completed the finishing touches on the pitch and shifted his focus to work on the South Tran proposal. He'd done so much research on the company and he felt very good about their bid. He sipped on his now lukewarm beverage and glanced over the documents. They were looking for a one-stop shop for the new app they were launching for one of their subsidiaries. The multi-year, million-dollar contract would be a major win for his company. Not only were they the fast-growing international conglomerate in the Eastern US, but they were expanding to Africa. He wanted to make sure that RoMac Technology got in on it from the ground up. Therefore, a woman was definitely not in the picture for the near future.

***

"Why were you giving Ms. Adolo the Ro stare?" Eseosa questioned Osaro as they rode home.

Osaro furrowed his brows and looked at the rearview mirror into the face of his niece. "The what?" There was no way he heard her correctly.

She shrugged and looked back at him. "Uncle Ehi said that when you look at someone for a long time with one of your eyebrows up like this…" She demonstrated by using her index finger to lift her left brow. "It's the Ro Stare."

Osaro didn't know whether to laugh or be annoyed that Ehi was telling her such rubbish. He looked in the mirror again and saw she was waiting for an answer.

It was his turn to shrug. "I don't think I did that. If I did, it might have been because I wanted to make sure you had a good day."

"I did. Ms. Adolo is very nice. I like her," Eseosa chanted.

Osaro focused back on the road. All summer he had heard about her first grade teacher in her former school. He wondered how many "Ms. Adolo this" and "Ms. Adolo that" he was going to have to endure now. It was bad enough the woman left a lingering impression on him; he wasn't up for being reminded about her every day.

"Uncle Ro, do you know she's from Nigeria, too?"

Osaro nodded. "Yeah, Baby Cakes."

Her name gave her away. He recognized it immediately because she happened to be from the same part of Nigeria he was from. He wondered what her immigrant story was.

Eseosa had never been to Nigeria, but Auntie Lizzy always tried to teach her different words in their language and made sure she knew about where they came from. She always said she never wanted any of them to forget their roots.

In the two years he was in Nigeria, his sister had started a relationship with a small-time drug dealer, Bongo, no matter how much her family tried to talk her out of it. By the time he got back Stateside, she'd moved in with Bongo. The relationship was toxic with them always fighting and getting back together in the name of what they called love.

Almost twelve years of her life was spent in a relationship where the man wasn't making any moves to make her his wife. Osaro remembered the night he almost went to jail, fighting Bongo to defend sister's honor, but she refused to leave the relationship. His sister was twenty-five when she had Eseosa.

After that, things calmed down between the couple, until that fateful night when the family got a call that his sister and Bongo had been killed in a crash on the interstate. They had been arguing. Eseosa was just two years old. The man's only family was his father who was in prison on a drug-related charge, so Osaro was granted sole custody of Eseosa.

Osaro willed the bile of guilt that threatened to rise any time he thought of those events back down. He pulled into the garage of his home and Eseosa rushed in through the adjoining door. He grinned, knowing she was headed straight to the kitchen for the after-school snack she was allowed to have.

"Don't forget to wash your hands first, then go and change out of your school clothes." He collected the mail and browsed through it as he headed into his home office. He dropped his things and jogged up the stairs to change. His nose tickled with the lingering aroma of the meal his part-time housekeeper had prepared. She came over three days a week to clean and prepare meals for them. He was used to cooking for himself, but there was no way he'd play with his niece's stomach like that.

An hour later, they'd checked in with Auntie Lizzy and Ehi, then settled down to dinner. He warmed up the pre-cooked dish of spaghetti and meatballs. Eseosa filled him in on the details of her day. The light that shone through her eyes lifted the weight of apprehension he had carried around for almost a year. The down side of it was that, as he had feared, all she talked about was Ms. Adolo.

The memory of the velvety raspy voice, which sounded like she was losing her voice, invaded his mind as he listened to his niece sing her praises. This was only day one. He had no idea how much of it he'd be able to endure. He looked up to the ceiling and tried bargaining with the Big Guy that she be exchanged for a less attractive, older woman. He wanted stability, but he wondered if his sanity could take the constant reminder of the sexy Ms. Adolo.

6

The first month of school passed by nicely. Itohan and most of the other teachers had been assigned teacher's assistants. She was glad a student teacher was assigned to her class. Students were still enthusiastic about teaching.

Last year, Itohan had to sub for a teacher who broke her leg and had to be out for a while. Her assistant then was a nightmare. Somewhere along the line, she'd lost the passion for teaching. It had turned into a paycheck. They'd bumped heads on the methods and her lesson plans. At the end of the day, what Itohan said was what went, since it was her classroom. However, constantly disagreeing with an older white woman wasn't something she was willing to do again. Her snide comments and backhanded compliments led Itohan to believe she had a problem with not only her methods, but also age, skin color and place of origin. The new assistant, Ms. Tisha Robinson, had been with her for a couple of weeks now and they were working out fine.

Presently, the kids were in their music connections class and Itohan was using the time to put the finishing touches on the recital her kids would be putting on before the Thanksgiving break. It was still a long way to go with it being early September, however, it was a coordinated effort with all the second-grade classes and she was chosen to lead it because none of the regular teachers wanted to deal with it. She had to design the plans for the ninety-minute production then have each teacher fill in the lengths and message of their parts. It was a huge production for the second grade every year and everyone looked forward to it.

"I've pinned up the pictures the kids drew about their families on the wall in the hall," Tisha said, approaching Itohan, who was plunking away on her laptop.

She looked up and focused on the younger lady.

"I think you should see this one." Tisha handed her one of the drawings.

Itohan took the piece of paper from her and looked at the lower right corner for the name first. She smiled when she saw it was Eseosa's drawing. She reminded herself to teach the child that the "Ese" and the "Osa" in her name was one word and should be written together and not apart. It was a beautiful name that meant "God's gift."

Her smile quickly faded when she studied the picture. There was what looked like wings on a woman and a man in a cloud. Then Eseosa drew herself in the middle of two men. One of them had to be the uncle she met because she drew his locs like plaits. Then there was an older woman, whose hair she colored white, that was waving with luggage in her hand. Itohan studied the picture and her eyes misted. At what, she didn't know, but the picture looked so sad.

Eseosa was a sweet kid. She was kind and respectful, although a bit on the quiet side and often having mood swings. Itohan had attributed that to her being in a new environment, especially since her uncle had stressed stability. Looking at the picture made her wonder if there was something else. The teacher-parent conference was in a couple of weeks. Seeing this picture, she didn't know whether to ask to speak to her uncle now or wait until then. There wasn't anything to be alarmed about, but this picture just tore at her heartstrings.

Something else bothered her about the picture... two men and Eseosa was in the middle. *Lord Jesus, please let this not be what I think. This man is too fine for that.*

"Itohan?"

"Huh?" Itohan looked up at her confused.

"You disappeared on me there for a minute," Tisha said. "Are you okay?"

"Yeah, I'm sorry. What did you say?"

"I was saying I wondered what her drawing meant. Maybe her parents are dead?"

"Yeah, maybe," Itohan responded.

She had to give it to him though. Mr. Ikimi was doing a great job. Eseosa's hair was always neatly braided and she was properly dressed. Maybe it wasn't what she thought, and he had a girlfriend that helped him take care of the little girl. The thought made her frown a bit. But why wasn't she drawn in the picture? She shook her head. How could she let this man get to her so much that she was trying to piece together his life from a six-year-old's picture?

"Do you have any plans for the next weekend?" Tisha asked.

"Nope and I'm so glad. Well just movies and chilling." Itohan packed up her papers. The kids would be coming back any minute.

"I have something you might be interested in."

Itohan turned around and Tisha had a flyer in her hand. She looked down at it and saw a Cross. She took it with some hesitation. She looked at it and returned her eyes to Tisha.

"I'm not sure if I'm allowed to do this in school, but my sister's church is having a Hurricane Relief event for the community…"

Itohan began to shake her head. No, she wasn't up for going to church. The internet services she attended when she felt like it, which was almost never, was more than enough for her.

"Err, Tisha, I don't think—"

"Before you say no, hear me out." Tisha paused and looked at her.

Itohan raised her brow for her to continue. She glanced at her watch again.

"It's not a service or anything. My sister said it will be a fun event. The men of the church are hosting a basketball tournament; the women are having a bake sale and the kids will be engaged in games. It's to raise funds and contribute items for the Food Bank while having some fun," Tisha said hurriedly.

Itohan nodded, folded the paper and put it in her pocket. "I'll think about it."

Tisha smiled at her and Itohan folded her hand across her chest. She hated when good people asked her to do things she wasn't too keen on doing. Tisha had been nothing but supportive of her, so she kinda felt uncomfortable telling her no outright. Saying, "I'll think about it" was the next best thing. If by next Sunday that turned into a solid, "I couldn't make it," at least she did think about it.

***

Later that day, as she drove home, Itohan decided to make a detour. She had no desire to cook anything for dinner, so stopped at one of her favorite Chinese buffets.

"Are you going to tell him?" Keni's voice boomed through the speakers in her car. She was in Spain and called to check in. Itohan had given her the run down on Eseosa and her uncle trying to get another opinion.

"Tell him what exactly?"

"Are you going to tell Mr. His-Locs-Are-So-Fine that his niece has mood swings? Then slide in a question about whether he's playing for the other team?" Keni asked, like what she just said was normal.

Itohan rolled her eyes. She regretted the day she told her sister and Ajoke about Mr. Ikimi and his dreadlocks. If she had known they would refer to him in the exact words she did, she would've eaten her words.

"I don't think there's any cause for alarm now. And stop calling him that. That's why I don't tell you anything." She paused. "Your other comment I'm going to ignore."

"You're just mad because you're undercover feeling the guy, but you're trying to stay loyal to your "all men are evil" foundation."

"Stop mocking my shame. At least I'm not changing men every second."

Itohan bit her tongue when that came out. Her sister went through a horrifying experience some years ago when she lost her fiancé on the battlefield. He was in the Nigerian Army. She hid her pain well by being a serial dater. She dropped every man after the second or even first date.

"Keni, I'm sorry. I didn't me—"

"I know you wouldn't intentionally hurt me, so it's fine."

"No, it's not fine. I really am sorry."

"You good, Sis. Back to you, first you have no shame because you weren't the cause of anything. Two, I'm not mocking you. I'm telling you to get over it," Keni retorted.

Itohan remained silent for a few seconds, then said, "Zogie thinks he came home some time ago."

"Please, don't tell me you're still thinking about Aidenoje. No, I didn't hear. If he flew on one of my flights, *I for don poison am*," Keni laughed.

"How are you telling me to let it go, but you want to poison the man?" Itohan laughed as she parked her car in front of the restaurant.

"That's because I am me and you are you." Keni paused. "On a more serious note, Sis, leave that man. He'll get his own and you'll sleep well because you had nothing to do with his karma."

It was easier said than done, especially since she had no idea why he did her that way.

"Itoh, have you prayed or been to church lately? The man broke your heart, humiliated you and took your money… yes. But you're searching for peace that Aidenoje's answers can't provide. Only Jesus can give you the peace you seek. It's been seven years. I know for you, technically, it's been four, but what's done is done."

Itohan sat stoic. That was the longest speech Keni had ever given her on the topic and she really didn't have the energy to talk about it.

"Open your heart, so people like Mr.—"

"Don't say it. I regret telling you that," Itohan said. Irritation took over, hearing Keni cackle as if it was so funny.

"Besides, I can't date my student's guardian."

"*Ah ah*, is there a law against it in America?"

"No, but it's not right."

"Says who?"

Itohan opened the doors of the restaurant. "Says me. Shouldn't you be sleeping? Don't you have a flight in the morning?"

"Stop running from the inevitable."

"Okay, I hear. Let me eat. I'll talk to you later. Call me when you touch down in Lagos." Itohan disconnected the call and looked in her purse for her credit card. When she got it out, it was bumped from her hand by a large figure.

"Ms. Adolo!"

Itohan turned and smiled at the person the jovial voice belonged to. "Hi, Eseosa."

Her uncle picked up her card and handed it to her. "I apologize."

Itohan was instantly engulfed by the husky, baritone voice and dark brown eyes that glanced over her body. She dropped her eyes and took the card from him.

"Thank you. I apologize." She turned to Eseosa, "I'll see you in school on Monday, right?"

The little girl nodded. As Itohan was about to excuse herself to the dining area, a second man appeared and patted Eseosa's uncle on his back. His grin was wide. *Maybe this was the man in the picture.*

"I apologize again. I didn't mean to bump into you. If you'll excuse me... you and your partner have a nice day," Itohan said.

"My what?"

"His what?"

Mr. Ikimi and the man roared in unison.

Itohan looked between both men. The glare on Mr. Ikimi's face could send her to the grave while the amusement in the other man's eyes had her questioning how far she had put her foot in her mouth.

7

His what? Osaro scowled at her. Malcolm thought it was hilarious, but nothing about the insinuation was funny to him. Was she high? She had to be under the influence of something to be that bold. Where in the world would she get an idea like that?

After he picked up Eseosa, he remembered he forgot a file in the office. Knowing they'd be out this weekend and he needed to work, he circled back to get it. That caused them to be caught up in traffic. Not willing to deal with getting back late and trying to heat up something, they decided to stop for Chinese food. Since Malcolm wanted the same and hadn't seen Eseosa in a minute, they decided to make an evening of it.

"Malcolm Bryson, my friend and business partner. Mac, this is Ms. Adolo—"

"Baby Cake's teacher," Malcolm cut his introduction short and extended his hand.

Ms. Adolo shook Malcolm's hand as Osaro continued to sneer at her.

"Oh my! I'm so sorry. I just assumed—" Ms. Adolo started.

"You know what they say when you assume right?" Osaro tone was curt. Despite his anger at her, he couldn't resist her allure and that incensed him more.

She rolled her eyes at him, smiled at Eseosa and turned away. Malcolm laughed so hard that Osaro picked up his niece and left him standing there. Malcolm caught up with them outside and it annoyed Osaro that he was still tickled. Osaro placed Eseosa in her booster seat and handed her the iPad, but noticed her eyes had begun to droop. It wouldn't be long before she was fast asleep. Closing the door, he turned to face Malcolm.

"Mac, cut it out, man. It's not that funny."

"It is funny. You're just mad because the chick you want to pretend you could care less about thought you played for the other team."

"Yeah, whatever man. When I try to at least like her because of Eseosa, she goes and opens her mouth on some random stuff."

"Whatchu mean try? Man, you do like her. That's why you're always irritated when Baby Cakes talks about her. You like her, but you don't want to," Malcolm said.

Osaro walked to the other side of his car. Over the past weeks, he'd had no interaction with Ms. Adolo at all. But she wouldn't leave his mind, especially since her name didn't finish in Eseosa's mouth.

Her scent, the ways her eyes shone when she looked at her kids and her curved frame was hard to push out of his mind. When he bumped into her, he felt an electric jolt, but it was a good thing she did put her foot in her mouth. It reminded him that he was right not to entertain the idea of getting to know her. The timing and situation were all wrong.

"She's my niece's teacher. That's it."

"That's not all you hope she can be tho."

"You going to the A this weekend?" Osaro asked, changing the subject.

"Yeah, going to chill with Grams a bit." Malcolm replied. His mom had passed giving birth to him and his grandma raised him until high school when he moved to Florida to stay with his uncle.

"Cool, say hi to her for me. I'm taking Eseosa to the County Fair and in turn she'll let me work."

"Bribing her already? Imma have to tell her that if you're handing out bribes they gotta at least be worth way more value."

"All right man, let me get her home and I'll see you on Monday." Osaro walked to the driver's side, and then paused. "You talk to Tex recently?"

"Erm, no. I was going to ask you the same thing. Always slipped my mind."

"Hmm. I'll try him again this weekend. That dude was supposed to hit me back a week ago to let me know when he'll be Stateside."

"He probably laid up with something warm, if you know what I mean."

"I do and on that note, I gotta go," Osaro said.

The friends dapped each other and went their respective ways.

About forty-five minutes later when they got home, Eseosa was wide awake, so they both changed into their PJs. He let her pick out a movie for them to watch while he popped some corn. Halfway into the movie *Sing*, she was out. He checked all the doors and turned off the lights. He picked her up and carried her upstairs. After tucking her in, he walked down the hall to his own bedroom.

One thing he didn't skimp on was his place, his car and his wardrobe. When he bought this house, he had the same designer that worked with Nancy for his office decorate this place. Eseosa's bedroom was done in a Moana theme, while his bedroom was done in basic grays, white and black. The living room and kitchen gave the house a family home feel, rather than the bachelor pad look of his former apartment. That had a lot to do with his auntie's input as well.

He walked into the attached bathroom and brushed his teeth, then prepared for bed. Peering at his reflection in the mirror, he chuckled to himself. It was a little after ten p.m. on a Friday night and he was about to call it a night. He had never been a party guy, but this was new to him. He slipped into his bed and turned on the television. He turned to ESPN to watch the highlights when his phone rang. He reached over and took it from the charging base. It was his brother.

"*How far?*" Osaro said, answering the call.

"*I dey o. Wetin dey happen?*"

Although they didn't grow up in Nigeria, Auntie Lizzy exposed them to their native tongue and Pidgin English. Osaro perfected his during his stay and taught Ehi all he knew when he returned to the States.

"Nothing much. So how was the meeting?" Osaro asked.

"It was okay. Got everything squared away and ready for

tomorrow."

"So, did you guys decide on what you're going to do?"

"Yeah, a while ago." Ehi paused. Osaro heard a garage door open, which meant his brother just got home. "It's on the flyer I gave Eseosa."

The police department was doing a fundraising drive for hurricane relief and Ehi was part of the organizing committee.

"I didn't even look at it yet. You got our tickets, right?"

"Yeah."

"Cool, so what y'all doing?" Osaro chuckled in anticipation of the crazy idea they came up with.

"We decided to have a donut eating contest and a wacky beauty pageant," Ehi said.

Osaro laughed harder. "So, the bright idea y'all came up with is giving the public a visual of the law enforcement donut eating myth."

"What myth are you talking about? Hollywood has given the public that visual for years with movies like *Beverly Hills Cop*. We're capitalizing on it."

The brothers laughed.

"So, you gonna make it?"

"Yeah. I'm taking Eseosa to the fair, but we'll stop by later."

There was a pause and smacking of lips. He hated when his brother did that while he was on the phone.

"Cool, Robin says what's up?"

"What's up with her? She must not be working tonight. Y'all smacking in my ear."

Ehi chuckled. "Yeah. Just a heads up, she's bringing one of her co-workers to meet you."

"Oh, man. Robin stays in my business. Is yours not enough for her to mind?"

Ehi laughed. "Chill on my woman. She's worried about you."

"Why though? I'm good."

Robin never liked his on and off again ex, Cassie, so was trying to hook him up before she reappeared.

Ehi remained silent and Osaro sighed.

He knew that Robin, who was close to his late sister, took it upon herself to try and do things for him that Ivie would've. During the first few months after Ivie's death, Osaro resented her gestures. In anger, he mistook it for her trying to take Ivie's place. He and Ehi bumped heads a lot because of it. In his head, he knew that wasn't the case, but his heart unleashed his guilt and anger on any available target. He let up a little, knowing deep down Robin was suffering just as much as he and his brother. She also carried some guilt around. Robin was the one who had invited Ivie to the party where she first met Bongo.

"Tell Sis to chill on the match making. It's all about Baby Cakes and me right now," Osaro said.

"Well, Baby Cakes will need a woman's influence soon. So, stop using her as an excuse."

"Says the man who had himself in the friend zone but panicked when Sis was trying to explore her options."

"At least I was in a zone. You have none. You need to get it together. Eseosa can't be your smoking mirrors, man," Ehi said.

Osaro shifted because he knew where his brother was headed.

"It's been four years, Bro. You couldn't have done anything otherwise. Ivie chose her path. I know you want to make up for whatever you blame yourself for doing to us by overcompensating, but stop."

"I messed up man." Osaro's tone was filled with regret.

"That was in high school. You've done perfect for yourself and us. It's unfortunate you blame yourself, but you did try. Yes, she started to change after you left for *Naija*, but there's nothing you can do about that. She got mixed up with the wrong man, but regretting that is regretting Eseosa and I know you don't."

Osaro listened to his brother. At some level, he knew what he was saying was right. Lord knows he tried to let it go. But as Ivie's big brother, he should have protected her. It was as though she was being brainwashed. If he had done what he should've, Bongo never would have had that chance.

"Eseosa is fine. You don't have to stop living because of her. Robin and I will babysit anytime. You still have Auntie Lizzy's until she leaves. Last resort, we'll hire outside help."

"I hear you, man. But I can't deal with a woman right now. Maybe once I clench this South Tran deal, I'll have the extra time to spend with one."

Osaro's mind drifted to Ms. Adolo. He wondered what her first name was. His lips curled up in a smile. There was something naughty and sexy about calling her Ms. Adolo. He envisioned her in her glasses and a schoolgirl uniform. He shook his head to get rid of the image. It had been a while since he was intimate with a woman, and he was now seeing things that weren't there. It was time to take himself to sleep.

"Okay, let's go with that excuse. See you tomorrow." Ehi said.

"A'ight, Bro. Later." Osaro was about to hang up when Ehi called out his name.

"For real though, I'm so proud of you and I know Papa and Mama would be proud, too. Don't sweat the small stuff. Love you, Bro."

"Thanks. Love you, too."

Osaro hung up the phone. He was no longer interested in watching television. He turned off the television and dimmed the lights. He never fully turned them off, in case Eseosa woke up at night and looked for him. He pulled up the covers, folded his arms across his broad chest and stared at the ceiling. He spoke to God for a few minutes in prayer, ending it with the same verse he started off with in the morning – Psalm 16:2. He made a habit of meditating on a verse a day.

Once done, he made a mental note to call the property agent in Nigeria tomorrow. His auntie had taken care of all of them. Now it was their turn to take care of her. She wanted a house in the GRA area in Benin and that's exactly what he and Ehi had given her. All that was left was getting it furnished and stocked with the basics and necessities. Thinking about it, he just might get a plot of land for himself. With that thought on his mind, he stretched out. Exhaustion rendered him immobile as he surrendered to sleep.

8

Sunday morning, Itohan used her spatula as a microphone as she danced around her kitchen to "I Wish" by Waje. It was one of those days where she woke up feeling like the songstress who wished she didn't possess a heart. She wasn't keen on it being filled with stone as the singer suggested. But if it meant she could forget the pain and despair that accompanied it being misused, she was all for it.

In her tank top and sweat pants, she rocked her body to the beat and scooped a mid-sized portion of the bean paste mixture. She tucked a strand of her hair back underneath her silk scarf then put the scoop into the hot peanut oil in the frying pan. She moved back to avoid the splatter.

After a hectic day, she cherished coming home to the relaxing feel of her apartment. She'd lived there for two years and simply loved it. The two-bedroom apartment was spacious with a living room, kitchen, small dining room and a self-contained laundry room. Her place wasn't too far from downtown, but it wasn't smack dab in the middle of it, either.

The moment she moved in, she knew her décor would be a mix of home and abroad. She achieved that with a mix of modern and African safari pieces. The pictures that hung on the wall were a blend of her own photos and African inspired art. Pictures of her family took position on her mantle.

After her marriage debacle, her parents contacted the Uwados, her godparents. They lived in Orlando. They and her parents maintained the friendship they started years ago when they schooled in Houston. Unlike her parents, they remained in America upon graduation. Itohan stayed with them for about a year before moving to St. Petersburg. They were nothing but nice to her.

After attending their Nigerian church and a couple of functions with them, she knew she had to get out of there. She left Nigeria because of "monitoring spirits." There was no way she was going to come to US and deal with them again.

Itohan fried up the remaining *akara* as the water for the custard came to a boil. Lifting the lever to the electric kettle, she poured and stirred, watching the white powder turn into the yellow pudding she loved.

Her thoughts turned to Mr. Ikimi. The person she met at the beach and the person who was in her classroom, as well as the one who used his eyes to stomp her into the ground in the restaurant were all different people. From Eseosa's contact form, Itohan knew they lived within a ten-mile radius of her. She'd never seen him before but now, he popped up everywhere.

The man had somehow managed to plague her mind all weekend. She should've listened to her church mind when it told her not to stick her nose in business that didn't concern her. When she'd sent him that email first day of school, he responded with his appreciation. The tone of his email was calmer than when they talked in person. For that, she was grateful. Things had been going well over the last couple of weeks. Occasionally, he'd ask her how his niece was adapting, and she'd respond with random pictures and brief updates.

She regretted reading meaning into Eseosa's picture. She had wanted the ground to swallow her when he looked at her like she had lost her mind. Not only did his stare make her feel extra silly, but his dark brown eyes seemed to search her soul for something. It was as though he was trying to read her. After apologizing and running off, Itohan's lips curved in a half smile as relief set in. He wasn't what she'd assumed.

That day, while scooping her lo mein noodles into the take-away Styrofoam, she allowed herself to go over the mental picture she'd captured. His locs weren't in the braided knot she'd seen before; they hung down on his shoulders. The red polo shirt he wore over brown khakis fit what she knew was a well-toned physic. Although she wasn't short, she still had to scoot back a bit to look at him without having to tilt her head. He had basketball height, six feet, five inches easy.

Men were trouble. She had that inscribed in her left brain. Now her right brain was taking over and she saw herself struggling to hold on to the mantra. Her heart quickened in fear as she was coming to the realization that her new student's uncle was about to mess up the system she had going.

"Jehovah *abeg*, please, I still haven't heard that Aidenoje's life has been destroyed. If he could buy his father a car, he's doing well. Since I'm still waiting on my payback, please keep this man from me…*abeg*," she murmured.

Blinking a few times to get her mind right, she dished and blessed her food before sitting down to eat with her *New African Woman* magazine. Minutes later, she was done and hurriedly cleaned up. If she calculated correctly, she was just in time to catch somebody's online ministry. She was a dedicated Bedside Baptist. She didn't have the energy or zeal to get up and go to church on any given Sunday. Itohan owned a Bible and knew key Scriptures, but she felt one *kain* – some kinda way – about being a diehard fan of the show *Snapped*, and hearing about forgiving those who made you snap. She knew she couldn't commit a murder like the women on the reality based show, but she understood what made them lose it. She read her Bible sometimes, but if she was being honest, it was more a "check off the righteousness box" kinda thing.

She finished up in the kitchen and plopped down on her plush, beige couch. As she reached for the remote, her phone rang. Itohan peered at the screen and silently pleaded to God for mercy. She missed home, but not that much. It was her mum.

"Mummy, good morning," she answered. Then she looked at the time. It was 10.a.m. "Oh, now for you it's afternoon. Good afternoon, Mummy."

"*Vbèè óye hé?* How are you?" Her mother spoke in Benin, their native language. Her voice was monotone, so Itohan knew exactly what was coming next.

"I'm fine—"

"Itohan, so if I don't call you, you will not call me?" her mother lashed out.

There it was.

"No, Ma. I just woke up. I was going to call you later." She hated lying to her mother, but sometimes it was way easier than saying, "*I don't call you often, because you stress me out.*"

"I have no idea when you turned into a liar, but I'll continue to try my best." Her mother began to sniff.

Itohan sighed. *O Lord here we go with the fake tears and guilt trip. Five...four...three...two*

"I didn't do this to my mother. I don't know why you're doing this to me," her mother sobbed.

"Mummy now, come on, we do this all the time. What am I doing to you? You and Daddy lived in America before. You know how busy it can get," Itohan pacified her mother.

"You make time for what's important. When you want to take pictures and teach at the same time, you have time, but not for your parents," she paused. "I have to pursue my oldest daughter up and down the place to talk to her."

Itohan knew how this movie ended. She'd been acting it for a while. "Mummy, someone hearing you now wouldn't know we spoke about four days ago. They'd think I haven't talked to you in a year."

Her mother continued to sniff but didn't say anything. Itohan rolled her eyes. She loved her parents dearly, but once she didn't toe the line, everything else she did after that seemed irrelevant. Even when she got her master's degree, that didn't even make them proud. She knew deep down they loved her, but she'd since concluded that until she married someone or went to the Moon they might never get over what she caused Aidenoje to do to their family name. Neither one of those things were happening any time soon so she would just keep being the prodigal daughter.

The fake tears stopped and Itohan decided to move the conversation on. She asked about her dad and listened to her mother tell her the latest *tafia* from her job. Her mom was the regional manager in one of the well-established banks in Nigeria. Itohan was always amazed at the tea she had to spill even at that level. She loved that job so much that Itohan often wondered what her mother would do when it came time for her to retire next year.

As time progressed, Itohan was enjoying herself. She laughed so much her stomach hurt. She wiped the tear that formed at the corner of her eye. These were the mother/daughter moments she missed. Once the laughter died down, there was a brief pause between them before her mother spoke again.

"Have you met any nice young man yet?"

Itohan closed her eyes. She should've known it was too good to be true. How could she think this call would end without that question?

"No, Mummy. When I meet one, I'll let you know immediately."

"Hmm. Don't be sarcastic, young lady," she said. "I hope you're not putting your nose up in the air at them because of that nonsense boy of before?"

Her mother sometimes acted like if they didn't talk about her failed marriage, then it never happened. It was a bad experience, but she still would have liked to be able to discuss it with her mum.

"His name is Aidenoje, Mummy. No, I'm not putting my nose up. It's where it has always been on my face." Itohan chuckled.

"It's funny, right? It won't be funny when I knock your head."

Itohan laughed harder. How exactly did she think she'd be able to hit her on her head over the phone?

"Anyway, don't be too snooty. Men hate when you act like you're better than them." She paused. "I want to be able to carry my grandchild soon."

Itohan grunted. She wasn't dumbing herself down for nobody. Aidenoje had taught her a lot of things not to do in a relationship. However, there was no need to argue with her mother on her male/female dynamic, so she didn't respond to that comment.

"Grandchild *ke*? Look to Keni and Zogie for that *o*. I don't even have a man," Itohan said.

"Itohan, you're thirty-two, you should be thinking about these things."

"Mummy, I'm not thinking about that *o*. But *last last*, if push comes to shove, I can go to a sperm bank if grandchildren is *hungering* you." Itohan giggled.

"A what? Why is your life like this? You just want to keep disgracing us. We didn't do this to our parents."

Itohan laughed and rolled her eyes. Time was up. It was time for her to get off the phone.

"Mummy, don't worry. You know I love you. Greet daddy for me *o* and I'll call before you call me next time. I promise." Itohan blew a kiss into the phone and hung up quickly.

"See what Aidenoje has turned my life into. A pop quiz wrapped into a counseling session," she muttered to herself.

Itohan picked up the remote and turned to Oxygen. She decided to bump online church; she was no longer in the mood. What she needed was a marathon of her favorite program – *Snapped*. With any luck, she'd find a way to snap Aidenoje's neck whenever she found him. Or give God some ideas on how she wanted her karma. Either way Aidenoje had to pay.

***

That same day on the other side of town, Osaro held on to Eseosa's hand as they walked into the sanctuary of The Lord is Good Ministries. The church had been his church home for about two years and was presided over by Dr. Zach. The church had a good sized congregation, but by the standards of other mega churches in the country, it was small. Sunday school had been cancelled, so all the kids were in the main sanctuary.

They got in the pew and he made sure Eseosa was comfortable. He handed her the children's book of Bible stories and opened the church bulletin the usher handed him on arrival. Seconds later, he felt someone looking at him, so he raised his head. His eyes met with Marcy's. She smiled at him and he returned the gesture with a head nod and a faint smile. What he loved about the size of the church was also what made him uncomfortable about it.

There wasn't the bottleneck that existed in bigger churches. If he had the need for his pastor, he didn't have to fill out numerous appointment books or have a pre-interview with an intermediary. As much as he loved that access, he was tired of fighting off unwanted attention. He was finally doing right and trying to maintain it.

The single ladies, however, assumed he was looking for a mate.

He got tired of smiling and politely refusing their offers for homemade lunches or helping with his niece. He didn't like to toot his own horn, but Osaro knew he was pleasing to the eyes. He shifted a stray loc that had escaped the low ponytail he sported. Using his index finger and thumb, he smoothed his thin mustache that was connected to his light beard. He always got special attention from ladies, but it shot up a lot of notches since the summer when his niece started living with him. He wondered if having her there placed an automatic "wife needed" sign on his forehead. He wanted one eventually, but now wasn't the time.

The praise and worship team started what he knew were the beginning chords of "Everlasting God" by William Murphy. It was one of Osaro's favorite songs. He clasped his hands together and said a few words of prayer to focus himself back on what he was here for – worship. He stood with the rest of the church. Not one for dancing, he swayed from side to side and lifted his hands up to the heavens.

When the song came to an end, Dr. Zach walked up to the podium. He greeted the congregation and received a loud response. He opened his Bible and notes and looked out into the sanctuary. After calling out a couple of people and welcoming them back from a mission's trip, he put his hands in his pockets and gave a dramatic pause.

"I was going to preach on seasons this morning. I had this great sermon prepared. I mean up until last night, that was my message. Then I ran into an old buddy. He and his wife used to be friends of my wife and I. Yesterday afternoon, I was at a gas station and he happened to be there." Dr. Zach paused and looked around at the church.

Osaro looked with him. The place was silent as everyone waited to see where this story was going. He would've preferred the sermon about seasons, since his had changed.

"We started catching up and he told me how he lost his family to his gambling habit. He was now on the road to recovery, but his one regret was that recovery came too late. I didn't want to inundate him with Scripture. Sometimes that's not what a person needs. We need people who can talk to us without all the bells and whistles. I talked to him a bit and then gave him Scripture to help comfort him. As I watched him leave, his shoulders were slumped. The Lord told me to change what I initially wanted to discuss. My message is titled, 'Hoarding is Hazardous.' Say it with me."

"Hoarding is hazardous," shouted the congregation.

"Some time ago, my wife and I decided we needed a two-day staycation. We were going to relax and do nothing. On one of those days, I woke up to my wife talking to the TV. I tried to see what got her talking to an inanimate object. All I saw on the screen was a room that looked like someone threw up in it. My wife explained it was a show called *Hoarders*. You know how you can get shocked and disgusted by something, but you can't take your eyes away?"

There was murmuring throughout the church as everyone agreed with him.

Dr. Zach glanced at his notes and continued. "That's how it was for me. We ended up watching the show 'til the end where they had an expert come in and help the person see their dysfunction. Turn to Ephesians 5:25-26 …*Christ loved the church and gave Himself up for her to make her holy, cleansing her by the washing with water through the word*. Follow me here – with the crucifixion of Jesus, past hurt, failures and regrets are no longer your emotional bags to own. If you keep holding on to or hoarding them, eventually you run the risk of becoming so bogged down, you fold under the weight. You can't grow, become stuck and can barely move or breathe. Hand it over to the Lord and take only the lesson. Why are you carrying bags that are not your own?

"So many people are carrying their regret and pain around like they are badges of honor. Guess what? They're not. There's nothing you can do about it now, so stop playing victim to it. Before you email me, listen clearly. I'm not belittling the event, what I'm saying is that…it is over. God did not intend for us to carry around such heavy burdens and baggage. It's the enemy of our souls that ties us down with such things. It's to keep us from living our lives in the freedom Christ offers and it hinders us from being all Christ calls us to be. Remember Romans 8:1, '*There's no condemnation for those who are in Christ.*' There are many great men and women of the Bible who did things that could have caused them to cower in regret. But guess what? If they did, God wouldn't have been able to use them the way He did. Remember, all things work together for the good of those who love the Lord. For those that don't know, that's Romans 8:28." Dr. Zach smirked, and the congregation laughed.

"Pray and ask God for His help to let go and move forward. It's a choice you must make. Accept things you can't change and allow God's grace to cover the situation. Let Him do what He does best—work it together for good in our lives. Or you can choose to hold on to the pain. Let it rule and dictate your life. Moses killed a man on his way to his destiny. We know he wasn't a cold-blooded murderer, so he must have felt guilt over his actions. What would have happened to the Israelites if he didn't move forward because of it?

Learn from the past, but move on and accept the freedom and gifts that Christ offers to set us free."

Dr. Zach walked to the podium that he had since abandoned and closed his Bible. Picking up the bottle of water, he went to his seat. For Osaro, after that, the rest of the service went by as a blur to him. He felt like the pastor just drop kicked him in the chest. He absently rubbed the locket of his necklace. He glanced over at his niece who'd made herself a makeshift bed with the vacant space next to her. He was carrying a bag that wasn't his. Not by raising her, but by the guilt he carried around as to why he had her.

He shifted in his seat when he heard in his spirit, *"So, when you have repented and turned to me again, strengthen your brothers"* from Luke 22:32. There wasn't anything that Ehi, Mac or Tex needed strengthening in, so why did that verse come to him?

As the benediction came to an end, Osaro picked up Eseosa and made his way out of the church. His stomach rumbled, and he could mentally envision Auntie's dinner spread. He hoped she made enough for seconds. He'd have to figure out Luke 22:32 later. Right now, what he needed was food.

9

Pat, clap, pat, pat… "Twenty-one." *Pat, clap, pat, pat…* "Twenty-four." *Pat, clap, pat, pat… Pat, clap, pat, pat…*

"Come on Eseosa, it's your turn. Three add twenty-four is what?" Itohan asked, nodding her head in encouragement. *Pat, clap, pat, pat…* It was Wednesday and the first day of parent/teacher conferences. She and her kids were having their final carpet activity for the day before it was time to go. The kids had early release day, allowing the teachers to prepare for the parents' arrival and to give the parents enough time to inquire about their child's progress.

Pat, clap, pat, pat… "Twenty-seven." Eseosa said, softly.

She was still shy, most times unsure of herself. However, she'd made tremendous progress from the start of the school year. She'd opened up more, but some days she shut down completely.

"Very good," Itohan said. She beamed at her before checking her watch again. "Good job, class." She stood, and her students groaned. They loved when they had carpet time and played games. Itohan tried to make sure she incorporated their learning of tougher subjects with play. It was a technique she used if more than a few of them were struggling.

"I'm so proud of all of you. Remember, when you get home to tell your parents or guardians to practice with you," she encouraged, clapping her hand together.

The kids got up from the mat. The sounds of shuffling back and forth could be heard as they hurried up and put the squares they had been using to practice away. Next, the kids raced around for their backpacks.

"Don't forget, there will be a spelling test on Friday," Itohan spoke over the commotion, erasing the stuff she had on the Smart Board.

Several minutes later, the bell had rung, and her kids had left for the day. Itohan sat at her table, waiting for her first parent. Soon there was a knock on the door. *Right on time.* She looked up from her table and stood with a smile on her face.

"Hi, welcome. You must be Mr. Valadez," Itohan said.

"Yes, I am. And you must be Ms. Adolo. Rico speaks highly of you," the man responded.

Itohan ushered him to the table she'd prepared for today's conferences. She brought out Ricardo Valadez's file and started going over the basics with his father. He was one of her stellar students. The beam on his father's face was identical to hers as she told him how well his son was doing in her class. He was way above his peers in the core subjects. He still suffered a bit with Social Studies but other than that, he was fine. It was also nothing extra one-on-one time couldn't take care of.

An hour and a half later, she was down to her last parent for the day. Or in this case guardian, Eseosa's uncle. She was so glad he opted for the last available appointment. After her routine weekend *Snapped* and *Deadly Women* marathon, she'd successfully buried whatever nonsense she was feeling for him way down in never-ever land.

Itohan glanced at the clock on the wall. She had exactly five minutes until their meeting. Her bladder wasn't going to make it through their fifteen-minute meeting, though. The large Coca Cola she'd had with her spicy Italian Sub for lunch was to blame. She quickly peeked into the class next door and that teacher was waiting on her parent, too. Itohan informed her she had to go the restroom and she'd be right back in case her last parent got here before she got back. She hurried away; her mission was to make it back in time. She was already on shaky ground with Mr. Ikimi and she wasn't in the mood for any more awkward moments that evolved into one of his intense stares.

Ten minutes later, Itohan quickened her pace down the hall to her classroom. As she approached, the trail of his cologne hit her nostrils, slowing her steps. She cursed under her breath. If only Principal Baker hadn't stopped her, she would've made it. She stepped into her classroom and he was over by the display board with his back to the door. She took a minute to observe him. The light pink dress shirt he wore over black khakis hugged his broad shoulders nicely. The sleeves were folded up to three quarters of his arm, showcasing how well the color contrasted against his dark skin. His hair was in individual plaits past his shoulders.

"Are you just going to stand there and stare at me or are we going to discuss how my niece is doing?" his deep voice jolted her. He didn't turn around.

She cleared her throat. "I apologize for being late."

Itohan walked further into the class. She mentally tried to conjure up an episode of *Snapped*. She hadn't been around him for two seconds and all the mental hard work she'd done over the weekend was already going down the drain.

He turned around. She was so happy he had shades on. She knew he could see her, but for a few seconds, she wanted to avoid the intensity of his stare.

"Good afternoon, Mr. Ikimi." She straightened her shoulders and gave him a faint smile. This was her classroom and she needed to take control of this meeting.

"Ms. Adolo," he said.

He took off his shades and put them atop his head. He inserted his hands in his pants pockets and walked toward her. Itohan felt his eyes assessing her. *There goes that stare again.* The pace of her heart accelerated. She took her reading glasses from her hair and put them on. Anything to keep her from looking at him. She nodded politely and with shaky hands, ushered him to the table she had been using all afternoon.

"Are you always late or just when it comes to your job?" He smirked at her.

"Excuse me?" She loved her students and for him to insinuate otherwise made her blood boil, no matter how attractive he was.

"The day of orientation, you didn't show up. Today I had to wait for you to show up." He shrugged. "So are you always this casual?"

"Not that I have to explain anything to you—"

"But you do. I'm your student's guardian," he countered.

Itohan rolled her eyes. She needed to focus on the task at hand and get this man out of here.

"For your information, I'm standing in for her actual teacher who had to be out at the last minute. I got the call after orientation. As for today, I'm sorry Your Majesty had to wait for five minutes while I used the restroom."

Mr. Ikimi stared at her with a grin on his face. Something told her he enjoyed seeing her riled up. She caught herself from going off on him any further. He was the guardian of her student. She had to be professional, although she already blew that. She didn't know the game he was playing, but she loved this job and it supplemented her income. God forbid, she be another disappointment and lose her job over a man. Besides, she didn't have very favorable news for him when it came to his niece and reading, so she still had another battle.

She took in a breath. "I apologize for losing my cool there, but I didn't like your assumption."

"It's not fun, is it?" He raised his thick eyebrow.

"Excuse me?" She furrowed her brows.

He chuckled. "Why do you keep excusing yourself? I'm pretty sure you heard me the first time."

Itohan ignored him and picked up Eseosa's file.

"It's no fun when people assume things about you, now is it?"

She got his meaning and lowered her head. He was talking about the incident in the restaurant. She'd hoped he didn't bring that up.

"Look, Mr. Ik—"

"Osaro."

"Huh?"

"Osaro, my name is Osaro."

"Oh...uhm...Osaro—"

"Don't I deserve the pleasure of knowing your name?"

"Ms. Adolo." She opened the red folder in front of her.

"You're Ms. Adolo to your students. What's your first name? Unless you want to teach me some things…"

Itohan felt her cheeks get hot. *This man cannot be flirting with me. I haven't had male attention in ages. I'm a live wire waiting to explode. Lord, You owe me. Take this temptation from my doorstep.*

"Let's call a truce. Eseosa's talks highly of you and I know I can be a bit much." He gave her a faint smile. "Besides, we're both *Naija*."

Itohan nodded her head with vigor. *So, the man can smile.* He should smile often. It was a good look on him.

"I said a bit, and for good reason. Don't get carried away," he warned.

Itohan saw the playfulness in his eyes. "Itohan."

"That's pretty. So now that we're on a first name basis, tell me about my niece."

Itohan didn't respond, but she started removing papers from the folder in front of her. Over the next couple of minutes, she focused on showing him his niece's work. With them being so close, it was hard to ignore the magnetic force between them, but she was determined to stay focused and get this over with. She showed him things Eseosa's did when she first got to her class, in comparison with where she was now. Osaro was very attentive and asked her clarifying questions along the way.

She got to the part she dreaded. It was always hard giving parents a negative report about their child. Their defenses shot up and they sometimes took it as a personal attack on their contribution to their child's education. She took out Eseosa's reading papers and handed them to him. Their hands brushed against each other and she felt the jolt of electricity. He felt it, too, because he looked up at her. They stared at each other for what seemed like eternity before Itohan blinked, breaking the uneasy pull between them.

"Eseosa is a very bright student. She's doing great in all her subjects, but reading is a core subject and she's behind her peers…"

"What do you mean behind? My niece is very intelligent." He frowned at her.

"Yes, she is. However, she's having trouble reading at the level of her peers."

Osaro looked down at the paper she handed him, and she explained where Eseosa was, as opposed to where she should be.

He continued to frown then, looked up at her. "So, what needs to be done?"

"I've placed her in a reading group that will help. But I need her to practice more at home every day." She handed him a list of books. It wasn't the school's recommendation, but hers, from years of experience.

Osaro remained silent and looked at the list she handed him. "You need to spend time reading with her every night. Make it fun and not like a chore. Also, have her tell you about the story. That way you can help her with her comprehension as well."

He nodded and Itohan braced herself.

"There's one more thing," she said.

Osaro's frowned. "What is it?"

"The school had to place her on probation."

"What! Why? She's just a kid." His jaw clenched in anger.

"Mr. Iki—"

He glared at her.

"Osaro, we know that. It's just school policy because she's behind, and not just by one level. It's just September. She has some time to get where she needs to be before the next testing."

Itohan remained silent. Osaro rubbed his chin with his index finger and thumb. His eyes searched her.

"What's your true assessment?" he asked, his tone now somber. He brushed his hand across his face.

"That was my true assessment." A beat of silence passed between them. "Eseosa is a young second grader. She just turned seven last week while her classmates were already seven when they got here. She just needs a little more time. I trust that with effort, she can do it, and this will be a thing of the past."

Osaro had a hint of scrutiny in his eyes. His gaze put her opinion to the test. "Okay, thank you." He took the papers she handed him to keep. Next, he signed the ones she needed for her records.

She noticed his hesitation in signing the acknowledgement of the conversation they just had. His body language changed the minute she mentioned it. She knew parents didn't take these things well, but he took it hard. Almost like there was something he blamed himself for. Once they were done, she walked him to the back wall to show the paintings and drawings the kids had made. It brightened his mood when he looked at his niece's drawing. He studied the picture of the family and Itohan slipped away to her desk to pack up her things. She was beat and all she needed was some food and her bed.

"Now I see where you came up with your outlandish assumption."

His voice caused her to stop digging in her purse for her keys and returned her gaze to him.

"May I?" He gestured toward the drawing.

She nodded, and he removed the tack that held it to the corkboard. She watched as he sauntered toward her. He stood before her. Any closer and his body would touch hers. She moved back, but he moved closer, until she was backed up against the Smart Board. Itohan decided right there and then, she was having a heart attack.

He stared down at her and she accepted his challenge holding his gaze. A vision of him taking her to the morgue because she'd died under the intensity of his gaze flashed through her mind. That could not and would not be her portion, so taking him on wasn't in her best interest. He was testing her, and she was bound to lose. She should be running and not entering the ring with him. Warning alarms went off in her head. This was a dangerous game, so she gave in. With nowhere else to go, she stepped aside.

"Did that feel like I play for the other team?"

She was stuck. When she told her brother the story, he told her she had inadvertently questioned Osaro's manhood. Right now, he was trying to prove a point and with the way her breath caught in her chest, he had accomplished his goal.

He bent down, putting his ear at the level of her mouth. "I didn't hear you, Ms. Adolo." His tone demanded an answer.

"No," she whispered.

"My niece is my late sister's daughter. That's who is in the clouds in her picture. The two men are my brother and I. The older woman is my aunt."

At his explanation, she lowered her eyes. "I'm…I'm…"

He pulled his full lips in, placed his right hand over his chest and bowed his head. "It's so hard…" he sniffed.

"I'm so sorry about your sister." *Was he crying?*

She looked around her classroom. She wondered why she did that because she knew there wasn't anyone there. "What can I do to help?" The words left her mouth before she could stop them.

Osaro straightened up, folded his arms across his chest and smirked at her. She rolled her eyes and hit him playfully on his arm. He had just played her like a native drum.

"Well, now that you offered…"

"You tricked me." She folded her arms across her chest

Osaro shrugged. "Hey, I use all arsenals at my disposal."

Itohan walked back to her desk and continued packing up her things.

"Am I your last conference for today?" He walked over and re-pinned the picture.

"Yes, and you've overstayed your welcome."

"You're kicking your fellow countryman out?"

"Yep." She put her bag on her shoulder.

Osaro chuckled. "Come on. I'll walk you to your car."

She pouted. "No, thank you."

The plan was to stay away from this man – not to owe him a favor because he tricked her into feeling sorry for him. She hadn't even had time to process that that sweet little girl no longer had a mother.

"Don't be like your seven-year-olds. Fix your face. I don't want people thinking I did something to you."

"But you did. You got on the last nerve I got today."

He laughed as he stepped aside for her to exit the class. They walked down the hall in silence. He walked her to her car. She unlocked it and flung her satchel into the passenger seat.

"You giving me the silent treatment?" he asked.

"No, I'm trying to get home."

"Don't be mad 'cause you now owe me a favor." He lifted her chin. "I'll go easy on you and let Eseosa choose what favor you can do for us."

Itohan rolled her eyes at him. "Fine."

Osaro closed her door for her and stepped back. She started her car and flew out of the parking lot like it was on fire. Her great resolve was dissolving and she didn't like that. Now she was stuck owing him a favor. Well, if Eseosa was involved, it shouldn't be too bad. She just had to keep chanting, *Men are trouble. Men are trouble.*

10

The sun shone brightly through the open drapes of his bedroom. With his eyes still closed, Osaro raised his hand to block the unwanted intrusion. The dip in his bed confirmed that his niece was on her Saturday mission to make sure he didn't sleep a second longer than she did. She had no concept of the term sleeping in. The pounding going on in his head made him wish that for once, more than anything, she did.

It had been a long time since he woke up with headaches. Her movements were aggravating the one he currently had. He only drank socially, so he wasn't suffering from a hangover. Instead, his misery was from lack of sleep. He received an email late last evening from South Tran. They wanted some additional information for the proposal he'd submitted – by Monday.

"Good morning, Uncle Ro." Eseosa bounced up and down on his bed.

"Hey, Baby Cakes. Uncle has a headache. Can you quit the bouncing?"

Her smile turned into a frown. "Sorry Uncle. You need medicine?"

Osaro wiped his eyes and gave her a faint smile. He drew her in for a hug and kissed her forehead. "No, Baby Cakes. I'll be fine. How was your night?"

"Good."

"Have you washed your face?"

"Yes." She nodded. "I can't find the remote, Uncle Ro. I want to watch Elena."

Osaro knew more about the Mexican Disney princess than any grown man should. Even when he wasn't with her, the theme songs of all Eseosa's shows played in his mind with little agreement from him.

He sat up and leaned against the headboard. "Before you watch TV, did you finish the book I gave you yesterday afternoon?"

"Uh huh, do you want me to tell you what it's about?"

"How about you tell me over breakfast?"

"Okay."

It had been a couple of days since the conference with her teacher and he was determined to do everything possible to help his niece get to and possibly above the reading level of her peers. After getting home that evening, he ordered the recommended reads online and had them shipped next-day delivery. He'd begun reading to her every night. She also read the book back to him at her own pace. Then he'd ask her to quicken the pace and time it. He checked her for accuracy and speed. The good thing was that they'd established a good rhythm and he knew with time she'd be okay. The only weakness he had was that the whole exercise put her teacher at the front of his mind.

Days after, the strawberry fragrance she wore still disturbed his thoughts. How did he go from not wanting a woman right now to thinking about one as often as he did? Maybe the mystery of her was what was drawing him in. Probably if he got closer to her or spent a little time with her, he'd find out there wasn't much there.

Smiling to himself, he knew he didn't even believe that. The unexplainable pull between them was more than his logical brain could explain. Osaro knew he made her nervous. He could almost feel the gears in her brain grinding against each other as she struggled to avoid eye contact. Truth be told, he knew he was no good for thinking it, but he found satisfaction in her nervousness. That meant she felt some kind of way about him, too.

"Uncle?"

"Yes? I'm sorry, baby girl, did you say something?"

"Yes… can I watch *Elena of Alvalor* since I've read the book and I won't tell you about it 'til breakfast?"

"Let's pray first," he said.

Osaro scooted to the edge of the bed. His niece got on her knees and he knelt beside her. That was one thing they didn't skimp on, no matter what he had going on that day. For the next couple of minutes, they prayed as he taught her. In thanksgiving and supplication, they prayed. Then they asked for protection and told the Big Guy their wants. After some seconds of silence, they stood.

"Uncle Ro, I want pancakes."

"Okay, but remember we're going to help out in the church this morning, so we gotta hurry up." He slipped his feet in his slippers and walked to the bathroom.

"Okay," she yelled and left his room.

Osaro had agreed to participate in a fundraiser his church was organizing for hurricane relief. He stared at his reflection in the mirror in his bathroom. Turning to examine his hair, Osaro concluded that he needed to get his edges shaped up and his locs retwisted. He'd been growing them since he was sixteen. There wasn't a deep reason behind it. It started off as trying to look good for the girls in high school since it started to become popular. Locs weren't typically a *Naija* thing, so his aunt almost had a fit but with time, she began to like them.

He brushed his teeth, washed his face and headed downstairs. He smiled when he entered the living room and saw that his niece had found a way to get the remote from the mantle and was now deep in an episode of Elena. He walked into the kitchen and took out the skillet and the Bisquick box.

"Baby Cakes, I'm ready. Come on," he called out to Eseosa.

Minutes later, she walked into the kitchen and sat on the barstool at the island. Like him, she was still in her pajamas. He put the Bisquick powder into the bowl and added the other ingredients for the pancake batter. Eseosa had her coloring book, puzzle book and her crayons with her.

"So, Baby Cakes, tell me what's been happening in school?"

"Uncle Ro, we talk about school every day," she whined. Her head was down and she was focused on what she was coloring.

"Yes, we do, and this is another day, so spill. First, tell me about the book you read." He turned on the burner and placed the skillet on top of it. He put in a little butter in it and turned around to face her, giving her the go ahead to continue. Over the next couple of minutes, he listened to her attentively tell the story. By the time she was done, he was whisking the eggs to scramble.

"We're having a recital in school and I need a fancy dress," Eseosa said.

"Any particular color?"

"Ms. Adolo said it should have some orange or brown in it. The paper is in my folder."

"All right. We'll check it out."

His thoughts strayed to her teacher. He remembered when he met her again in that classroom. He was determined to avoid her because he'd anticipated exactly what was happening now. Now, he'd resigned himself to the fact that it was fruitless, especially with the way Eseosa was always talking about her. One thing he knew for sure was that he wouldn't spend an indefinite part of the school year in this state. The conclusion he came to earlier was what he was going to stick to; get to know her, satisfy his curiosity, and maybe find out there wasn't much there.

Soon after, he dished their pancakes, sausages and eggs. He took his coffee while letting her wash her food down with orange juice. Once they were done, Eseosa insisted on washing dishes with him. Osaro pulled a stool closer to the sink and put her on it. Allowing her to get her hands wet at intervals, he observed her. The cheerful demeanor had gone and she seemed sober.

"What's wrong, Baby Cakes?"

She remained silent for a moment. "Will I ever have a mommy and daddy again?"

He froze. The question took him by surprise. They'd talked to her about the tragedy, although he wasn't sure how much of it she understood when they did. It was only right that she'd become more curious as she got older. Osaro dried his hands and picked her up. With her little hands around his neck, he carried her to the living room and sat with her in his lap.

"Baby Cakes, a person gets only one mommy and daddy. You can, however, have many people that love you so, so much and will take care of you."

She nodded with her eyes still downcast.

"Remember what we discussed about mommy and daddy going to be with Jesus and they won't be coming back?"

"Yes. But who will go to all the things I do in my new school? My friends have mommies and daddies."

Osaro paused, carefully gathering his words. "You may not have your mummy or daddy there, but you'll have Uncle Ehi, Auntie Robin and Nana Lizzy." He paused. "I miss your mummy, too and I know she's looking down on us and is very proud of you."

He stared at her, trying to read her comprehension of his answer.

She frowned. "You're not coming, Uncle Ro?"

He chuckled, realizing he omitted himself in the lineup. He rubbed his nose against hers. "I'll always be there for you. Always."

That smile he was used to reappeared and she wrapped her small arms around his neck. He kissed her forehead and stood. Transferring her to his back, he ran up the stairs and his heart warmed at her giggles. Osaro made his way to her room for her to pick out her outfit. The sun was already out, and its full effect would be felt in a couple of hours. Since they were going to be outside for majority of the day, he made sure she picked out the appropriate attire. Minutes later, she handed him some capris and a t-shirt. He took it to the ironing board.

"Okay, Baby Cakes, go get started on brushing your teeth. I'll come help you out in a minute."

***

An hour and a half later they were dressed and headed to the garage. Osaro placed the cartons of canned goods he'd purchased in the trunk. The venue of today's activities would be the expansive church grounds. There were supposed to be games, sales of baked goods, entertainment, lunch and care box preparation. It would be like what Ehi and the police department did the other weekend, but on a smaller and more intimate scale. His family was supposed to meet them there.

"You ready to spend the night with Nana Lizzy?" Osaro asked Eseosa. She was in the back seat with her eyes glued to her iPad, playing games. Since she needed her hair redone, Eseosa would go with his auntie after the event.

"Yes, you'll get me after church tomorrow, right?"

Osaro chuckled. "Yes, after Sunday dinner. But what's up? You don't like it there?"

He glanced in the rearview mirror to make eye contact with her. She met his eyes and he tried to read her expression.

She shrugged. "I do. It's just that Nana Lizzy doesn't let me watch Elena when it comes on sometimes. They show the new Elena when Nana's program is on."

Osaro laughed. The program she was referring to was *Law and Order: Special Victims Unit*. He sometimes wondered if that wasn't what influenced Ehi. His auntie has been watching that show since forever. Osaro and Ehi didn't discuss their clients or cases. But Osaro always got a kick out of how his auntie would listen to the news, hear a crime and try and tell Ehi how it should be solved based on her knowledge of her television program.

For Osaro, after being stung by hackers in his first year of business, he never talked about his clients. That error cost him a huge deal. If he ever talked about his clients, it was in very general terms. That was because he was dealing with the security of their intellectual and sometimes financial information. He didn't want the information to get into the hands of hackers ever again; at least not by his carelessness. He trusted his family wholeheartedly, but he decided to form the habit of remaining silent about who he was working with. That prevented him from slipping up and discussing them where he wasn't sure of who was listening.

"I bet you that Disney would show the new Elena a million times more after tomorrow. You can watch something else on your iPad."

Osaro pulled into the church parking lot and the place was packed. He parked, popped the trunk and got out the carton he had with him. The humidity made him glad he decided to go with Capri jeans, a simple white tee and a pair of Nikes on his feet. His snapback secured his hair that was in a low bun off his neck. He got Eseosa out of the car, balanced the carton on his left arm and grabbed her hand with his right hand. Walking over to the long table that was set up, he put the box down. He looked around, pleased that members of the church had indeed answered the call.

Osaro felt Eseosa tug her hand to be free. He glanced at her and followed the direction of her excitement. He saw his family approaching, so he let her hand go.

"Be careful," he called after her as she ran to his brother.

Eseosa ran to his auntie, greeted her and then jumped into Ehi arms, drawing Robin in with her small arms for a hug. Osaro smiled. He has glad Robin's schedule was free for today. He walked toward them and pulled his auntie into a hug.

"Auntie, *Ób'ówie*. How are you?" Osaro kissed her cheek.

"Good morning, my son. I'm fine. How are you?" She looked up at him. "You were supposed to call me back three days ago," she scolded.

Osaro tried to remember why he didn't. Then it came to him. That was the day that he got the unsettling news about Eseosa and her reading. He was so focused on getting the books and doing homework because she had to go to school the next morning. Nothing else was more important to him than that.

"Oh, Auntie. I was busy with your grandchild," he answered.

Both of them turned and smiled at the same time at Eseosa who was relaxed comfortably in Ehi's arms.

"Put that girl down. Why are you guys always picking her up? Between both of you, she'll be spoiled rotten," Auntie Lizzy fussed.

"That's my job…to spoil her," Ehi said. "Osaro can do the disciplining."

Auntie Lizzy turned to him and gave him a stern look. He raised his hands in surrender and winked at her. She knew there was no way he could bring himself to be that hard on her. Robin walked over to him and Osaro wrapped his arm around her.

"Sis, *na ya eye be dis*?" Osaro asked, referring to having not seen her in a while. He talked to her last Sunday, but he hadn't set his eyes on her in about three weeks.

"I know. You know it's all love. I've been working doubles for a minute. You know trying to get that paper." She rubbed her fingers together. "Any extra time is for my boo." She showcased her thirty-two teeth, letting him know how deep her love went for Ehi.

"Is that right? So, bump the rest of the family?" Osaro raised his brow at her while walking over to his brother who used his free arm to dap him. "Hey, Bro."

"I'm good, man. Stop harassing my woman," Ehi said. "Of course, I come first. I been telling you to get yours."

"Ms. Adolo!" Eseosa screamed, wiggling out of Ehi hands.

Osaro looked up to the sky. *You trying to tell me something?*

He had to ask God, because the timing of Itohan's arrival after Ehi made his comment didn't go unnoticed. His family had turned to see the object of Eseosa's affection. Truth be told, his too. Osaro was already facing her, so took a minute to take in her appearance.

As usual, she was flawless in a simple pair of ripped, faded jeans and a pink t-shirt she gathered up to the side in a knot. On her head was a baseball hat that said G.L.O.W. Her eyes were covered with oversized sunglasses, but he could feel her stare.

The other stare he felt was his auntie's at his side, but he refused to meet it. Although he tried not to give her the satisfaction of knowing it, she knew him better than anyone else and he wasn't up for questions. Itohan bent down and hugged Eseosa tight. They talked for a few seconds, then his niece grabbed her hand and started pulling her toward them.

"That's her teacher," Osaro whispered to the group.

"Uh hum...," Auntie Lizzy nudged him with her shoulder and he paid her absolutely no attention. Now wasn't the time.

"Hello, everyone," Itohan said when she got to them.

"This is my Nana Lizzy; this is my Uncle Ehi and my Auntie Robin and my Uncle Ro." Osaro watched Eseosa make the introductions like the young lady she thought she was.

Itohan walked closer to Auntie Lizzy. "*Ko ỳe*, Ma." She curtsied and bowed slightly at the same time.

"*Ko ovbi mwen*, my daughter. How are you?" She put her hand on Itohan's shoulder and glanced over at Osaro.

He intentionally didn't talk about Itohan with his family, so they didn't know that she was Nigerian, or more specifically that she was from Edo State like they were. He was a bit thrown off that she greeted them in their native language and it was kinda sexy to him.

"I'm fine, Ma. Thank you." Itohan turned to Ehi and Robin. She'd yet to acknowledge Osaro. Whether it was intentional or not, he wasn't sure.

"So, you're my niece's *teacher*," Ehi said. It wasn't really a question and with the way he drew out the word teacher, Osaro knew what he was getting at.

"That would be me. I get the pleasure of spending time with this lovely little lady, five days a week." Itohan smiled down at Eseosa who was still holding on to her hand.

"Well, thank you for all you do. Glad that Baby Cakes is in good hands. This is my wife, Robin."

"Baby Cakes, huh?" Itohan tweaked Eseosa's nose and she busted into a fit of giggles.

"Hey," Robin said. She gave Itohan a side hug.

"Hi, nice to meet you."

Osaro liked that Itohan was comfortable around everyone, but he was also irritated that she seemed to be taking her time getting to him. He folded his arms across his chest and decided to see how long she'd be able to drag this out.

"Same here; I love your hat. That's dope." Robin complimented her.

Itohan smiled and shared where she got it from at Robin's request. There was an awkward silence, then Itohan walked over to Osaro.

"Hello, Mr...Osaro," Itohan said.

Before he could respond, one of the church women came over and dragged his aunt away. She visited his church whenever she came to see him over the weekend, so people knew her. As the two older women walked away, Osaro gave Ehi a knowing stare. His brother got the message and left with Robin who peeled Esesoa away with the promise of a lollipop.

With them alone, he faced Itohan and stared down at her. He noticed her shift from one leg to the other.

"You're not speaking today?" she asked.

"It took you long enough to get to me. I didn't think you really wanted to speak to me," he said, his voice monotone.

"Well, truth be told I didn't, but it would be rude not to…considering—"

"Oh, so I'm an afterthought?" He placed his hands in his pockets and nodded his head.

"Err…"

He took off her glasses and put them in his breast pocket. "Nah, be a big girl and take these off when you trying to be smart."

She squinted a few times, adjusting to the direct sunlight. He caught the amusement in her eyes when they landed on him.

"I don't know about you, but my mouth and eyes aren't connected," she sassed.

"Okay, I see this mouth gonna be a problem."

"You seem to bring it out, so the cure might be to watch the company I keep." She shrugged.

"That's two strikes, woman. Don't go for a third."

Osaro smirked when she raised her brow, but he raised his higher, silently daring her to challenge him. She relaxed, and he smiled.

"Now was that so hard?" he asked.

"Ugh." She turned her head to look around. "Is this your church?"

"Yes, and I haven't seen you here before so…"

"My teaching assistant invited me. Was gonna decline, but seeing how important it was to her, I decided not to."

"Well, I'm glad you didn't."

"Good morning. Please gather 'round."

Osaro heard Mr. Parker, the head of the organizing committee started speaking over a megaphone.

Osaro took Itohan's hand and started to walk toward the spot where everyone was gathering. He did it out of habit as a protector, but was glad when she didn't withdraw from him. In comfortable silence, they walked the short distance to the middle of the church grounds. Over the next couple of minutes, Mr. Parker announced the agenda for the day.

"Have fun everyone and thank you for volunteering your Saturday for the needy and displaced," Mr. Parker said.

Once he was done speakers boomed with "Overcomer" by Mandisa.

"I'm preparing care boxes. You wanna join me?" Osaro asked as everyone dispersed to the stations that had been set up. He watched his aunt and Ehi move in the opposite direction to the lunch station. Robin and Eseosa went to the station where clothes and shoes were inspected, making sure they met the standard before being accepted.

Itohan looked around. "I don't know where Tisha is. She invited me and might want me by her side."

"Come on. She'll see you by the table if she's looking for you." He took her hand again and led her to where they'd be stationed. Osaro was beginning to like the feel of her hand in his. What he liked more was the fact that she seemed to like it, too.

Over the next couple of hours, they put together care packages for families of four. As they worked with other church members, the duo talked about a variety of topics. From politics – Nigerian and American – to food, culture, favorite things and TV shows. He got to know that she went to school back home, was a photographer, and a homebody. Osaro shared as much as he could with her, careful not to shed too much light on the demons that haunted him. When he talked about his siblings, he found himself almost drifting to a place he knew would ruin the moment. He must've stopped talking as the next thing he knew, he was jolted out of his memory when he felt her hand on his arms. She was rubbing him in a soothing manner.

"How many of these do you have?" She pointed to the tattoo on his arm.

He stretched his arms out. "I have two arms, like most people."

"I mean tattoos, smarty." She absently traced the design with her fingers.

He was enjoying the contact, but knew she wasn't really aware. He decided to flex his muscles to mess with her. The way she jolted and withdrew, like she was caught stealing, was comical. Osaro chuckled and she avoided his eyes.

"I have three of them; one on each shoulder and one that only my future wife will get to see." He winked at her.

Itohan's eyes grew big like saucers and he laughed. The look of shock and embarrassment was priceless. He was having so much fun teasing her. Itohan rolled her eyes at him. She turned and continued putting the care boxes together.

"So, what's your story?"

Itohan looked around. "I don't have a story."

"Everyone has a story." He motioned for her to pass him a can of corn.

She handed him the can and he placed it in the box. "Even if I did, this isn't the place to tell it."

"Are you asking for some alone time with me?" He raised his brow.

"What? Huh? And you came up with that how?" she asked.

"You still owe me anyway."

"You tricked me," she countered.

"I've no idea what you mean." He feigned innocence.

Before, Osaro knew he wanted to get to know her, now he

craved it. He wasn't searching for a woman. However, the time they spent together had accelerated him past mere curiosity and any fight he had left. Besides, he'd always prayed for the right person, but at the right time. It wasn't the right time for him, but he'd learned a long time ago that life was too short to misuse the opportunities God places in your lap.

Lean not to your own understanding. Osaro sighed. God was making His plan known loud and clear as he heard the verse from Proverbs 3:5

"So, where are we going?" He grinned, but she didn't respond. He was about to ask again, but the announcer called for all the players that signed up for basketball.

"That would be my cue," he said.

Itohan furrowed her forehead. "Huh?"

"The men of the church have a basketball game. Just for fun," Osaro said.

She looked around and he knew she was trying to make up an excuse to leave. He hadn't had enough of her yet.

"Come watch me play. I need my personal cheerleader."

A crease took over her forehead. She was either getting ready to object or say something smart and he wasn't trying to hear either.

"Do it for the cause." He took off his shirt and gave it to her. "Don't leave. Besides, we got unfinished business."

He ran to the makeshift court that was set up for the six-man game. He turned back and looked at her clutching his shirt. She could easily give it to anyone in his family and vanish, but he wished she would stay. He hadn't had a sufficient dose of Itohan Adolo for the night and he wasn't ready to let her go.

11

The sweat on Osaro's skin made it glisten as the sun kissed it at a perfect angle. Itohan stood mesmerized at the perfection of God's creation. His locs were now hanging and kept together with a bandana tied around his head. She had intended to give his shirt to his brother and make her exit, but she couldn't will her legs to move.

The noises and cheers from the crowd brought her out of her trance. The makeshift scoreboard had #TeamRo leading by two points. She reached in her backpack for her camera since she never left home without it. The sight before her was too good to pass up. She took off her hat. Removing the lens cap, she brought the camera up to her eye and clicked away.

She captured Osaro with his hands on his knees studying his opponent's move; another of him offering a hand to someone who'd fallen. She captured him sitting, hands covering his face, scowling and slightly smirking, perfectly normal, candid moments. She continued to take pictures, clicking away, she was in a world of her own. Until she noticed he was posing for her when a ball passed him by.

Itohan laughed at the face he made. She lowered her camera and focused on the crowd who was now chanting Osaro's name. Despite his distraction, his team won. He sauntered over to her. With each step of his approach, she felt her body temperature rise. Whether the rise was caused by his effect on her or her nervousness of photographing him without permission, she wasn't sure yet.

"You have the tendency to get me in trouble." Osaro took the face towel he had hanging from his back pocket and wiped his face.

Lost for words, Itohan giggled.

"You got some good shots?" Osaro asked.

The scent of his cologne mixed with his sweat sent her senses into a frenzy. She backed away some. He smiled and extended his hand. She removed his shirt that was hanging over her shoulder and handed it to him.

"So, did you?" He put his shirt on.

"Erm…yeah I did. Sorry I didn't ask first."

Osaro took off his bandana and replaced it with his snapback. "Don't worry about it. Come on. It's time for lunch." He led her to the table at the corner where sandwiches were set up for the volunteers.

Everything within her screamed that getting too close to this man was bad news. But his charm mixed with the mystery of him drew her in like a magnetic force she couldn't ignore.

"I should probably look for Tisha. She invited me and I haven't seen her."

She looked around her and saw Tisha on the other side of the church lawn. Their eyes met. Tisha waved and began walking towards them. Itohan felt bad about not checking in.

"Is that her?" Osaro asked.

Itohan nodded.

"She doesn't look like she's upset or ready to go. Let me go grab us something to eat and you talk to her." He began to walk away, but then stopped. "You wouldn't sneak away, now would you?"

Itohan giggled. "No, I won't."

Osaro smirked and walked away.

"Hey, Itohan," Tisha said when she got to her.

"Hey, Tisha, this is great. Thank you for inviting me."

"I'm so glad you could make it. I didn't see you when I walked in," she said.

"I was by the care package table."

"Are you leaving any time soon? And I see you've met Ro." Tisha pointed to Osaro.

At the mention of Osaro's name, Itohan's curiosity was piqued.

Tisha didn't act like she knew Osaro when she showed her Eseosa's picture. She wanted to know how she knew him, so asked.

"Oh, my sister pointed him out. You know this is her church. She said that Ro is the man to know." Tisha glanced over to where Osaro was. Itohan felt a twinge of unwelcome jealousy.

A few seconds later, someone yelled out Tisha's name. She turned to the person, waved and then turned back to Itohan. "I gotta go. Thank you for coming." Tisha hugged her before walking away.

Minutes later, Osaro approached her, "You ready?"

Itohan nodded. The thought that women vied for his attention unsettled her a little; as fine as he was, of course they did. But she still didn't like it.

"Come on. I got us a spot by the trees."

Itohan followed Osaro to a shaded area. He had a blanket laid out for them and a few hand-picked flowers tied together by a little string. They sat, and he took one flower out of the bunch and handed the rest to her.

Itohan took them from him with a faint smile. "Thank you. How did you pull this together?"

He detached the flower from the stem and stuck it on the right side of her hair. "I make things happen for what I want."

"And am I to assume what you want is me?"

"No need to assume. I'll tell you right out, I want to get to know you," Osaro said, his eyes never leaving hers. His voice held a certain authoritative confidence that scared and reassured her at the same time. Even with that, the sirens in her head went off when she remembered Tisha's comments.

"Are you asking me on a date?" She raised her brow. "And don't you have a girlfriend or enough attention?" she snapped and immediately regretted it.

With a blank expression, he took her hands and blessed the food. Not letting go of her hand, he spoke. "Do I have a girlfriend? No. Did I have one? Not really, it was an off and on affair that ended a year ago. Now, hear me when I say this next thing. It doesn't matter whose attention is on me because my attention is on you."

Itohan removed her hand from his and rubbed the back of her neck. Her breath hitched as she tried to get it back to its regular rhythm.

"Now that we got that covered, will you go out with me?"

"I can't. You're my student's guardian."

He furrowed his brow. "And? Is there a rule in your handbook that says that's forbidden?"

"No, but it's the principle of it all." She unscrewed the cap of her water bottle and drank.

"If you're going to turn me down, I need a better excuse, woman."

"I don't want Eseosa to be confused."

Osaro studied her. She knew he didn't believe her, but for now, that was her story.

"I'm a persistent man, Itohan, but we'll change the subject for now," he said. They ate in comfortable silence for a few minutes.

"What drew you to photography?"

"I adore all things beautiful. I marvel at God's creation, human or otherwise. So, when I come across something that just takes my breath away, I want to capture it."

"Wow, you spoke with so much passion. Before you noticed I was posing, you were lost in the moment. That's sexy. To live without the passion for anything is inexcusable." He drank from his bottled water. "By the way, I'm glad I take your breath away. You take mine away, too."

Itohan's cheeks flushed. She saw him as more than beautiful, but those thoughts she'd keep to herself for now. Instead of giving him a response, she changed the subject.

"You were great out there. It's almost like you played professionally."

He remained silent and for a minute and stared off into space. He gave her a contemplative look, as though he was struggling with how much to tell her.

"That was my dream." he said softly.

The shift in his mood gave her chills. Itohan regretted asking him, but couldn't resist the need to know more.

"Was?"

Osaro told her the story of his basketball ambition in high school and the pressure to provide for his family.

"I was so excited and terrified at the same time, that I made a stupid decision that changed the course of my life."

Itohan waited for him to fill up the holes in the story. She knew they were there because she also knew how to tell a story, but not really tell it. That's how she got by for years without people knowing she was of royal lineage. As a child, she was confused on what her royal heritage meant. But her father was quick to educate them that it could be likened to the British, Monaco or any other monarchy in the world. Although her father wasn't in direct linage to the throne of Benin, she was still a princess and her father always insisted she carry and conduct herself different. All that went out the door when Aidenoje entered the picture.

When Osaro didn't fill in the holes of his story, she decided to let it go. "I'm so sorry to hear that," Itohan said.

"Have you always wanted to be a teacher?" Osaro asked, changing the topic. They had finished eating and began gathering up their mess.

"Yes, for as far back as I can remember. I used to be the one that taught my siblings after school." She finished off her Strawberry Kiwi Snapple and set the bottle down. "My brother had a hard time with math at a point in secondary school and I took it as a personal challenge to make sure he got up to speed. No brother of mine would lag behind."

Osaro laughed. "That sounds like me. Something about being the oldest, right?"

Itohan unwrapped the bite-sized brownie and nodded. "In my opinion, if you're the firstborn in an African home, you've already completed a course on leadership." She bit into the brownie.

Osaro threw his head back in laughter. "It should definitely qualify as experience."

Their laughter faded into a hypnotizing gaze. He lifted his thumb and swiped the chocolate remnant from the corner of her mouth. Her body shivered under his touch, but her eyes couldn't detangle themselves from his. He licked the chocolate off his thumb, drew her chin in and softly brushed his lips against hers. When he let her go, it was as though energy had vacated her body. This shouldn't be happening. Yet, as much as she told that to her mind, the heart she thought she had frozen shut was beginning to thaw. But what did her heart know? It'd been crushed by someone who was supposed to protect it forever.

***

"It's like I see him everywhere now. I'm telling you when he took off his shirt, I almost fainted," Itohan spoke into her Bluetooth. School was over, she'd gone home to change and was now on her way to fulfill the commitment she made to herself at the beginning of the year – work out at least two times a week. She loved her size ten frame but wanted to tone up more and get rid of the small pudge around her stomach.

"Itoh, if I didn't know better, I'd think you're smitten by the guy," Ajoke said

It'd been three days since the church fundraiser and this was the first time they could have a conversation. Keni was all the way in China and Itohan wouldn't dare mess up her sleep pattern by calling her.

"I don't know about smitten. He seems cool, but you know that's where it ends for me."

Ajoke sucked her teeth and Itohan knew she was also rolling her eyes. "So, wait oh, what is your game plan for your life? Are you going to be on this man strike for two more years? Three? A lifetime? Let us know so we can govern ourselves accordingly."

"I can't deal with the *wahala*."

"You can't, or you won't? Itohan shame the devil and start living your life again. You're merely existing, my friend."

"Both. I'm scared, Joks…I'm scared. You know how much I gave Aidenoje. If he could do that with so many years between us, I just don't have the power to try with anyone else." Itohan spoke truthfully. The idea of being in love was where it ended for her. She couldn't go through that again. Osaro had the ability to destroy every wall she'd erected and she couldn't allow that to happen to her again.

"Love is risky, but this is deeper than that. You still hate Aidenoje and hating him means that you care. You're still emotionally vested and until you deal with that, you can't move on."

"How? Everyone says move on. How? When I don't even know what the heck I did to deserve his actions. You're right Joks, I hate him. I hate what he did to me." Itohan pulled into the parking lot and began to sob.

"Come on, Itoh. Don't cry. You know neither Keni nor I are there. Please don't cry. But girl, this is not healthy." Ajoke chuckled.

"What's so funny?" Itohan was irritated. She was hurting, and everyone wanted to make light of it. Her mother acted like it didn't happen. And her friend and sister acted like she should just sweep it under the carpet.

"I know this is the wrong time, but do you know that this is the first time you've actually spoken about Aidenoje and said exactly what you felt. In all these years, this is the first time!"

"No, it's not."

"Yes, it is. You cried once or twice, but never spoke about it. After that it was, 'I'm fine.' That's all we heard, 'I'm fine.' You refused to confront it ever," Ajoke said.

"So? What's funny?"

"If you being around this man…what's his name?"

Itohan rolled her eyes. Ajoke was terrible with names. "Osaro."

"Oh ok. If Osaro could get you to cry and be open, it's because you're ready to try again. Your heart is, but your mind is speaking a different language. The best way to start healing is to confront. You can't heal from what you avoid." A beat of silence passed between them.

Itohan wiped her wet cheeks. Ajoke was right. The pain Aidenoje inflicted on her cut deep and she never wanted to experience that again. Since Saturday, she'd been unable to get Osaro off her mind. The way she felt now after spending time with him was way more intense than their initial run-ins. Her mind played their lunch over. Their conversation, his laughter, how gentle and caring he was with her and persistent. Very persistent. She didn't agree to a date, but she knew, somehow, that wouldn't be the last she saw of him in that regard.

"Now that you've at least admitted that you hate him, you can heal from it. So, you can fill your heart with the love of another occupant."

"I don't know how I can heal without getting closure or retribution," Itohan said.

"*Abeg*, Itoh, that's your wounded pride talking. You're still watching *Snapped*? Leave this revenge thing alone. God will avenge. Let Him deal with Aidenoje. God might have just saved you from marrying a buffoon. So just take the lesson and move on," Ajoke pleaded.

Itohan laughed manically. "People love quoting Scripture when the atrocity wasn't done to them. My father almost disowned me because I stood for my love for Aidenoje. Hundreds of people came for the traditional ceremony – all for what? For him to have the nerve, three years later, to ask for his dowry back. That he doesn't want me anymore. Oh, God! I could just die. Me? To get returned like unwanted merchandise.

"I was literally disgraced from Benin from the shame. My mother couldn't go anywhere without her fellow women pointing at her in gossip. Don't get me started on the financial loss." She sighed. "Then you hear people say, just thank God. Thank Him for what? I'm angry. Then my favorite, God will repay, vengeance is His…okay if it is, what is He waiting on?"

"How do you know He hasn't done something?" Ajoke asked softly.

"Because I would've heard about it. *Last last* through the grapevine back home," Itohan insisted.

"You can't even find him, so how're you going to hear when something bad happens?"

"Because humans, being who we are, like to spread bad news."

"I'll keep praying for you, Sis. I'll never say I know how you feel, but it is time for you to live again," Ajoke said.

Done with the conversation, Itohan glanced at her watch. She'd been in this car for twenty minutes of her gym time. Suddenly, Itohan could hear shouting and a thud in the background.

"My godson is really active tonight," Itohan said.

"Jesus is Lord. Let me go and see what's up. I hope he hasn't tricked his daddy into giving him candy this late."

"Okay, let me blow of some of this steam on the treadmill."

The friends said good night with a promise to check in in a couple of days. Itohan put her head against the steering wheel. She would never hate on her friend. She was genuinely happy for her. But her heart ached when she thought of how she was robbed of a family. She felt tears well back up in her eyes and she let them fall.

Moments later there was a knock on her window. Not thinking about her appearance, she lifted her head and was staring into the face of the man she least expected to see. She was trying to run away, so why did they keep running into each other?

Osaro made the gesture for her to wind down her glass with a frown on his face. She dabbed her wet cheeks with her palm while letting down the window.

"Whose behind do I need to kick for making you shed a tear?" Osaro asked with no single hint of amusement. His jaw was clenched like he was ready to hurt someone.

She gave him a faint smile, lowered her eyes and got out of the car. As she was gathering her gym bag, she took in a deep breath. *Father God, a person should never be this fine now. Ehen? Why?*

"Hey, Osaro. What are you doing here?"

"Hey, yourself, but I asked you a question." He gave her a stern look that told her he meant business.

Itohan glanced over him, committing his appearance to memory so she could get lost in it in the privacy of her bedroom later. Sweatpants, a snug white tee and Air Force Ones never looked so good. His hair hung down, tied in place with a bandana.

"It's nothing. I'm fine. How is Eseosa?"

"You saw her today, right? So, this is my time." He raised his hand to wipe the residue of her tears from her face. "You're too beautiful to be shedding tears. If I find out it's over a man, we'll have serious problems. Your man is supposed to keep a smile on your face, or at least make that his priority every day he draws breath."

They began to walk to the gym entrance.

"What are you doing here?"

"I came to fry fish," she teased. "What do people come to the gym to do?"

"Woman, why are you always so difficult?" he joked. "Is this how it's going to be with us?"

"Us?"

"I didn't stutter, did I? But back to my question. You better not be trying to lose any weight." He paused, and she looked at him. "You're perfect the way you are."

Itohan didn't know how to respond to that. She opted for "Thank you."

"No thanks necessary. It's the truth."

"I'm just trying to be healthy and toned."

"That I can get with, but I better not see a pound missing."

"What is it to you, *sef?*" she asked

Osaro laughed. "Is that what I do? Make you break out in Pidgin English?" He opened the door. "I like my woman just the way she is."

"Huh?"

"Once again, Beautiful, I didn't stutter. Go exercise and I'll see you when you're done."

She'd had enough shock for the last ten minutes, so didn't even bother responding. She faced the treadmills.

"Itohan." He pulled her back.

"Don't let any man in here get whooped on your account," he whispered in her ear and kissed her forehead.

"You need help."

"I know and I'm glad I got the right woman for the job." Osaro walked a couple of steps and paused. "Aye, come get me when you're about to leave."

Itohan shook her head and watched him walk to the back without waiting on her response. A part of her wanted to turn around and leave. She knew he'd come find her, though. She taught his niece, so if he wanted to, he could make up any number of reasons. She would stick tonight out, but she was considering changing her membership or switching days.

12

"One…Two…Three…" Malcolm counted.

"Argh," Osaro yelled out as he replaced the weight back on the bar.

"Good job, man. You on one hundred today. What's up?" he asked.

He and Malcolm worked out about three times a week. They normally met at six p.m. but Osaro had been running late trying to get Eseosa situated with the nanny. It must've been God's providence because he always beat Malcolm to the gym. His tardiness, however, was the only reason he ran into Itohan. Normally, he'd walk right past the treadmills where he now knew she spent her time. The haphazard way she parked drew his attention to the car. What confirmed that it was hers was the "Powered By Coffee" bumper sticker he noticed on there Saturday when he walked her to her car.

The protector in him became angry and irritated at the sight of her tears. The thought that a man might be behind it was driving him crazy. Why did the thought that she might have a man or that they were recently broken up never cross his mind? Now that it did, it wasn't sitting well with him because the fact that she might be crying over him meant she hasn't gotten over him. Or he still had a chance to slide back in.

The old him wouldn't have cared about another man. He would've shot his shot regardless. As a Christian, he wouldn't do that, so he had to find out where her mind was at as soon as possible.

"It's Itohan. I barely know her and she's driving me crazy," he confessed.

"Is she here?"

"Yeah, at the treadmills." Osaro stood and walked over to the dumbbells.

Malcolm stretched his neck toward the glass partition. "Man, she's been driving you insane since you met her."

"True, but now that I've spent time with her it's gone up a couple of notches." Osaro chuckled.

Malcom shrugged. "So, ask her out."

"I did. But now that I think about it, I didn't even ask if she got a man or not."

"So what did she say?"

"She gave me the whole "your niece is in my class" spiel. But I told her I wasn't having it. But now, maybe…"

"If she had a man, she would've straight shut you down. Come on man, you know a woman don't go out with another man when they're seriously seeing someone else," Malcolm said.

"That's what I thought, too. I can't stop thinking about her so I was ready to put in the work, but seeing her in tears knocked me off my square."

"You sound like you really interested."

"I am and if she doesn't have a man, she's as good as mine. All that stuff I said about a woman not being the move right now…" Osaro shook his head. "After spending time with her Saturday, I just knew man. I'm telling you, I want her. And I'm not trying to date just to date. I'm hoping to build something." As he spoke the words, Osaro realized how true they were. There was a calm and unsettling in his spirit at the same time.

Over the last three days, he'd come to realize that acknowledging the truth also had a way of pissing him off. He still was anticipating very busy months ahead at work. With his schedule, taking care of his niece and working on getting his auntie relocated in a couple of months, it was still true that now wasn't the ideal time to date. However, what was also clearer now was the fact that, in all that, Itohan was just going to have to fit in. He couldn't envision not having her smart mouth, witty attitude and soothing laugh in his every day.

"Do what you gotta do, player."

"Yeah, Imma have to," Osaro muttered, more to himself.

As they worked out, the men discussed business. Osaro lay on the bench and closed his eyes. He placed a small towel over his face when he felt a pair of eyes on him. His stomach summersaulted and he knew who was responsible for it. He took the towel off his face and caught her eyes.

"Hey, we didn't have a proper introduction the last time. I'm Mac," Malcolm walked over to Itohan and extended his hand.

Osaro sat up and observed her. The bun on her head was now messy with loose tresses. She still had on her running tights, but had exchanged the t-shirt she had on earlier for a sports bra. He silently willed her to use the running hoodie around her waist to cover up. He'd been doing good with the absence of physical intimacy. Not being near anyone he was remotely interested in, cold showers and morning runs helped. But she was a different story. He needed all his self-control and the Holy Spirit to help him out.

Itohan placed her hand in Malcolm's. "It's nice to meet you too and I'm sorry about what I said the first time we met."

"The only person you owe an apology is me. But we already established how you gonna make it up to me, right?" Osaro walked up to them. She pulled her running hoodie over her head and he sent up a word of thanks.

"Ugh…I'm ready to go home. Just came to let you know," she said.

"Good girl. I see you follow instructions."

Itohan folded her hands across her chest. "Not because I wanted to. But I don't want you popping up in the bushes somewhere. Since you seem to pop up everywhere."

Malcolm laughed.

Osaro shook his head. He found Saturday that he loved teasing her because the annoyed look and pout she sported was the sexiest thing ever.

"I see your smart mouth didn't learn from Saturday."

She lowered her eyes. If she were lighter, she would've changed color with the way she was blushing. He had warned her that she had one more strike, but after their lunch, she decided to test him. He'd tickled her until she was in tears and begging. She must be remembering the kiss he placed on her lips before letting her up.

"What happened Saturday?" Malcolm asked.

"Nothing really. He was being mean and bossy." Itohan rolled her eyes at Osaro. Then she turned back to Malcolm with a smile. "How do you deal with that?"

"He knows who to boss up on. Don't worry. I'll keep him in check." Malcolm winked at her.

"Don't be winking at her and making false promises. Mess around and hurt her feelings when you can't fulfill them." Osaro packed up his bag.

"You just can't help yourself, can you?" Itohan asked him.

"When it comes to you, no. You ready?"

She ignored him and turned to Malcolm. "Have a good night, Malcolm."

"Call me Mac, and you do the same, beautiful."

Itohan turned back to Osaro, frowned and headed toward the exit.

"Okay, I see both of you testing my gangsta." Osaro walked over to Malcolm and dapped him.

"You got a fire cracker on your hands, Bro," Malcolm whispered.

"Yeah, and you steady gingering her. Let me go see about her. As stubborn as she is, she just might get in her car and drive off."

Malcolm laughed. "Handle that. I'll see you in the morning."

Osaro walked out of the gym. Normally, he would take a quick shower, but he knew Itohan had to be in school the next day. He didn't want to keep her out any longer. He walked her to her car and leaned against the driver's door. She followed suit by his side.

"You feel better?" he asked.

"Yes, thanks."

"You wanna talk about it?"

"I'd rather not."

"I'm a good listener. I promise."

Itohan rubbed the back of her neck. "Maybe…someday."

"Oh okay, she's considering seeing me again." He rubbed his hands together. "I must be doing something right."

She giggled. "Osaro, can I go home now?"

"What I tell you about calling me that?"

"I'm not going to call you Ro. I'll call you Osa, how about that?"

"As long as you call me," he smirked.

Itohan chuckled. "Oh my gosh. That's so cheesy. Does it work?"

"I've been outta practice, woman. Give me a break." There was a beat of silence between them. He didn't want to dampen her mood, but he had to know. "Was a man the cause of your tears?"

She looked at him with her brows furrowed. She was probably contemplating how much, if any, she wanted to share.

"I was crying over a bad experience. I don't have time for men or a relationship right now."

Osaro kept his expression blank, but he was doing cartwheels of happiness inside. He knew that "no time for relationships" song. He wrote the lyrics and the good thing was that he could rewrite them.

"Fair enough."

"I'm going to head out now," she said.

"Okay, I know you got school tomorrow."

Itohan placed her hand over her chest and bowed her head. "Why thank you, kind sir."

Osaro gave her a warning look. "While you giving me a hard time plug your number in here." He handed her his phone. She hesitated. "Come on, I need to know you got home safe."

"Sure…" She took his phone and did as he asked.

"Thank you. That wasn't so hard, was it?"

Itohan chuckled and unlocked her car. He picked up the gym bag she had placed on the hood of her car and tossed it in the back seat. He opened the driver's door for her.

Osaro leveled his eyes against her for a few moments. He caressed her cheek with the back of his index finger. "Have a good night, beautiful."

She beamed, warming his heart. "You do the same, Osa."

He watched her back out and waited until her car disappeared onto the street. An unfamiliar leap in his chest confused him. He was in trouble and he knew it. He never had his thoughts dominated by a woman he hadn't taken out on a date yet.

13

The next day, Itohan stood under the shade, watching her students have fun during recess.

"Be careful, Jordan," she yelled at one of the students.

Itohan made small talk with the other teachers. Her mind, however, was far from present conversation. It was on her conversation with Ajoke and the encounter with Osaro the previous evening. Mulling over the chat with her friend, she realized that she had, for four years, bottled everything up inside. To hear out loud the intensity of her admission of animosity and hatred for Aidenoje shook her to tears. Then to crown it all, she tossed and turned all night at the terrifying realization that Osaro had the ability to disrupt the way she'd learned to cope with the invisible shackles that kept her heart safe.

"Ms. Adolo, Ms. Adolo, Eseosa is crying." One student tugged her.

Itohan threw all other thoughts aside and took off running to where the little girl pointed. Over the weeks, she had developed a soft spot for Eseosa. The feeling intensified when she got to spend time with the little girl and her family. Itohan bent over Eseosa where she lay on the grass holding her knee. Itohan's heart skipped as she saw the blood that trickled down her leg.

"What happened?" Itohan asked.

Osaro was so protective of this little girl that she was sure he'd pitch a fit if he was called to come get her. The way it looked, she was sure he'd be receiving a call.

"Jordan ran into her and she fell on this rock," Isabella said. She pointed to a small rock in the grass. She must have fallen hard to draw that much blood.

"Jordan, did you apologize?" Itohan asked.

"Yes, Ms. Adolo." Itohan saw remorse in the boy's eyes and nodded. She was sure he didn't set out to hurt Eseosa

"Eseosa, sweetie does it hurt a lot?"

"Yes." She had stopped crying and was now whimpering.

"Okay, I'll help you up. Ms. Tisha will go with you to the school clinic." Just then the bell rang and recess was over.

Itohan escorted the rest of the students into the class while Tisha and Eseosa went the opposite way.

Hours later, school was over and Itohan was packing up to go home. Eseosa never returned. The nurse had sent for her backpack when Osaro came to take her home. Itohan got in her car and put the key in the ignition. Before she started the car, she pulled out her phone and turned it back on. She'd texted Osaro earlier to find out how Eseosa was doing. Her heart beat with anticipation of his response. The phone dinged signifying it was on and she went to her texts messages. Her heart fell when she read the response.

Fine.

She refreshed this screen. Maybe all the messages hadn't loaded yet. But sadly, that was it. Irritation washed over her. What was his problem? She took in a breath. Maybe he just didn't feel like texting. He did tell her that texting wasn't his thing. She shrugged off her annoyance, started her car and drove off. She had to make a trip across town to get a replacement part for her new camera, so she had little time to think of Osaro now.

A few hours later, she stopped at Zaxby's and got a salad. She had no energy to cook. Food, shower and bed, in that order, were all that was on her agenda when she got home. Itohan knew she had pictures to edit, watermark and send out from the fiftieth birthday celebration she recently covered. She also had an application to fill out for a corporate photographic job she came across. However, with the day she had, none of that would be happening when she got home.

When she wasn't subbing, she conducted business from one of those monthly subscription office spaces downtown. But in a few months, she would be able to lease a small studio she'd had her eyes on for a while.

Later that evening, Itohan paused the movie she had playing and tossed the remote on the couch. She threw back the covers and walked into the kitchen to throw away her trash from dinner. She took out a cold Coca Cola from the fridge and returned to her spot. Sleep didn't come as easily for her when she got back home, so she decided to relax with the television.

Her thoughts were all over the place. They'd been nagging her all evening and she knew that unless she gave in, this was going to be another restless night. Osaro's one-word response bothered her more that she would've liked it to. She sighed. *This is why I like staying unbothered.* Against her better judgement, she decided to call. He'd stressed the "I'm a grown man line in her ear," but if he was ignoring her, he wasn't grown – he was petty.

"Hello," he answered.

"Uh, hello," she said. Itohan wasn't sure of his tone. "Osa?"

"Yeah, what's up?" his tone held no warmth.

"Err, nothing I was just calling to check on Eseosa. She was pretty shaken up and I wanted to make sure she was okay."

"She's fine… now." His tone was accusatory and that made Itohan's blood boil.

"You do know it was an accident, right?"

"That shouldn't have happened if she was being watched properly." His response was curt. "I had to step away from important clients because of it."

Itohan closed her eyes and removed the phone from her ear to gather herself before she responded. How dare he?

"I'm so sorry the almighty Mr. Ikimi had to step away from work to pick up his niece…"

"That's not the point. I wouldn't have had to if she was being supervised, preventing the whole thing."

"Are you saying I was negligent?" Her hand itched to meet his face, but for the phone. For someone so smart, he was acting dumb.

How had she allowed a relationship with her student's guardian get to the point where he could totally bring her out of character?

He remained silent. She could hear him clicking away on what she assumed was a computer keyboard. But before she hung up, she had something to say.

"You do realize she's a kid. Her getting hurt is bound to happen from time to time. In fact, she won't stop getting hurt into adulthood. You need to back off and give her room to grow."

Every other day, he wrote her a note about his niece. He wanted to know every detail of her day. It was smothering and she'd wanted to tell him for a while that he needed to loosen his hold.

"Yeah, ok," came his disinterested response.

Itohan hung up the phone. She was done. She needed to go back into her shell. It was a mistake to entertain him in any capacity in the first place. Now all she had to do was remember his rudeness when his handsome face tried to invade her mind.

***

Friday night, Itohan discarded her silk robe and stepped into the bubble-filled tub. When she was in Nigeria, showers were more her thing. They kind of still were. But with the kind of week she'd had, she deserved to put her claw-foot tub to good use. One of the things she loved about her apartment was that she was given full range to paint on moving in. She was restricted from performing any construction changes, but she didn't have time for that anyway.

Itohan felt a shudder ride through her body when she sank into the hot, Jasmine bath. She rested her head on the tile and allowed the melody of "Jamb Question" by Simi to fill the room. The standoffish attitude of the songstress to male attention should've been what she practiced when she saw Osaro. Now she had allowed him into her thoughts and couldn't get him out.

The day after she hung up on him, Eseosa came to school like she had no care in the world. The incident was the furthest thing from the little girl's mind as she, Jordan and Isabella got right back to being the playful kids they were.

And here she had been arguing with her big-headed uncle over what should've been a trivial issue. The next day, he sent an email sneaking in an apology into his request for her to keep an eye on his niece. The only reason she responded to him was that above all else, she was still Eseosa's teacher. Just as he had done, she gave him a one-liner.

Will do.

After that, he didn't contact her and she was just fine with that.

What had her bothered now was the job she had to do on Sunday. When Itohan got the email request for a photography job some weeks ago, it said "dedication reception." The problem now was that earlier, she got an email from the new mother stating that the service would start at 10 a. m. Itohan knew she didn't sign up to go to anybody's church. If she had known the job also included the service and not just the reception afterwards, she wouldn't have taken the job. When she sent an email back for clarification, the lady said her husband filled out the form wrong and it should've been church and reception dedication. All morning, she'd been wrestling with the unease of visiting a church after not being in one for so long.

In the years when she used to be a staunch churchgoer, God always had a way of making the message about her. She wasn't ready for that, especially when she hadn't gotten her pound of Aidenoje's flesh. She'd thought about it all day but couldn't in good conscience cancel at the last minute.

She sighed, stepped out of the water and got into the shower for a quick rinse. Her hot bath was supposed to relax her, but her anxiety about Sunday made its way back to the forefront of her mind. And Osaro refused to leave it, too. Itohan popped open her Tylenol PM and took two pills. She was in dire need of a restful sleep, eager to shut off her emotions at least for a good eight to ten hours. It was the weekend and she intended to sleep in and forget all about the hamster wheel her life had become. Before she met the dread-head man, her life was perfectly stuck in place.

14

"And then the snake stood up and slapped me. I landed in Africa."

"Hmm, that's good." Osaro twirled his pen between his fingers.

"Ro! What's wrong with you man?"

Osaro blinked. "What?"

Malcolm and Nancy, his assistant, sat across from him in his office. His eyes went to Nancy who had an arch in her brow.

"What?" Osaro repeated. The way they stared at him rubbed him the wrong way. It was late Friday and he really didn't want to be bothered.

"Do you need to leave?" Malcolm inquired.

"No, we're good. My bad. Continue," Osaro said.

His friend observed him for a few seconds and continued to break down the balance sheet and income statement for the third quarter. It was the end of September and they were going over their forecast for the fourth quarter against the estimated versus actual earnings for the present quarter end. South Tran had sent a memo, apparently to all prospective bidders, that the product launch had been moved to the beginning of the next year, but they were still on track to choose their new web partner after Thanksgiving. Since they had thought the decision would've been made and a first payment down, Malcolm had to adjust the forecast.

"Nancy, please make sure we send out a memo to those clients whose sites we have to renew next quarter confirming the contracted down time," Osaro said.

"Okay, I'll get on it." Nancy walked to the door. "After that I'll be leaving. Is there anything else I can get you?"

Osaro shook his head. "No thank you and have a nice weekend."

"Thanks, Nancy but I'm good as well. Now go before that husband of yours starts calling," Malcolm said.

Osaro looked at the time. It was past 6.p.m, but he was in no hurry to leave. If he'd been able to control his temper, he probably would've had plans. This was their final meeting of the day and Eseosa was spending the weekend with Ehi and Robin.

Malcolm leaned back in his chair and folded his arms across his chest. Osaro wasn't ready for the lecture he knew was coming, especially since he'd let his current situation interfere with business.

"So, are you going to speak, or do you need me to actually ask?"

Osaro groaned inwardly and stood. With his hands buried deep in his pockets, Osaro walked over to his open windows. He looked out over the view of Tampa Bay, but only saw her face. He had put his foot in his mouth big time and had quickly found out that Itohan was just as stubborn as he was, if not more. The minute she hung up on him, he knew he had sent himself back to ground zero with her.

His annoyance with himself didn't let him call her back, so he tried the next day with an email. Her two-word response told him she had seen right through him. He couldn't blame her, not in the least. But he had to do something to fix it.

Ehi and his aunt always talked about his overprotective tendencies and he had been doing better, but getting that call from the school nurse threw him for a loop. He was already having a bad morning with a client who wanted a third web design revision when all he offered was two. The fact that he'd already done so much work, and RoMac was still a growing company, were the only reasons he didn't walk away. One bad experience told to the right person could be detrimental.

When he got the call about his niece, he was taken back to the day he got the call about his sister. Eseosa, being a kid, had acted like the world had shut down and that frustrated him more. He never meant to take it out on Itohan. But he did and had to figure out a way to climb out of the hole he'd dug for himself.

Osaro took a deep breath, and turned to face Malcolm.

"What's going on?" he asked.

Osaro frowned and walked back to his desk and rested his body on the back of the chair. "Just having a bad couple of days."

"That, any blind man can see. I'm asking what's up?"

Reluctantly, Osaro trudged over to the front of his chair and sat. He ran his hand through his hair that now hung loose. He spent the next few minutes telling his friend what happened after he left that afternoon to pick up his niece. When he was done, Malcolm didn't respond. After a few more seconds, his friend's silence annoyed him.

"How you gonna ask what's wrong then be quiet when I tell you?"

"Whoa, you need to be mad at yourself, not me." He paused. "Look man, we've talked about this for years. Ivie's death isn't your fault. Until you truly accept that, this will continue to happen with Eseosa. You can't bring her mother back by holding on to her that tight. It's cute now that she's a kid. But if you continue, when she grows older, she'll resent you and won't be able to share things with you. Also, you'll never deem a woman fit to take care of her. No female dealing with you is going to put up with walking on eggshells when it comes to your niece."

"I get that." Osaro sighed.

"Do you?" Malcolm chuckled.

"I don't see nothing funny, man."

"How you go from not wanting a relationship to stressing over a woman? I didn't get it at first, but I'm starting to think maybe you should have kept your distance. How you lose something that's not even yours yet?" Malcolm snickered.

Osaro frowned at him. "Ha, ha, ha; very funny. Well, what's done is done. So, unless you trying to help, keep your opinion."

He should have just kept his problem to himself. He wasn't in the mood to be analyzed. What he needed was a way back to Itohan. Staying away from her was no longer an option. Osaro packed up some papers that he needed at home.

"You know I'm just messing with you. What does she like? What's she into? Think along those lines. You've not known her for long, but you should use the information she's shared to make her an offer she can't refuse."

"You're quoting Scarface now, so I know it's time to cut this conversation short." Osaro pushed back from the desk and Malcolm closed his laptop and stood.

"I'm serious, man. She sounds as stubborn as you, so you gotta come strong. No lame flowers and candy. Remember you're the one in the doghouse in this situation. She holds all the aces."

Osaro nodded. Malcolm, who was headed out of town early the next morning, also left to go to his office and pack up. The friends wished each other good night and went their separate ways.

Osaro put a little more pep in his step as he walked to his car. He grinned because talking to Malcolm had opened his eyes to what he'd overlooked. The two things he knew she loved were teaching and photography. When he thought of teaching, nothing came to mind. But with photography, the options made even him excited. He rubbed his hands together, unable to contain the smirk that formed on his face. He got in the car and pulled out. He had some research to do and he silently begged God for favor. He knew exactly the offer to make that he was sure she'd never refuse.

15

It was almost eight o'clock in the morning and Itohan should've taken her shower by now, but she was still standing in front of her closet deciding on what to wear. She could just hear her mother now, "You get your clothes out for church the day before."

Itohan shook her head and felt the tightening in her stomach. She had stayed up watching episodes of her favorite show she'd DVRed, and now she was planning to go praise the Lord. She wasn't really going for herself, but the mere fact that she would be in the vicinity and holy water might sprinkle on her when the baby was being baptized made her shudder.

"Oh jeez, I'm turning into a heathen," Itohan whispered to herself as she shifted from one leg to the other. She wasn't stupid. Itohan knew that holding on to her past was unhealthy and some days, she wanted to let everything go. Her hesitation was simple; she just didn't know how. How could she serve God when the anger and pain haunted her heart? She'd since concluded to stay away.

Itohan reached for a multicolored, Ankara, off-the-shoulder top with a flared waist and some dark blue, skinny jeans. The attire was nothing like what she would have dared wear to church if she were back home. She looked down and got her nude butterfly heels to go with her outfit. She opened the backpack that contained her camera and added her ballerina flats and flip-flops. Minutes later, she turned from side to side in front of the full-length mirror glancing over her frame. She gave herself a nod of approval and picked up her bag.

Entering the kitchen, she picked up a banana and a bottle of water. She had spent so much time undecided in front of her closet that she didn't factor in that she would have to eat. It was going to be a long day and she knew she was going to pay for that mistake.

When she arrived at the church, she spotted the couple in the parking lot immediately. She grinned at the sight before her. The husband had the baby in his arms while the woman fussed with her appearance in the car window. All the while, Itohan could read the man's lips, telling his wife she looked fine. She brought out her camera, hung the strap over her neck and quickly took some candid shots. She had gotten some pretty cool shots by the time the couple caught on to her. Itohan put her keys in her backpack and put it on her back.

"Hey Carol, you look great." Itohan complimented when she reached the couple.

"Are you sure?"

"Yes," Itohan and her husband, Ben, said in unison.

They shared a laugh and were joined shortly after by the rest of their guests and family. As the celebrants stepped into the church, Itohan hung back taking pictures. The church, Salt & Light Ministries, seemed like a medium-sized church. She found her place a couple of pews behind the new parents. A couple of minutes went by and she got up to take pictures. After a couple of shots, the usher told her she could only take pictures during the actual dedication. Itohan was annoyed because this meant instead of being busy, she'd have to sit through the sermon.

Soon after, church dancers got in formation on the sanctuary floor and started to mime to "Here to Sing" by Frank Edwards featuring Chee. As the song continued, she massaged the back of her neck at the edge of her hairline. A feeling of unease came upon her. The melody commanded surrender and reverence – things she had since forgotten how to do.

Itohan looked around and saw tears in the eyes of some. She adjusted herself in her seat as the song continued to play. She tapped her fingers on her camera that sat in her lap, breathing a sigh of relief as the performance came to an end. Next came prayer, then the collection, which to her, took forever, although it was in rapid succession.

An older man of medium build dressed in a tan suit came out next. Itohan shook her head. Only President Obama should ever be allowed to rock a tan suit. *This man just looks awful.* When he stepped up to the podium, Itohan heard someone by her whisper that they were glad pastor was back from his travel. Itohan quickly glanced up at the ceiling. Just in case thunder decided to strike her for talking about a pastor, she'd see it coming.

"Good morning, church," the pastor said.

The church responded to his greeting and he followed with a quick update of his travels and what he and his team accomplished while away.

"This morning, we have baby dedications. These proud parents are giving their babies back to the Lord." He clapped. "Congratulations."

The congregation responded with applause and cheers.

"So, let me tell you what happened to me over the weekend. Yesterday on our way back, we were at the terminal waiting to catch our flight. When they made the call for first class passengers, as I was about to step forward, this burly fellow cut me off and said, 'Excuse me, they called first class'."

The congregation gasped. Itohan wasn't shocked. She'd had experiences of people thinking she was less than because of how dark her skin was.

"I had just finished a two-week intensive work sharing the news of Christ and all I wanted to do was to come home. So, I didn't have a lot of God in me at that moment. My pride was wounded. How dare he insinuate that either I couldn't afford it or that I didn't belong there? Who did he think he was? I wanted to show him." The pastor's eyes roamed the congregation before he continued.

"Don't look at me funny, I'm telling the truth. Newsflash, when you become a Christian, the things that are naturally in you don't disappear. Your love for Him and reliance on His sovereignty pushes them to the background. It's a daily fight to die to self. Don't let anyone fool you that because they accepted Jesus, they are pristine and all their issues have disappeared like magic. Your spirit gets saved way before your mind does. That's why we're supposed to feed it with the Word of God. To combat the things that in our might, we can't. Well, I didn't do that yesterday. I did what the young kids call reading. I read the man."

The church hollered in laughter. The pastor raised his hand to calm them down.

"In a semi holy way of course. However, after I sat down, I realized my wounded pride caused me to want revenge. However little it might be. It caused me to think of Hannah. All she wanted was a child and Peninnah wounded her pride every day by taunting her. How would the story be different today if after she was given the child, she went and rubbed it in Peninnah's face? It would've felt good, but would she have been blessed? We're told to live peaceably with all men as much as it is in our power. My incident was little; Hannah's lasted a little while longer. Joseph could've had the ultimate payback, but how would that have changed his destiny?

"When we got settled on the plane, Romans 12:17 popped in my head. It says to live peaceably. *Repay no one evil for evil, but give thought to do what is honorable in the sight of all* and I repented. Now am I saying be a coward and let people walk all over you? No. I mean we don't have to attend every battle we're invited to. That is Christian living, representing Christ. I want to challenge these parents with new babies today, to lean on God to help raise them in His ways. In fact, church for this week, I challenge you to make Romans 12 your study chapter. May God's peace be with you."

Itohan let out a sigh of relief when the pastor wiped his bald head with a face towel, signaling the conclusion of the sermon. The church applauded and the pianist played a tune. Despite all the ruckus, Itohan heard, **Pray for your enemies, bless those who mistreat you.** She turned as those words played in the atmosphere. Her atmosphere. No one else seemed to hear the words but her, so she faced forward again.

Put your trust in Me. Itohan heard the voice again. She rubbed her neck and checked the time. It was almost ten-thirty.

"The church closes by eleven o' clock. Just thirty more minutes of this," she muttered to herself.

The new parents were called to the front for the dedication ceremony. Show time. Itohan took her camera and went to the front of the church to do what she was paid to do. As she clicked away from all available angles, she felt the goose pimples cover her skin. She shuddered. Only one person caused that reaction lately. Her eyes roamed the church quickly, but there was no sign of him.

Once the ceremony was over, Itohan took a couple more

pictures outside and left the church. She promised the couple she would see them in half an hour and went to her car. She needed to get out of this place. She needed air. She had run from God and all these "turn the other cheek" sermons. Hearing another one made her dizzy. For a few seconds, she wondered whether the thousand dollars booking fee was worth it. She cranked her car and here came the voice again…***Harden not your heart***.

"Okay, that it!" She sighed in frustration and raced out of the parking lot.

***

Itohan took off her heels and replaced them with her ballerina flats. She now had her curly hair up in a messy bun atop her head. She'd been at it for the past thirty minutes and her body was shutting down. Normally, a full day of taking pictures was nothing to her. The fact that her conscience continued playing the pastor's words in her brain was what was irritating her soul. She hadn't even found Aidenoje, had no idea of what his life was like, so she wasn't sure what punishment he deserved. At least until she got those details. Why couldn't she push the pastor's words from her brain as she had done everyone else's?

Itohan walked up to her client. "Carol, do you want to go put on your last outfit change?"

"Oh yes, yes. Today has been fantastic and I'm sure the pictures will be great. Did you get anything to eat yet?"

Itohan shook her head. "No, I wanted to finish."

"Oh no, please go get something. I want to clean Emily up a bit before I change her." Carol bounced the nine month old baby on her hip.

Itohan lifted her hand and caressed the baby's plump cheeks with the back of her hand. "Ok, how long will you be?"

"I'll be ready in about twenty minutes. I know your time is almost up and I'm so grateful. You went over and beyond what I thought today."

"Thanks. And no problem. I loved being a part of your day," Itohan reassured her.

"We'll be right back," Carol turned and walked to the staircase.

Itohan took a couple more shots of guests then headed to the space where the food was kept. She looked at the table and decided she didn't have a taste for anything there. What she craved in the moment was Amala and Ewedu. During the time she lived in Lagos, she fell in love with the dish. After weighing her options, Itohan settled for a salad only so she'd still be hungry when she got home and have room for what she really wanted. She cooked stew the day before and had some leftover Ewedu soup, so turning the Amala flour was the only thing left to do.

With her camera hanging on her neck, she picked up a bowl and put the vegetables together. As she was about to pour ranch dressing over it, she heard that voice. After slowly drizzling the dressing over her salad, Itohan replaced the container and shut her eyes.

"I'm sorry, Ben. I was at the church, but late. However, I had to make a quick stop at home," Osaro said.

Itohan took a breath and looked up at the ceiling. *Why now, ehn? I was just about to eat this salad and escape. Why now?* She questioned God.

She took her food and headed in the opposite direction of his voice. If she got through these few minutes waiting for Carol, she just might be able to escape any unnecessary conversation. No sooner had she sat on one of the chairs in the corner and lifted a forkful of lettuce to her lips did another man she had been dodging all afternoon step to her.

Without being invited, he sat next to her. "I see you're just now getting to eat something."

Itohan grunted and put the food in her mouth to prevent her from speaking. She wasn't trying to be rude, but her mind was troubled by two men and she hated it. The first one was in her past, and the second one was around here somewhere and she was trying to stay hidden at least for a while. She had no desire to entertain a third one.

"You should've let me get you something to eat when I offered before," he said.

Itohan cupped her hand over her mouth and gave him a polite smile. She slowed down her chewing to occupy her mouth a little bit longer.

"So how long have you been taking pictures? It's kind of not a profession you would see a woman in every day."

Itohan raised her brows at him. *Father God, if you get this man away from me I promise I will read that chapter twelve the pastor talked about.*

"I disagree, but you can say that I'm not like most women. I started about two years ago," Itohan replied. She had lost her appetite now, so she set the salad aside.

"So," he said coming closer to her. She leaned back. "May I have the pleasure of taking you out some time?"

Itohan rubbed her hand on the back of her neck.

"Hey baby, sorry I'm late."

She heard his voice from behind her but didn't react until she felt his lips on her neck. She turned around and looked at him. He winked at her and came around the front to her admirer. Itohan watched with her eyes bugged out as Osaro stretched his hand to introduce himself to the man. The man she now knew as Henry, in turn cut his eyes at her as if she had betrayed Jesus. She couldn't deal with the foolishness of their nonverbal testosterone battle. She picked up her salad and turned to leave when Osaro gripped her waist. He kissed her cheek.

"I'll be over in a minute, baby." He smirked.

Itohan had a vision of her hand landing across his face and slob flying out of it to the other room. She quickly dismissed the teasing vision because she knew there was no world in which she could slap Osaro. She pursed her lips together and nodded before turning to leave the two men standing there.

Thankfully, by the time she got back from dumping her uneaten salad, Carol was ready. She wanted a few more shots next to their faux fireplace and outside. In no time, Itohan was done and started to put her things together. She spotted Osaro talking to a group of men by the bar. She hugged Carol and slipped out of the door. She got to her car, grateful that she wasn't blocked in, opened the back door, put her bag in and exchanged her ballerina flats for her flip-flops. As she opened her driver's door to get in, she heard him.

"Is that how you dip on people that save you?"

Itohan put her head against the open door and took in a breath. *I promise God I won't talk about pastors again.* Itohan plastered on a smile and looked up at him.

He leaned against the car and folded his arms across his chest. He looked GQ delicious in the black blazer he wore over a blue cashmere V-neck sweater with brown khakis. If he weren't irritating her so much, she would've told him that. She was no longer angry with him, but she didn't want to be around him either.

"I didn't need saving—"

"First of all, you can plaster on a smile for everyone else except me." His eyes burned into her.

She scowled.

"That's better. I prefer a genuine expression than that fake stuff. If you're mad at me, which I know you are, let me know that. Second, I know that when you rub your neck, you're nervous or uncomfortable."

"That may be, but I didn't need saving from him."

"Oh, that was for me. I wasn't about to let you go out with anyone else before I made you an offer you couldn't refuse." He smiled at her.

She rolled her eyes. "You're quoting Scarface now?"

"Desperate times."

"Mr. Ikimi, what do you want? I'm hungry, tired and I need to go home. I have school tomorrow."

"You've been mad for just a couple days. How am I back to Mr. Ikimi?"

"Isn't that your name?" she challenged.

Itohan watched Osaro lift himself from the car. For someone in the wrong, he was awfully confident, but truth be told, that was one of the traits that attracted her. He walked around the open door and closed her in. He leaned in on her. His lips were so close to her earlobe that one move and they would brush up against it.

"I'm gonna let you have that since I messed up, but I'm still Osa, baby." He used his lips to tug her earlobe then stood to his full height. "Understood?"

Itohan nodded when her voice failed. Her body tingled. Some of her body parts probably thought she was dead after all these years. But this man was changing that at a pace she couldn't understand but was fighting with all her might.

"Now that we've reestablished that, may I take you out on a date? I want to apologize properly." He gave her back her personal space.

She started to shake her head and he came closer. Itohan turned her head, suddenly aware that they were still in the front of someone else's yard.

"What do you say?"

She held out her hand to stop him from coming any closer. "Ok, call me later. I really need to go."

He caressed her cheek with the back of his hand. "That's my girl."

Osaro stepped aside and allowed her to get into the driver's seat. He closed the door behind her and tapped on the hood. Itohan backed up and headed out of the subdivision. She shrugged when she regained her normal breathing pattern. She was tired of fighting him. She knew the date would be a lame dinner or movie date. Once she got it out of the way, she would tell him that at least she gave him his date and be done with him and his *wahala*.

16

The following Friday evening, Osaro stood in front of the bathroom mirror and brushed his facial hair. He set the brush down, inspecting himself. He rubbed his hands together in anticipation of the evening. He turned his head from side to side as he checked out his freshly twisted locs. He had them in two single braids down his back.

He couldn't believe his luck when he walked into Ben's child dedication ceremony and saw Itohan talking pictures. He shook his head and adjusted the collar of his baby-blue dress shirt. Take that back – luck had nothing to do with it. It was the favor that he had asked God for days prior. He made sure his shirt was properly tucked into his navy-blue khakis and left the bathroom. Waking out to his adjoining bedroom, he picked up his tan blazer and keys and headed out.

Effortlessly navigating his SUV, his mind travelled back to last Sunday. He'd been late to the church because at the last minute, Robin decided she'd bring Eseosa back in the evening instead of that morning as previously agreed. After a dismal weekend, he was eager to get his niece back. But the Big Man upstairs had other plans.

When he got to the church and saw Itohan, he was glad his niece wasn't there. He was sure Itohan would've agreed to anything if Eseosa pressured her enough. However, he wanted her to agree to see him because of him – not Eseosa. After church, he dipped because he got a call his house alarm was going off. The false alarm annoyed him, but what got his blood hot was seeing that Henry guy trying to encroach on what he'd since claimed as his.

After convincing Itohan to give him another shot, they'd kept in constant communication all week. He chuckled remembering how she initially gave him grief when he demanded she let him know she got home safe at the end of each day. After fussing about being fine before she met him, he quickly told her that old things have passed away. She gave up the fight when he didn't relent.

Osaro pulled into her apartment complex. He put the car in park and walked up to her door. He pressed the bell and waited. His chest tightened like he was a schoolboy on prom night.

"Hi Osaro, please come in," Itohan said, opening the door.

He handed her the flowers he brought for her. "Hey, you. These are for you."

She took them, sniffed and stepped aside for him to enter. When she smiled, Osaro felt his heart lose its steady beat.

"Thank you. I'll put these in water, get my purse and we'll be on our way."

Osaro walked into her living room and browsed over her décor. He liked it. Immediately he returned his gaze to her. He leaned against the couch and took in her profile. Her hair was in big loose curls that stopped at her shoulders. The sway of her hips as she sauntered around the open kitchen had him mesmerized. The knee-length, loose fit, red, Ankara dress did nothing to hide her curves. It also gave him a distractingly perfect view of her shapely legs. He loved what she had on and knew for sure he wouldn't be the only man mesmerized. But he wouldn't hesitate to check anyone that looked at her with a bit too much admiration.

"Okay, I'm ready." Itohan said, breaking his thoughts.

Osaro stood aside for her to walk ahead. He took the keys from her, locked the door and gave them back. Placing his hand on the small of her back, he led her down the short steps. He helped her into the car, made sure she was buckled in properly and walked over to his side.

"You still won't tell me where we're going?" she asked as he backed up.

"Nope," he responded.

"You said dress casual, so I hope I'm good?"

He glanced over at her. "You look beautiful. Sorry I didn't say that earlier. I was concentrating on other things." He winked.

"Okay o. If I'm underdressed, I'm killing you."

He laughed. "I'll gladly take your hands on me."

"I see you. Nasty. I thought you were a Jesus boy."

"And? Where do people get this notion that Christian men are somehow lame?"

She shrugged. "Isn't the talk or insinuation of sex taboo?"

"I have no idea who your pastor is, but to answer your question, no. Our sexuality is part of who we are from the moment that we're born. As a matter of fact, the mere knowledge of that sexuality is what made you desirable to me. If not, I'd be home doing something else. My sexual desires are there by God's design. Wasn't it Him that didn't think it wise for Adam to be alone? That was not only for her to be a companion but also to procreate." He felt her gaze fixed on him and he chuckled. "He wanted them to get it ooooonn."

Itohan gasped. "Get it on? Who says that anymore?"

"I just did."

"Your age is showing." She giggled.

The sound of her laugh was like a sweet melody in his soul.

"Woman, I'm only thirty-three, but let me finish my point."

Itohan raised her hand in mock surrender.

"So where was …?"

"Getting it on." She chuckled.

He gave her a warning look and was amused when she tried to stifle her laugh.

"We all have desires and sexual needs are just one of them. Because of Jesus, I know how to pump my brakes before they get outta hand." He glanced over at her and waggled his eyebrows. "Same reason I know my body, like yours is a temple. You can't let every spirit access it even if they desire it. Why it's such a taboo topic is beyond me."

"You sound like you've given this a lot of thought."

"It's stuff I've lived through since I became celibate a year ago. Those urges don't go away because you've been dipped in water at baptism." Osaro chuckled. "My gripe, though, is the church shies away from talking about something as natural as sex. Truth be told, that's why we have all this internet porn addicts and all these undercover sexual crimes. That's why my pastor is perfect for me. He breaks it down in a relatable way and I meditate and study the Word for myself."

Osaro cut his eyes from the road and glanced at Itohan. She was doing her thing with her neck.

"Which part of what I said made you uncomfortable?" he asked.

"None of it, actually. I'm not close enough to the topic to comment, but I see your point."

"Not too close to what? Sexuality or God?"

"At this point both, unfortunately," she whispered, looking out of the window.

He reached for her hand. "Don't turn away from me. You wanna talk about it?"

The sexuality part, probably was associated with the not having time for men stuff she said earlier. What he didn't understand was the God piece. Osaro knew there was no way she grew up in a *Naija* home and didn't have a relationship with Jesus in some capacity. He remembered when he was growing up, one of his classmate said they didn't believe in God. He looked at them like they had lost their minds because he didn't even know that that was an option. Auntie Lizzy would hammer the Jesus in you. By fire by force, you were believing in God. So whatever had happened to Itohan must have taken place in her adulthood.

"Maybe some other time." She lowered her head.

"Look baby, I don't judge. Do I want you to know Jesus like I do? Of course, but my job isn't to force salvation on you. My job is to lead you to Him through my actions. Once you get there, He'll take it from there."

She didn't respond, and he didn't press her further. He wanted her to have fun tonight and he knew that when they got to their destination, she'd do just that. He gave her hand a gentle squeeze and gave her a reassuring smile. The rest of the ride was made in comfortable silence.

He pulled into the parking lot and she squirmed in her seat. Osaro put the car in park and chuckled as she bounced up and down.

"It's a lie. It's a lie." She looked over at him and cupped her hand over her mouth. "The tickets to this place are sold out three months in advance!"

"Hang on, baby." Osaro got out and jogged over to her side to open the door. He helped her out and took her hand in his.

They walked to the entrance of the MasterCraft Art Tour & Exhibit. When he decided he'd bring her here, one thing made it impossible. The tickets were sold out for months. He had connections, but he didn't know anyone in this sphere. At least he thought he didn't. One night while he was expressing his frustration to his friends, Tekena came to the rescue. He had a friend in the circuit who could help. At that point, Osaro could care less how expensive the tickets were. He got two immediately. After he got the tickets, he called in another favor. Again, it was the favor of God because his next surprise wasn't even supposed to be in Florida this weekend.

Osaro nudged Itohan's shoulder as they were escorted to where their tour guide would meet them. She'd been eerily silent after her initial reaction.

"Are you all right?" he asked.

"Err...yes. I'm just speechless."

"You're kidding me. You, speechless? I must've done good."

She beamed at him. "You did great!"

He pumped his fist in the air.

"There's no one else here," Itohan said. "Are we the only ones taking the tour? That can't be."

"Yeah, maybe they're on the way." He shrugged.

She leaned her head slightly on his shoulder and he put his arm around her waist. He looked up and saw one of the male attendees looking at them. He followed the man's gaze and it landed on Itohan's legs. Osaro frowned and it occurred to him that with her posture, her dress rose a little.

He raised his brow at the man, issuing a nonverbal warning and the man looked away. Osaro looked around to see if there were any others.

"Err baby, I love the feel of your head on my shoulder. But I am anti-jail and if another man stares at your legs, I might end up there," Osaro said.

"Don't be silly."

"You call it silly, I call it taking precautions." Osaro looked over her and saw his big surprise walking toward them.

Itohan turned around and her mouth dropped. Osaro chuckled and took her hand. The man walked up to him. He and Osaro dapped each other while Itohan remained frozen.

"Hey, beautiful. You must be Ms. Itohan Adolo," Mitchell Clay said.

Mr. Clay was a renowned, new age photographer. Osaro knew nothing about the guy, but when he started to do some research, he was intrigued by the man's stats. Mr. Clay's expertise was in his passion for the wonders of creation. According to Google, it birthed the multiple awarding winning "In the Beginning Series" which he started when he was just sixteen. His travel was extensive and his work was only displayed in select galleries with this being one of them. Osaro understood why Itohan thought he was dope.

Itohan remained silent. Osaro waved his hand in front of her. "Baby?"

She turned to him. "Do...do...you know who this is?"

Osaro chuckled again. "Yes, I do baby and by your expression, so do you. But watch it, the only man that should make you speechless is me."

That brought her out of her trance as she hit him on his shoulder. She turned to Mitchell Clay. "Mr. Clay, I'm a huge fan of your work."

Mitchell nodded his head. "Thank you. I've seen some of your work as well and you're quite talented."

Osaro smiled as Itohan blushed. "You've seen my...my pictures?"

Mitchell nodded and turned to Osaro. Itohan looked at him and a tear formed in the corner of her eye. Osaro thumbed it away and she hugged him while burying her face in his chest. Osaro kissed the top of her head and pulled her away. Her eyes held gratitude. He kissed her forehead and whispered. "You're welcome."

After Malcolm talked to him about things she was interested in, he remembered her mentioning Clay. The way she gushed over him almost made him jealous. He didn't know Clay personally, but knew he was related to one of his clients. It cost him a free client consultation, a redesign and enhancement for their website, but the look on Itohan's face was worth it. When he was finally connected to Clay, he showed him Itohan's website where she had her pictures.

"Today, I'll have the pleasure of being your guide," Mitchell said. "I'll take you behind the scenes and then you can ask me questions about my own private collection. Sounds good?"

Itohan nodded and before Osaro could comprehend what was happening, she turned to him and kissed him full on the lips. She wiped his lips with her thumb, rubbing off her lipstick.

Itohan cupped his face in her hands. "You'll never know what this means to me."

"Your happiness is my life's mission."

Mitchell cleared his throat. They both smiled, and then hand in hand, they followed his lead.

***

"I feel so silly and stupid," Itohan said.

"Don't say that about yourself." Osaro glanced over at her. They had left the gallery about an hour ago. Itohan was so excited that she told him she'd take a raincheck on dinner. If he had known she would be so full on emotions, he would've fed her first. She pleaded that she was fine and he didn't want to come off as bossy, so he let her have her way. But he couldn't let her starve so he took her to a Suya Joint he recently found out about. He bought several sticks of the spicy, skewered, lean meat and something for them to drink. It was now a quarter to midnight and they'd been in his car with their seats reclined, talking. They discussed light topics that made them laugh and tease each other. Everything was good until she asked and he told her exactly how his parents died.

"I'm so sorry. That's horrible. Them being taken away like that, and from you at such a young age. Meanwhile silly me, here I am, I have parents, but I dodge them any chance I get," Itohan said.

"Why do you?"

"I haven't always lived up to the expectation or standards they set for me and they never let me forget it. So instead of dealing with it, I just let them be."

"Take it from me; don't let the distance go on too long. I love my auntie, but you only get one set of parents. Talk to them. It might not be that bad."

"Hmm…I'll try again," she said.

Osaro turned his body to look at her. He reached over and tucked her hair behind her ears. "You're so beautiful."

She lowered her eyes. "Thank you."

"My own Chocomilo." Osaro caressed her cheek.

Itohan laughed. "What do you know about Chocomilo?"

Her dark skin reminded Osaro of the cube-sized confectionary made from the Milo energy drink. He was introduced to the treat during his stay back home.

"A lot, smarty." Osaro paused.

"You're easy on the eyes as well. Very easy as a matter of fact. I see myself in serious trouble."

"We'll be in trouble together." A beat of silence passed between them. "You sure there's no man I should be worried about?"

She studied him for a few seconds. "No, there's no man. But you've asked me that before."

"Yeah, and you never gave me a straight no. You gave me the 'I don't have time for men' line," he said. "That tells me you're hurting or recently been hurt; like you still have feelings for this person."

Osaro studied her face for a confirmation of his suspicion. Her expression was blank.

"I have been hurt. No, I don't have feelings for this person. I did. But I'm not ready to talk about it."

"When you're ready to talk about it, I'm all ears. As long as I'm not competing with a ghost." Osaro ran his hand through his hair. On Itohan's insistence, he'd let his hair down earlier. She claimed she wanted to touch it. Her hand in his hair felt so good, but he had to stop her before they got carried away.

"Tell me about Cassie," Itohan said.

"What do you want to know? You know she and I had an off and on thing. We were convenient lovers."

"Why did it end?"

"Simple – as I got older, we wanted different things. It was never about love, but familiarity and convenience."

"Explain?"

"I want to settle down eventually. I want a family with the woman who'll trust me to lead, love, protect and provide for her and our family."

Itohan's brow shot up. "Provide for? Like barefoot and pregnant?"

"No baby, my woman making her own money is sexy, but we'll be spending mine. That's what I mean by provide for." He winked. "A relationship that thrives on mutual respect with one who will walk beside and not behind me, make me a better version of myself as I'll make her. One I can laugh with and argue with, but we both know we're in it for forever. Because we're committed to each other," Osaro finished.

Her expression told him her brain was churning.

"You...what do you want?"

Itohan shrugged. "Pretty much the same thing and consistency, an inconsistent man shakes my trust. I have no problem submitting, but I need to see something to submit to."

Osaro banked her response in his memory.

"Can I ask you a question?"

"Sure," Osaro responded.

"Why do you hold on to your niece so tight?"

He turned away from her and said on a low whisper, "Because I killed her mother."

Itohan broke out into a coughing fit. Osaro turned around and took the Fanta Orange she had out of her hand. He knew the beverage must have gone down the wrong way with his confession. He patted and rubbed her back.

"You what?"

The way her eyes bugged out at him, he knew he had to explain himself quick.

17

"No, I didn't mean it like that. I mean, I'm the reason she died."

"Same difference. Explain." Itohan turned her body to face him, folding her legs under her. Her heart raced anticipating his response. They'd had an amazing night. He rendered her speechless with his surprise. Once she stopped resisting him and relaxed, she found out that he – underneath his no nonsense, take charge, pseudo aggression – was a nice, caring gentleman.

"If I'd done what I was supposed to do, she'd still be here today," he said calmly.

"Osa, you just told me that you killed your sister or were responsible for her demise. So, stop taking in parables and tell me what happened." Itohan placed her hand on the back of his and massaged it gently. She knew whatever happened wasn't intentional. That much she knew of him and if she was wrong, then she'd totally misjudged him.

Over the next several minutes, Osaro told her what she considered a heck of a story.

"If I hadn't taken those steroids, I could've played ball professionally, my family would've moved out of the hood, and she wouldn't have fallen into the wrong hands if I'd been here. I was responsible for protecting her. Me!" His voice was shaky as he hit his chest repeatedly.

Itohan sat in awe. His anguish pierced her heart. She couldn't believe he blamed himself and to think he had carried the guilt around for years. She knew the responsibility first children carried in Nigeria and being a boy, there was a lot of pressure. But he was a kid, a sixteen-year-old kid. He shouldn't have been responsible for anyone. He refused to look at her. He placed his cupped hands over his face as his shoulders shook slightly. She felt helpless. She tried to pry open his hands, but he didn't let up.

"I should've just said no. I should've said no. I could do it. I knew I could, but I panicked. When we were kids, the one thing I always promised her and Ehi before we slept was that I was going to take them out of the neighborhood. I promised. I promised!"

Itohan couldn't take it anymore. She opened her door, not bothering to put on her shoes, walked around to the driver's side and opened his door. Only then did he look up at her, confusion etched on his face. He turned to face her, putting his legs out of the car. Itohan got between his legs and held on to his face. He lowered his eyes.

"Osa, look at me," she commanded. He did. "I know someone must've told you this before, but the way you just wept shows you haven't let it sink in. Letting it go in one ear and out the other. I'm so sorry about your sister. But…hold on." Itohan placed one of her hands over his ear. She then bent to his other ear. "You're not responsible for her death. You're carrying a burden that isn't yours to carry." She blocked his other ear with her other hand and straightened herself. She moved his head slightly from side to side.

His glossy eyes carried a faint smile confirming that he caught on to what she was doing. Her heart fluttered in relief. Despite his present anguish, she'd placed a smile on his face. He circled his arms around her waist and hugged her. Unsure of what to do in that moment, she lifted her hands and massaged his scalp.

"If you're about to say anything else and you want me to hear or understand, you better stop." Osaro grumbled, not lifting his head.

Itohan giggled and tried lifting his head. He resisted at first then gave in. She figured he was probably embarrassed at crying in front of her and was trying to play it off.

"What, woman? I was comfortable with my head where it was."

"Osa, did you hear what I said?"

"You blocked both my ears to make sure it didn't get out, so I'm sure it's in there somewhere."

"I'm serious."

"Look, baby, I didn't mean to break down. It's been four years and I haven't cried like that ever." He looked up at her. "You see what you do to me? You're the only woman I've ever shed a tear in front of; you're quickly becoming my safe place."

Itohan massaged her neck. Their connection was taking on a life of its own. His words made her lightheaded. But then Aidenoje was the exact same way in the beginning. The fear that overcame her was crippling. She could feel him staring at her, but this time she was the one who didn't meet his stare. She cleared her throat and stepped back.

"Baby, if you don't tell me what's going on, I can't fix it," Osaro pleaded.

"You can't save everybody Osa."

"Wow…okay," he said, his tone annoyed.

"I'm sorry. Sorry, I didn't mean that." She paused, meeting with his scowl. "It's just that I don't need you to fix anything. I'm fine. Can we drop it?" Her eyes pleaded with him.

"For now," He caressed her cheek with the back of his hand.

"It's getting late. I should go."

Osaro reached over to the passenger side and got her shoes and purse. "You wanna put these on?"

Itohan took her purse from him then contemplated her shoes. She hated heels, but they were a necessary evil. She always carried her flats, but since this was a date, she didn't. This was the first time in years she had been on one. Before she could say anything else, Osaro got out of the car and lifted her bridal style. He used his hip to close his door and headed to her apartment.

"Osa, what are you doing?"

"Carrying you. You were taking too long." He narrowed his gaze at her eyebrows.

It was a good thing he was carrying her. Because any time he gave her those intense stares, she had to catch herself from buckling at the knee.

"My nosy neighbors might see you. Put me down," she said in a hushed whisper.

"I'm not understanding how that's a problem. They better get used to seeing me here." He responded to her in the exact same hushed whisper. "Protest again and I'll kiss you."

That threat shut her right up. She surprised herself when she kissed him earlier, especially in front of someone else. But she couldn't help herself when she saw Mitchell Clay. The feel of his lips still lingered and for her sanity, that wasn't anything she wanted to play around with.

"I see that shut you up. Go figure." He got in front of her door. "Where are your keys?"

"You can put me down now."

"I like you in my arms. Where are your keys, woman?"

Osaro held on to her like she weighed nothing as Itohan opened her clutch and got the keys. He unlocked the door and opened it. Osaro entered and put her down.

Itohan took her shoes from him and threw them to the corner and her clutch on the sofa.

"I had a great, exhilarating time. Thank you. Thank you. You made my day," she said.

"I aim to please. Anything to keep that smile on your face, baby."

Itohan shifted from one foot to the other. Osaro's dark eyes narrowed, intensifying his stare. As much as she tried, she couldn't pull her eyes away. He stepped closer to her and drew her in by her chin. She felt her legs move, although she had no idea where the will came from. He brushed a stray curl from her face, lifted her chin and raised his brow. Even with the intensity of the moment, he still asked her permission. She gave a slight nod and he pressed his lips to hers. His lips remained on her mouth for a few moments, then applied soft kisses in rapid succession ending his assault on her cheeks.

"Lock up, beautiful and I'll call you."

Speechless, Itohan nodded.

Osaro chuckled and left into the dark of the night…or wee hours of the morning.

***

The next day, Itohan rubbed her eyes and blinked a few times. She rolled over to the other side of the bed and reached for her watch on the side dresser. She narrowed her eyes and focused. It was one o'clock in the afternoon. She reached for her phone next and smiled. She had four texts from Osaro that started at noon.

She smiled for two reasons. One, when they first met, he hated texting. But since she loved it, he adjusted. Two, the tone of each text became more and more agitated. The last one asked her to call him ASAP or he was coming over to check on her. It also accused her of avoiding him. She made a mental note to text him as soon as she got out of the shower.

She yawned and fanned her nose. She needed to handle the morning breath, immediately. It was all those Suya spices. Her brush-before-bed routine was quickly forgotten last night as she floated on cloud Osaro. The other missed calls were from her sister, Ajoke, and her brother.

Itohan laid her head back on the pillow and stretched her body. She hadn't slept this peaceably or this long in years. She kicked off the covers and sat up with her feet firmly planted on the floor. Memories of the day before bombarded her and sent warm and fuzzy sensations through her.

She stood and walked into the bathroom to take care of her hygiene. Minutes later, fresh out of the shower, she put on a pair of yoga pants and a tank top. Itohan made her way into the kitchen and opened her pantry. It was already afternoon, so she decided on a plantain omelet. She put her earphones in her ears, plugged into her phone and began rocking to "Mad Over You" by Runtown. While the music played, she cut, salted, and fried the plantains. Next, she worked on the eggs, soon after, she sat down to eat, and texted Osaro.

Hey Osa, how are you? Wasn't avoiding you. I just woke up.

Immediately after, her phone rang. She smiled and answered, "Hey."

"Hey, yourself. You had me worried there for a minute."

"Don't be. I just saw you some hours ago. I needed my full eight hours." She giggled. "So what you up to?"

"Nothing much. I'm working, and your student is around here some place."

"What are you working on? You haven't told me how the whole web design/developer thing works. Are your clients local or are they all over?"

"Slow down, now. Someone would think you're actually interested."

Itohan chewed what was in her mouth. "I am."

He gave her a quick rundown of the functions of a designer, developer and a webmaster. Itohan was fascinated by Osaro, the geek, and admired how smart he was.

"I don't really talk about my clients. It's just a habit because of security. But basically, my company offers the wing-to-wing graphics, design and cyber security for our clients," he said.

She never knew there was a difference between all roles. The fact that he was a master of all three, but outsourced often showed how business savvy he was.

"That sounds hard."

"So does running after unruly kids all day, but you do it."

"Yeah, I guess. How did you go from basketball to computers?"

"I've always loved computers and basketball came naturally to me."

"Seeing you, no one would ever believe you're an undercover geek."

Osaro laughed. "See, you get a pass at calling me a geek because I like you."

"Yeah sure." Itohan chewed.

"What are you eating?"

"Nosy."

"Chocomilo, answer my question."

"A plantain omelet."

"What is that? Something you made up?"

"No silly. It's basically plantain and eggs."

"So why not just say that?"

"Because it's called an omelet."

Over the next several minutes, Itohan remained seated at her island while they chatted. Then he had to go and attend to Eseosa. Something about her pinkie finger getting caught in the dresser. She stayed on until he got to her. It wasn't bad, but she was whiny, so they hung up with a promise to reconnect.

Itohan tidied up the kitchen. She turned on her stereo and found herself jamming to "Brand New Me" by Alicia Keys as she started cleaning her house. As she went through the motions, all she could think about was Osaro. He was everything she could now admit she wanted, but was afraid to have. She could see herself falling for him, but scares from the past had her trust set up wrong.

Despite her fear, Itohan resolved to commit to the process and trust him. She hoped he'd not give up on her along the way.

18

The playlist in Osaro's SUV was a collection of Afro Beat and American sounds. "Skintight" by Mr. Eazi blasted from his speakers as he made it down the highway. The two years he stayed home forever changed his perspective on his culture and the country. He knew some things about Nigeria because of his auntie, but staying there was a whole different, enlightening experience. One he'd never take for granted. Although he lived majority of his life in America, he stayed connected with the news and in about five years, he hoped to expand RoMac Technologies to Lagos or Abuja.

Osaro took in the clear, early November sky as he turned down the access road to Itohan's apartment complex. No one could tell him there wasn't a God. The last six weeks proved, once again, that He was a miracle worker. They'd become closer with each passing day. With prayer, his actions, and her willingness to let him in, he was breaking down her walls. He was so proud of her because he could feel her fear, but admired her bravado.

What happened to her had to have cut deep. She still hadn't shared, but he was committed to fixing her banged-up heart. They spent most weekends at the movies, museum or park with Eseosa. Wednesdays and Fridays were reserved for just the two of them. They worked out together, went to dinner, took walks on the beach and rode the skyline.

Osaro smiled at their skyline adventure because he had dared her to get on and she couldn't resist the challenge. After the ride, she became sick with a queasy stomach. That night cemented his growing feelings for her. Seeing her too ill to care about hiding her vulnerability did something to him. He hated her being sick, but she was totally dependent on him, and that felt good. He didn't want a weak woman; he could deal with strong ones. His auntie raised him better than that.

But Itohan was so good at hiding her need for him that he sometimes questioned it himself. That night, they stopped at Walgreens and he got her some Pepto-Bismol. He took her home, helped her get into bed and made her drink some ginger ale. His save-the-day cape was stripped off him when she threw up. He helped hold her hair back but soon after, she kicked him out because according to her, she looked terrible.

Despite her willingness to give their budding relationship a chance, one issue remained – her mood swings. Some days, she'd act like she couldn't be bothered with him and some days she wouldn't let him get off the phone. His attachment to her scared him for nothing else but that reason right there. He was sure of his feelings for her. It might not be love, but they were way past mere like. He didn't want to be out there by himself but he couldn't shake her, even if he tried. He could feel she was holding back and that kept him up most nights.

Osaro parked, activated his locks and walked up to her apartment. He put his hand on the bell and the door opened almost immediately.

"Err, hi," Osaro greeted the lady sizing him up.

She had what he assumed was coffee in one hand and was clad in a woolen night robe. He looked back at the apartment number. It was the right one.

"So you're *our* boyfriend?" She moved aside.

Osaro chuckled inwardly and walked inside. This was, without a doubt, Keni. In the picture Itohan showed him, she had black hair. Now he was looking at a golden blonde. He hadn't met Itohan's "girls," as she called them, but he talked to them once over the phone. Her sister was the firecracker of the group, followed by his baby. He wondered how Ajoke kept up with them.

"You must be Keni. I'm Osaro, nice to meet you." Osaro extended his hand.

She gave him a firm shake. "I see why my sister can't stop talking about you."

He walked over to the sofa and sat.

"After we chat, I'll tell you whether it's nice to meet you too. Itoh is getting ready." Keni sat on the chair opposite him.

Osaro needed Itohan to make an appearance. He wasn't prepared to deal with Keni by his lonesome. She sat with her legs under her and leaned on the armrest. Her intense gaze would've intimidated the ordinary man. *She must have watched too many of those cop shows.*

Once he was told Itohan was late as usual, he settled in for her attack. This would be part two. They'd had part one over the phone.

"Fair enough. When did you get in?" he asked.

"Last night. I wanted to surprise my sis. I'll be outta here tomorrow night *sha*." She sipped on her drink and eyed him.

"I see you've lasted a while. That's means she's feeling you… seriously. Don't hurt her Osaro." She drew her earlobe – a gesture Auntie Lizzy did often to stress the seriousness or importance of her statement.

"You just love giving me *wahala*. We've talked about this over the phone, right?" Osaro asked.

"*Ehen*? You can tell me anything over the phone. I want to see *ya* eye when you say it. *Oya, repeat am*."

Osaro chuckled but gave Keni what she wanted. "Itohan and I are getting to know each other. I'm not here to play with her. I wanna build with her."

Keni put her mug down. She sat with her elbows on her knees. "Osaro, Itoh has been through a lot. If there's the remotest chance that you might not be there for the long haul, *abeg leave am now*." She spoke in the calmest tone he'd ever heard her speak.

"She means a lot to me. I've shown her all of me. I wish she'd open up to me but—"

"She will, in her own time. Be patient with her," she said.

"Keni, are you playing my parent again?" Itohan said, walking up on them.

At the sound of her voice, Osaro turned and stood. He buried his hands in his pockets and allowed his eyes roam over her frame.

The way her curves stacked drove him insane each time he saw her. She had on an Ankara jumper and her hair was in a head wrap but the top part was open so her curls spilled over. He chuckled at the stern look she gave her sister and the unbothered one Keni returned.

"You know she's always late *abi*?" Keni asked him.

Osaro looked over at Itohan and smirked. She walked over to him and he snaked his arm around her waist and kissed her forehead. He felt her continue to stare at him waiting for his response. Keni knew she was correct, but wrong for trying to get him to cosign and he wasn't falling into that trap.

"Why are you looking at him like that? It's true, now." Keni laughed and picked up her mug and sipped.

"Hey, you," she said, ignoring Keni.

"Hey, yourself. You ready?"

"Osaro, don't worry. I know you can't answer me, but we know what is what." Keni grabbed the television remote on the coffee table. "Let me see whose pastor is on television since this one didn't go to church and has been hoarding the television with this nonsense *Snapped* show."

"Keni, shut up. Ugh." Itohan tapped him, "Please, let's go."

Itohan's harsh response confused him. He also noticed she cut her eyes at her sister who, again, didn't seem moved, but stuck her tongue out at her. He already knew Itohan didn't go to church regularly and he was praying constantly for her. Sometimes he got her to watch the replay of some services with him.

They said their goodbyes and Osaro walked Itohan to the car. After helping her in and getting himself situated, they hit the road. They'd been on the road a few minutes and there was an uncomfortable silence between them. He didn't like it. He glanced over at her. She was looking out the window, apparently lost in thought. When he let her in the car, her body stiffened at his touch. He didn't like that, either. He was lost as to what could have happened from the time she came out of the room until now.

"You okay?" Osaro glanced at her, then returned his eyes to the road.

"Yeah, why?"

He shrugged. "You seem preoccupied."

She looked over at him and rubbed his arm assuredly. "I'm good. I'm sorry. I hope Keni didn't give you a hard time."

"No, she was cool. Wanted to make sure I was good to you."

Itohan smiled.

"But I can see something got to you. Why are you upset? I know about you and church." He paused. "Now that program she was talking about, I know nothing about."

Itohan remained silent. "It's not important." A beat of silence passed between them. "So, I get to meet the whole family again. Am I presentable enough?"

"It's a little late to be asking that question, isn't it?"

"Osa!"

"I'm teasing, baby. You look beautiful and anyone who doesn't agree is answerable to me." He grabbed her hand and continued down the road. Now the silence between them was comfortable. He still felt she was a little agitated, but decided not to push. It was Sunday. He was taking her to his family. *Love is patient...*he coached himself.

***

"And this is where I used to sleep before I went to live with Uncle Ro."

Osaro heard his niece as he climbed the stairs to look for his girls. He and Itohan had arrived about an hour ago just as his auntie was about to fry some goat meat. He reintroduced Itohan to everyone again and his auntie kidnapped her and headed to the kitchen where Robin was. He turned to follow his brother to the living room, but not before catching the thumbs-up his auntie threw his way. He shook his head at her silliness and took a seat.

His brother handed him a controller and they played a spirited game of Forza Motorsport on the Xbox One. They always kept a game system at their auntie's for when they visited.

Osaro got closer to the bedroom and leaned on the doorframe as he watched Itohan brush Eseosa's hair as his niece told her stories of what he assumed was Princess Elena.

He cleared his throat and smiled at them when they looked toward him.

"Uncle Ro!" Eseosa ran toward him. He picked her up and kissed her cheek. "Nana Lizzy said it's time to eat. Go wash your hands." Osaro put her down.

"Okay." She turned and ran down the hallway.

"Stop running," he cautioned.

Itohan walked up to him and he trained his eyes on her. His lips curved up in admiration.

"You're good with her, Uncle Ro," she teased.

He pulled her to him by her pockets. He wrapped his arms around her waist and she curved hers around his neck. "Thank you. There are many things I want you to call me...Uncle Ro is not one of them."

"Hmmm, what would you want me to call you?" she said seductively.

He lifted his brow at her rare boldness. "Don't play with me, woman. Let's go eat." Osaro removed his hand from her waist and took her hand.

"Don't play with you? Why do you say that?" she asked in a whiny voice.

He stopped at the landing and squinted his eyes at her. "Did you drink something?" Her boldness continued to surprise him.

"No, silly. I just want to know."

"Itohan, you aren't ready for me. When you are, I'll make you mine and you won't have to ask what I want you to call me."

He wanted to be called her man, her protector and somewhere down the line, her husband, but there were so many walls up around her. He was willing to be patient since he could tell she was feeling him, too. But he also had to be careful. When he loved, he loved hard and he didn't want to go there if she was unsure.

They gathered around the table and held hands while Robin led them in giving the blessing. After that was done, they sat down to eat. Lively conversation mixed with the chatter of silverware against the dishes filled the room. Osaro loved how Itohan conversed freely with everyone, and Auntie Lizzy seemed to take a special liking to her. The conversation centered a little bit around everyone's jobs and the week that just went by. As usual, he and Ehi gave the general gist without details. Robin had just concluded a vacation, or a staycation, as she called it, and was headed back to work. Itohan was preparing for the play that Eseosa couldn't stop talking about.

"So Itohan, how does it feel being the only one here in America? Osaro tells me that everyone else is back home." Auntie Lizzy said.

Osaro reached under the table and squeezed her hand. Why she was the only one here was something she didn't discuss with him in detail. All she told him was she needed a fresh start and her parents sent her to her godparents. He did know she felt uncomfortable talking about it.

Itohan looked over at him. "It's okay, Ma. It does get lonely, but I talk to them every weekend. My sister visits often and my brother will be here to do his master's soon."

"Oh really? That's nice. Did Osaro tell you I'm thinking of relocating back?"

"No, he didn't, Ma." Itohan looked over at him and punched him playfully on his shoulder.

"Ouch, woman, that hurt." Osaro rubbed the area in feigned pain.

Ehi and Robin laughed.

"You can kiss it and make it feel better, Ms. Adolo. Just like you did me when I was hurt," Eseosa offered.

"Yes, kiss it and make it feel better, Ms. Adolo." Osaro repeated. He laughed when he saw the warning look she gave him.

"I'll kiss it later," Itohan told Eseosa sweetly, but kicked him under the table. The look she gave him dared him to say anything.

Since he was expecting real kisses later, he decided he had pushed her enough.

"What area would you be staying, Ma?"

"GRA."

"Oh, that's a nice area. That's where my family lives in Benin," Itohan said.

Osaro looked over at her. GRA was one of the affluent areas in Benin City and nothing she had shown him remotely expressed that she came from money. To get his auntie a house there, he and Ehi both had to chip in.

"I heard about how armed robbers kidnapped one prominent man last week and there was a curfew in the city." Auntie took a sip of her water. "I hope you heard from your parents?"

"Yes, I called them yesterday, but they had a function. My dad was supposed to call back today and I'm waiting for his call," Itohan said.

The group conversation drifted off into lighter topics and they shared several laughs. Some minutes later, Itohan's phone rang.

"It's my dad. I have to take this." She looked around and Osaro knew she was looking for where she could talk in private.

"Baby, you can go into the kitchen or upstairs," Osaro said.

She nodded. "Excuse me."

Everyone nodded, giving nonverbal consent.

She stood, answered the phone. "*Lamogun*, Sir," she said, walking into the kitchen.

Auntie Lizzy's eyes followed Itohan until she disappeared into the kitchen. "I like her for you, Osaro. But when were you going to tell me that you're dating a princess?"

Osaro choked on the plantain he had in his mouth. He reached for the glass of water in front of him and guzzled it down. "A what?"

Auntie Lizzy furrowed her brows at him. "A princess?"

"Like a real-life princess, princess?" Robin asked, her eyes bugged out. His auntie nodded.

"How do you know that?" Osaro asked.

"That greeting she just used means she is a royal descendant." Auntie Lizzy paused. "I'm not sure how far her lineage is from the throne, but she's no different from those British princesses."

"You didn't know, man?" Ehi asked.

Osaro shook his head slowly.

"I guess she wanted to see if you're worthy like Eddie Murphy did that chick in *Coming to America*." Ehi laughed and turned to Robin. "Babe, what's that chick name in the movie?"

"Lisa," Robin replied.

Ehi snapped his fingers. "Yeah, that's it."

Osaro was frozen in place. His confusion was quickly replaced by anger. He had opened himself to her. Shared things he hadn't with anybody and she couldn't tell him that she was a princess. He didn't have time for these kinds of games. Now more than ever, he wished he followed his head and stayed away from her in the first place. Now his heart was in it and he wondered if it was too late to let her go.

19

If he clenches his jaw any harder, the veins at the side of head will pop.

Itohan glanced over at Osaro. He had been driving for about thirty minutes and hadn't said more than two words to her. Instead, the veins at the side of his head and his knuckles showed the strain of his annoyance. She'd asked him what his problem was once she got into the car, but he said nothing. She hadn't entertained a man in forever, but even she knew when they needed time to stew a little bit before saying what was up.

Itohan turned and smiled at Eseosa who was now sleeping comfortably in the back seat. The little girl took a bigger piece of her heart day by day. Itohan wondered if she'd be as great a mother as she was a teacher. Recently, she asked herself that question more. At the beginning of the year, she couldn't see any scenario where she'd have kids because men were a no go. Now it was plausible. Being in this car now confirmed that.

Itohan turned back around and adjusted her seatbelt. She looked over at Osaro again and couldn't take the silence anymore. She'd had a great time and thought he did too, but now he was beginning to get on her nerves. *Tell me the problem or get rid of the attitude.*

"What is your problem, Osa?" Irritation laced her tone. "You've been giving me the cold shoulder since we left…or rather since I got back from speaking to my dad."

"Not now."

His tone further irritated her. Was he talking to his child?

"O—"

"Itohan, my niece is in the car. Not now."

Itohan folded her arms across her chest and turned her face to look out the window. With nothing better to do, she took out her phone.

Are u still awake?

It was only eight p.m. but Itohan knew that Keni had to leave for the airport by three a.m. She really hoped her sister was awake. She needed someone to talk to; her emotions were all jumbled up.

No, *wetin* happen?

Too much to text. On my way. Need to talk.

No *wahala*. You want to eat something?

Itohan smiled. That's what she loved about her sister. She had her back always – well before telling her about herself if she was in the wrong. But she had her back, regardless.

I'm full but thanks sis.

Itohan turned her phone face down and continued to look out the window. She could feel Osaro burning a hole in the side of her face, but she was no longer interested in what he had to say. Then she noticed he wasn't headed in the direction of her apartment.

"Err…sir, where are we going?"

"To my house. I need to drop off Eseosa and we need to talk." Osaro said, not looking her way.

A few minutes later, they pulled into what she assumed was his home. Over the several weeks they'd been dating, they always went to public places. Osaro parked and got out. He opened the back door and picked up Eseosa, then he rounded the car and opened the door for her. Itohan followed him inside.

"Make yourself comfortable. Let me put her to bed. I'll be right back."

Itohan walked over to the living room. She surveyed the area and loved it. It wasn't a typical bachelor pad. She saw the effort he put into making the space, especially the living area, child friendly. It felt more like a family home.

She walked to the mantle and studied the pictures he had on it. She saw one of him and his siblings. Eseosa was a replica of her mother. The other pictures were of him and Eseosa. There were a couple of her school pictures and his whole family. She walked toward the one she assumed was the one of his late parents. Her heart hurt for him, for his family. A weary smile covered her face as she thought about how proud they would be of their kids. Because of Osaro, she no longer thought of her parents with so much angst. Their relationship was better, and she accepted them for who they were. When she didn't fight so much, she was able to listen and in return, they listened to her. Osaro did that for her.

"When were you going to tell me that you were a princess?"

Osaro's voice washed over her and instead of the tingling feeling that went along with it any time he spoke to her, her heart accelerated. His tone dripped with disappointment. She closed her eyes and inhaled. Letting out a heavy breath, she turned around. *That stupid greeting.*

"It was never the right time," she whispered. She stood in place and folded her arms across her chest.

Osaro walked from the bottom of the stairs and placed his hands on the back of the couch. He bent his head and his locs fell all over his head. He lifted his head and stared at her.

"Respect me enough not to lie to me. Not to my face." He clenched his jaw.

"When was I supposed to tell you?"

"Are you kidding me? How about when I gave you a rundown of my past, present and future? I trusted you with my vulnerability. Why is it so hard for you to do the same?"

Itohan remained silent.

"So again, I ask you, why didn't you tell me?"

Itohan shrugged. There was no way she was telling him about Aidenoje and how her royalty played a huge role in her father's reaction to him. How he played her and made her look so stupid. She wasn't ready to reveal that layer. Besides, although she was royal, her family wasn't in line to the throne. So, what difference did it make?

"You didn't tell me because of this." He pointed to her.

"What?"

"This, your closed off nature. The way you cross your arms every time shows that you want to remain hidden. You're so scared of being vulnerable to anyone that you can't allow yourself to experience love, joy...to live."

"How dare you judge me? I do have joy and have those I love."

"You don't have joy. You make yourself happy. There's a difference. And I'm not judging you. I'm opening your eyes to your flaws, just like you did for me. Your flaws make you beautiful." He paced.

Itohan's hands shook uncontrollably. She needed to get away from him. She thought she was ready for the emotional exposure being with a man would entail. But maybe she wasn't. He was staring at her like he could read her deepest, darkest thoughts.

"I need to go." Itohan walked toward the door.

"I always thought of you as courageous. My niece adores you and I really, really like you. But I can't do this if you're not willing to meet me halfway."

She stopped in her tracks. Her heart pounded. In that instant, her mind went through all scenarios where he wouldn't be in her life. He hadn't been there long, so logically, she saw no reason why it would be that hard if he left. However, the panic that overtook her told her she wasn't sure she was ready to find out.

"Osa, I don't know what's happening between us. You're right. I'm a coward. I'm scared, and I can admit that."

Osaro walked over to her. He took her hand and led her to the couch. He sat her down and occupied the space beside her. Still holding on to her hand, he lifted her face with the other.

"Baby, I never said you were a coward…"

"Same difference. I'm a teacher, remember?"

He shook his head. "You can't live scared. God didn't give you the spirit of fear. Walking around and avoiding risk means you aren't living the abundant life you're supposed to be living. That's not how God intended it or who He created us to be. You limit yourself from any meaningful existence."

"Osaro, I told you before, you can't save me," she said, in a bare whisper.

"I'm not trying to save you. I'm trying to love you, woman."

Itohan looked up at him. His eyes were searching hers, probably for a similar expression of emotion. She had nothing for him other than shock. She wasn't oblivious to their chemistry – but love? She debated whether she could trust her vulnerability with him. Another heartbreak would kill her…literally.

"Love me?"

"Yes, what did you think this is? I'm too old for games. I told you that." He paused. "I want to be the one that uplifts you, protects your body, mind and soul. Your consistent security. I want to be your biggest cheerleader and your toughest critic. I won't offer you perfection, because in love it doesn't exist. I will promise you that I'll always be straight and true with you."

Itohan remained silent. A tear rolled down her cheek at the words he just spoke. Goose bumps overtook her arms and she shuddered. Osaro thumbed away her tear, took the throw blanket from the arm of the chair and wrapped it around her shoulders. She looked up at him, confident that in this moment, she'd lost the battle to keep her heart.

"Look, I know something happened in your past. I'd be a fool to be oblivious to that fact. I won't push you on sharing it, but I'm asking if you can give us an honest chance. Stop over analyzing and fighting me."

After a couple minutes of silence, Itohan spoke. "My family comes from the Akenzua lineage in Benin. My life as a royal has been one that I've embraced with mixed feelings. I'm not ashamed of who I am, but the fact that I am the first girl and royal added to the expectations that my father has for me. How I carry myself and who I eventually settle down with."

For the next several minutes, Itohan gave Osaro a rundown of her life. All she told him about her ex was how long they'd been together and that they split up. She figured he knew he was the reason for her present hiccups because of the way his jaw clenched in anger. Osaro didn't ask for his name and she didn't offer. Because it'd been such a long time and she hadn't dated in so long, Osaro asked whether she still had feelings for her ex. She answered with a resounding no. They talked a bit more and she told him about her own future plans. He told her that he had confidence that she could do anything she set her mind to.

"I have to get home. Keni will kill me."

"Why? She knows you're with me."

"Yeah, but I kinda told her you were being a jerk and I needed to talk to her."

He shook his head. "You know that girl is borderline crazy and suspicious of me already. Why did you tell her that?"

"'Cause, you were." Itohan pouted.

"You know I can't remain mad at you for too long." He kissed her pouty lips. "Let's go. Let me get you home."

"What about Eseosa?"

"She's coming with. She's knocked out anyway and you don't live too far from here."

Itohan watched him take the stairs two at a time. There was a new-found peace that settled in her belly at the progress they had made tonight. It was time for her to let Aidenoje go

20

The following afternoon, Osaro and Malcolm were in the pizzeria in their building lobby having lunch. The waitress had taken their orders and Mac stepped to the restroom. That left Osaro alone with his thoughts. He rubbed his temples, trying to ease the tension headache he felt coming. He'd endured a restless night because of Itohan.

Last night had thrown him way off. Although he felt somewhat accomplished when she opened up to him, the fact that she was okay with hiding such a vital part of herself from him still nagged him. If his aunt hadn't mentioned it, he knew for sure she wasn't going to. His auntie always used to say that when you find one cockroach, there's bound to be others. So, he knew there was still more Itohan wasn't telling him. He, in no way, expected her to bare her whole soul to him so soon. However, the things she hid were major foundational blocks. That scared him. If things didn't work out with them, his niece would be affected. That was something he wasn't willing to take a chance on.

When he took her home, she apologized, and he did sense the sincerity in her apology. But he couldn't shake the feeling that he was in this by himself. Apart from the women in his family, he'd never told a woman he loved her. The fact that he almost voiced that emotion to Itohan yesterday was messing with his mind. He hadn't discussed his relationship with his friend in any detail. But he needed to vent. Malcolm was going to be his makeshift counsellor.

The waitress retuned with their lunch of two subs and drinks, just as Malcolm made it back to the table.

"You good, man?" Osaro asked after blessing his food.

"Yeah, on my way back, my grandma called. Imma have to make it down to Atlanta again this weekend." Malcolm took a bite out of his Italian sandwich.

Osaro knew that the strain of running back and forth from Atlanta to Florida had on his friend, however, his grandma refused to move to Florida. Being that he was her only grandson and caretaker, Malcolm had no choice.

"Have you talked to her again about moving to Florida?"

Malcolm shook his head and he sipped on his Coca Cola. "You know that's a battle I've been fighting forever. She loves that nursing home up there. But something is gonna give real soon."

Osaro nodded and the friends ate in comfortable silence. Osaro's had his eyebrows furrowed together as Itohan came back to his mind.

"Okay, so what's up? I know we didn't come down here to eat sandwiches. We could've done that upstairs. So, talk to me," Malcolm said.

Osaro looked at his friend. "I love Itohan, man. She's the first thing I think about when I wake. When we're together, I can't keep my hands off her. When we're apart, I feel like I'm suffocating. I don't know, man."

"So, what's the problem? Have you told her how you feel?"

Osaro sighed in frustration. "No, if I do, she might run for the hills. She's so closed off emotionally. I think something happened in her past and she hasn't let that stuff go. How do you love half a person? I feel like she's one foot in with me, but she's keeping her other foot on solid ground just in case something happens."

"Has she told you that or you're assuming she's hiding something?"

Osaro massaged his temples. He told Malcolm about her being a princess and their talk. Narrating the story again made him upset. Seconds ticked by as he waited for his friend to say something.

"I see where you're coming from, Ro. But you can't force the time in which her heart opens up for you. You must be willing to be that consistency she needs. Enjoy her when she's open and be patient with her when she's closed. If your assumption is correct, that means her ex did her dirty. We both know that if that's the case, like it or not, you're the one that's gonna pay for it. The question is, do you wanna stick around and heal her damaged heart or do you want to bump it? Just maintain the guardian/teacher relationship y'all got and keep it stepping."

"How do I know she'll ever get to where I am? I'm not trying to be in it by myself."

Malcolm waved him off, "If you love and respect Itohan, you'll be patient with her. I know you ain't no pushover, so I'm not asking you to be a lap dog. But I'm telling you to think about it. If you think loving her is hard now, try forgetting about her. That will help you make your decision. Besides you've only known her for a little over three months. Give the woman time to trust you with her heart."

"Yeah, I guess you're right." Osaro took a few minutes to digest what his friend said. He knew he wasn't walking away from Itohan, but he was skeptical of the secrets. Since he couldn't control her actions, he would just make sure his were strong enough to wear her down.

Malcolm's phone rang and they both looked at the screen. It was Tekena. Malcolm answered and put it on speaker.

"What's up, Tex?" Malcolm answered. "I got Ro here, you're on speaker and we're out in public."

"So? Why you explaining all that?" Tekena asked.

"Watch your mouth!" Osaro and Malcolm said in unison.

Osaro laughed because his friend had no filter at all. He was one of the bluntest yet nicest men he'd had ever met. There was no one more solid than Tekena. You had to know him to love him or you'd hate his guts.

"First of all, last I checked, none of y'alls name is on my birth certificate so I ain't gotta do nothing. Two, those people don't feed me. I can say what I wanna say. Three, I know that dread-head ain't over there laughing and not answering my calls. It was him I called first and he didn't answer the phone." Tekena rattled off.

Osaro pulled out his phone from his pocket. He did have one missed call. He put it back in his pocket. Tekena was the youngest of the three and wildest. Osaro was just glad he took his wild and crazy tendencies out on the racetrack rather than the streets. He was almost headed there if it weren't for the grace of God.

"Whatchu looking for me for? Do I owe you?" Osaro asked.

"I see you talking slick now after I done gotchu the tickets you were crying for. As a matter of fact, I recorded how you were crying and I'm playing it for your girl."

Malcolm laughed.

"Man, be quiet. I wasn't crying."

"Evidence speaks, Bro. But bump that. Tell Auntie Lizzy, I'm coming for Thanksgiving in two weeks. I'm going to *Naija* real quick and see my fam, then I'm coming your way," Tekena informed them. Presently he was in Argentina with his sponsors.

"That's dope, man. Just let me know when you're getting in."

"A'ight bet." Tekena said.

Malcolm reached to end the call when Tekena spoke again. "Oh wait, hold up. For the week I'm there, Imma need Geek One and Geek Two to drop the geekiness and show a brother a good time. Mac, I don't wanna hear nothing about no numbers and Ro, you bet not talk about no designs either."

Osaro and Malcolm laughed. "How you gonna be our friend and don't wanna know about what we working on?"

"I didn't say all that. I know what y'all working on. You got ten minutes when I get there to give me any new developments. But after that, I don't wanna hear about it. In fact, y'all need to have some honeys lined up."

"I don't do honeys. I do grown women and Ro practically married," Malcolm said.

Osaro punched Malcolm on his arm. He hadn't even been ready to talk to Malcolm about Itohan. Adding Tekena to the mix was just bad. He wasn't ready for the constant teasing.

"Married? Ro, you holding out on me, man? Let me find out she ugly and that's why you didn't tell me."

"You're so stupid, man," Osaro chuckled. His baby was far from ugly.

"It's okay Ro, as far as you like her, we love her. But before you cuff her, think about the future li'l Ro's and Ro'ettes – how they gonna look. You an all right looking dude, but I'm not sure your genes strong enough to have them looking good."

"Tex, shut up man. I'm not talking about Itohan with you."

"Itohan? Oh, the chick with the art tickets. Why didn't you tell me that's who you talking about? You didn't wanna talk about her then. Y'all rocking like that now? I gotta see this chick. You still celibate, becau—"

"Hang up on that fool." Osaro said.

Malcolm was doubled over laughing. If Osaro wasn't so irritated, he would have laughed, too. Tekena had no kind of sense whatsoever, but he was one of the realest men he knew. He would bend over backwards for those he cared about.

"Aye, don't do me like that, man. We go way back from elementary school days," Tekena said. Osaro could tell from his voice that he was in a full-blown laughing fit. This was always the case. Malcolm was the instigator, Tekena was the clown and he was the serious one.

"Yeah, you gonna make me forget that if you keep messing with my girl." Osaro said. He no longer had a taste for the sandwich. His phone vibrated in his pocket. He took it out and saw a text from Itohan.

If you can make it, I have an I'm sorry meal waiting for you. 7:30?

Osaro smiled, but quickly wiped the emotion off his face. He didn't need Malcolm to pick up on it and then tell Tekena and the teasing start all over again. It was one in the afternoon, so he'd call her when he got back to the office. He and his friends talked a little bit more before Tekena hung up.

Walking out of the pizzeria minutes later, Osaro felt lighter than he felt in the past several hours. He was glad he could connect with his boys. With their schedules, it was very difficult being in the same place at the same time. Osaro was already anticipating all three of them being back together again in two weeks. Just like high school.

***

After ensuring her homework was done, she was fed and making her promise she wouldn't give the sitter any problems when it was time to go to bed, Osaro kissed Eseosa on her forehead and left his house. Less than thirty minutes later, he was at Itohan's door. When she opened the door, her smile sent shock waves through his body. Malcolm was right, as stubborn and guarded as she was, he would just have to be patient and wear her down. The alternative was just unfathomable. He said he was trying to love and build with her and that was exactly what he was going to do.

"Hey, baby. These are for you." He handed her some flowers he bought.

"Thank you. They're beautiful."

"Not as beautiful as you." They both stared at each other before Osaro tore his eyes away. They had a long evening and he wasn't about to make either of them uncomfortable.

"Thank you." She walked toward the kitchen and he went into the living room.

"It sure smells good in here. Hope it tastes good as well," Osaro teased.

"Are you trying to *yab* my cooking?" She put her hands on her waist and smirked at him.

Osaro shrugged. "I don't know. It is *yabable*."

"*Yabable*? Wow, you just make words up as you go, don't you?"

He laughed and picked up the remote. She had some reality program on and her house or not, he wasn't about to be subjected to somebody's scripted reality. He flipped the television to the ESPN Sports Center. Basketball season was back, and he was more than ready. He was probably watching for a couple of minutes when he felt Itohan's soft hands massaging his shoulders. It felt so good and so natural. All his inhibitions of earlier were totally washed away with the gentleness of her touch. After kneading his shoulders for about five minutes, she kissed his cheeks.

"Come on, food is ready."

Osaro stood up and put his hand in her outstretched one. He liked this Itohan. Normally, he would be the first one to initiate any kind of contact between them. As much as he hated to admit it, he desperately needed to feel that she needed him just as much as he needed her.

She led him to kitchen and turned to face the stove. "Wash your hands. Let me dish the food."

Osaro looked over and saw that she had a steamy pot of catfish pepper soup and boiled yam that screamed his name. He went to the sink and did as he was told. He watched Itohan put a couple pieces of yam in a deep bowl then scooped the soup and poured all around it. She did the same in a second bowl.

"Here, take the bowls and I'll bring the water. I figure you'd want to sit in front of the television and watched ESPN."

Osaro walked back into the living room and placed the food on the coffee table. He drew the table close to the couch. Itohan put their water down. Osaro held out his hand, she placed hers in his and he said grace. They watched and ate in an easy silence. The soup was very spicy, so they were both careful not to choke.

"This is so good," Osaro told her.

"I'm glad you like it."

"So, the princess cooks."

Itohan frowned and Osaro chuckled. He was going to have so much fun teasing her.

"You see why I don't tell people?" Itohan pouted.

"Quit whining, woman. I was just playing with you. Besides you can be their princess, but I'm trying to make you my queen."

"Aww, that was so sweet." She puckered her lips and he brushed his against them. "Do you cook?"

"Yeah, a little bit, just enough to survive. Auntie Lizzy made sure we could fend for ourselves. She always used to say we should know how to cook so no woman could make *shakara* for us."

"I think that's a Naija thing, because my mom says the same thing to my brother all the time."

"I already know how your day was, but how is the preparation for the recital coming?"

"It's going great. I'll be glad when it's over. You'll be there *abi*?"

"Two of my favorite ladies will be there, of course, I'll be there."

They finished their food. Osaro took both bowls to the kitchen and cleaned up, while Itohan scooped them some frozen sorbet. Minutes later, they were enjoying dessert at her kitchen island and talking.

Osaro set his cup down. "Come here."

Itohan stood from the barstool she was on and walked to him. He spread his legs, so she could stand in between them. He stared at her for a few minutes until she lowered her head.

"I enjoyed my 'I'm sorry' dinner. I enjoyed this with you."

"I'm glad you did." She smiled at him.

"Since my sister died, I haven't allowed myself to have this...calm."

"I'm glad I could bring that for you."

"What about you, baby? Are you going to let me be that for you? Your shoulder, your listening ear? Your protector and your covering?"

Osaro looked at her eyes dance for a few seconds in uncertainty and he also saw a little fear in them.

"You have to trust me, baby, that I won't do anything to hurt you. Intentionally. I'm not perfect, but I'll try my darnedest with you."

"I'm happy with you. I promise to be like an open book." She laughed and he pulled her in for a kiss.

"Now I have a favor to ask." Osaro twirled her hair around his fingers.

"What is it?"

"Come to church with me or at least Bible study on Wednesday."

Itohan shook her head. "Osa, I don't know."

"Think about it. That's all I ask for now. Our bond will never be as tight as it should be if God isn't at the center."

"Okay."

"Thank you." Osaro hadn't expected her to give in so easily. He cupped her face. "I love you. I love you, Itohan Adolo, and your heart is safe with me." He kissed her lips and she stared at him in shock, but remained speechless.

Before tonight, that would have scared him, but not anymore. He wanted to stay longer, but he knew they both had early starts in the morning. "Come and lock the door and I'll talk to you tomorrow.

Minutes later, he cruised down the highway back to his home. The grin he wore on his face was so big, that he could feel his cheeks tighten.

21

"Oh my gosh, you're so out of touch. How can you not know who RMD is?" Itohan asked.

"Because I didn't know about Nigerian movies until you introduced me to them." Osaro replied, glancing over at her.

It was three days before Thanksgiving. School was out and Itohan was no longer Eseosa's teacher. Her regular teacher had come back from maternity leave and Itohan was now focused on her business full time. They were on their way to the airport to pick up Tekena. Keni would arrive the next day while Ajoke was spending the holiday on an impromptu trip her husband put together.

Itohan had a new-found peace about her relationship with Osaro. She knew now, without a doubt, that she loved him, but she had yet to find the courage to tell him. Any time she opened her mouth to tell him, she chickened out.

Fear that her admittance of the emotion she'd forbidden herself to feel for so long would suddenly change the dynamics of their relationship hindered her from saying anything. Sometimes the anxiety that he would take his love away because she refused to give hers consumed her. But he'd shown her time and time again that he was here with her because it was where he wanted to be. He'd asked her to allow him to love her and that was what she was doing.

Eseosa was spending the week with her Nana so they'd had enough time to themselves. Their evenings ranged from time at his place or hers for dinner, or them going out. She loved their evening drives to nowhere in particular. She even got him to agree to an impromptu photo shoot.

"There are so many more talented actors. RMD is our Denzel. In fact, I'm going to put you on to game. I can't have you disgracing me in these Florida streets. *Naija* man talking about you don't know about Nollywood." She sucked her teeth. "Ta! Not on my watch."

Osaro threw his head back in laughter. He laughed so hard she thought he was going to drive them off the road.

"All right, you win."

"Of course I win. Africa is taking the world by storm with music and film. They even play Afro beats in clubs in Florida." Itohan said. "Haven't you heard the phrase 'Naija no dey carry last?' Meaning we excel in what we do. So, if it's crime, we excel too." Itohan chuckled, but the truth was, for a long time, Africans in the diaspora were ashamed to say they were from Nigeria.

But things were changing, and the country was producing the biggest names out of the continent. With the guy in the TV show *Power*, the woman in *Insecure*, the Oyewole guy that hung with Oprah and so many more, Nigeria was no longer synonymous with scamming. The country even now had the first ever women's bobsled team to compete in the Winter Olympics.

"Clubs? Don't get in trouble." Osaro voice brought her out of her thoughts. He had a scowl on his face.

Itohan laughed at him and rubbed his shoulder. "Aww, someone's jealous?"

"You're treading too close to the doghouse. When did you go to the club?"

"Bruh – that's how they say it, right?" Itohan waited for him to answer, but saw he wasn't going to until he got an answer to the club comment. "Anyway, Bruh, cool down for Jesus. I didn't go to the club. I was playing one of Tekno's songs in the parking lot of my school a while ago, getting ready to head out, and one of the teachers asked me about the song."

Osaro gave her a warning look. "I see you itching for punishment. That's how they say it, but call me 'bruh' one more time."

She laughed. A comfortable silence took over as he drove the rest of the way. She reached over and massaged the back of his neck.

It was something she'd started doing and he seemed to get lost in the feel of her fingers.

"You're going to put me to sleep, woman."

She removed her hand. "We can't have that, now can we? How is the big deal you never want to talk about coming along?"

"I do talk about my job; I just don't talk about my clients." He reached over and took her hand. "But the South Tran deal is going good. Now, we're just waiting. But my source told me that we have the deal in the bag. There's just a bit of a delay."

"Oh baby, that's wonderful. We should celebrate."

"We'll celebrate when we actually get it." He paused. "I love how happy you always are for me."

Itohan lifted their hands and kissed the back of his. "That's how it's supposed to be. You taught me how to do that. Before you entered my life, I was broody and had no cares to give about anyone except my siblings and friend. Even my parents weren't high up my 'let me take your feelings into consideration' chain."

"Don't forget mean," Osaro said, focused on the road. He turned into the airport arrival lane.

"Huh?"

"You forgot that you were mean...okay keep going. This is good for my ego."

"Lord knows your ego is large enough, so let me stop. You good people."

Osaro laughed and the sound was like a balm to her soul. The first couple of times she saw him, he always had that evil eyebrow raised. Laughter seemed to be a forbidden, but now, his eyebrows were always level and he was more carefree. He gave her a reason to live again. As they approached the airport terminal, Itohan saw the guy she now knew to be Tekena Tamuno.

If her man wasn't in the car, she would've given God a shout for "great things He hath done." Tekena was fine with a "ph." Nothing or no one compared to her Osaro, but this man right here was very close behind. And they all went to school together. How did those girls deal? He was tall, well-built with a honey brown complexion and a clean fade with bushy, wild curls at the top. He had a diamond stud in his ear and was clad in Nike. She loved her own chocolate thunder, but this light-skinned lightening wasn't bad.

The men dapped each other and laughed about whatever it was they were talking about. Osaro walked over to the trunk, popped it, and seconds later they entered the car.

"Tex, meet my lady, my love, Itohan. Itohan, my boy Tekena or Tex." Osaro beamed and Itohan blushed.

She turned around in her seat to say hi. Tekena took her hand and kissed the back of it. "It's very nice to meet you. Has my boy told you that you're very beautiful?"

Itohan looked over at Osaro. He wasn't paying them any attention. He was trying to get them back into the moving traffic, so they could get out of the airport. She decided to mess with him a little.

"No, he hasn't, but I assume you will."

"I don't slack like that. You are beautiful." Tekena looked toward Osaro. "He's been keeping you all to himself because he knows there's serious competition out there."

"Thank you. And, erm… you're probably right," Itohan cosigned.

"Both of you are about to get put out of this car, watch," Osaro warned.

They laughed at him.

Finally, they got on the highway and made their way Itohan's apartment. She was looking forward to this weekend. The good thing was Keni wouldn't be watching her like a hawk thinking she'd crumble since she didn't have a man.

"So Tekena, Osaro tells me that you're a professional racecar driver. That's so cool. So I know a celebrity."

"Oh please, babe, don't gas him up. His fans do enough of that already," Osaro said.

"Well, if he's good, they should."

"What you mean by 'if' Sis? Of course, I'm good." Tekena frowned.

Itohan gave Osaro a knowing glance. Now she understood what he meant by not to gas Tekena up.

"Oh, excuse me." Itohan put her hand to her chest in feigned shock.

Tekena smirked and waved her off. "You good because of my boy here. When you know better, you do better."

"She ain't the one man," Osaro warned.

Tekena chuckled.

"You see I was trying to get to know you, so I could figure out whether I wanted to hook you up. But now I don't know," Itohan teased.

Tekena laughed. "It's all love, Sis. Ro over there, is about ready to fight me. What you do to him so fast?"

"Baby, we will not be playing cupid. I don't want anybody coming to you when they have problems before I have to check them," Osaro said.

Itohan rolled her eyes and turned to Tekena. "Anyways…how was your flight? You're coming from *Naija* right?"

"It was all right except one rude air hostess I wanted to strangle. If my mama didn't raise me right, I would've been in the news."

Osaro and Itohan looked at each other. She was sure they both had the same thought. But it couldn't be. Keni wasn't supposed to come in until tomorrow.

"You flew first class, right? What did she do?" Osaro asked.

"Yeah of course, always. So, you would expect the service to be impeccable, right? Check this out, I got on the plane and wanted a vodka and cranberry juice. Shorty was nice, smiling and grinning. You know your boy is fine, right?"

"No, I don't. But I know you think you are. Just tell the story, man," Osaro said.

Itohan listened to their banter and couldn't contain her laughter.

Now she knew where Malcolm fell into this equation. He must be the mediator. Malcolm was their Ajoke. Her man and Tekena were two extremes.

Tekena went on to tell them about how after tasting the drink he ordered, he decided he no longer wanted it. He remembered that it might not be a good idea to mix alcohol and a semi empty stomach. So, he told the air hostess he wanted apple juice. When she brought it, he saw that the cup looked dirty, so he asked her to give him a water instead. Itohan laughed as he told the story like he didn't see how sending the poor hostess around like a maid wasn't cool.

"Man, she gonna have the nerve to tell me I had to make up my mind about what I wanted to drink. Then sent over another hostess back with the water."

"Well, she's kinda right." Osaro turned into her apartment complex.

"Yep. But all that went down the drain with the delivery. She sucked her teeth and rolled her eyes, then turned her back on me when I tried to tell her, 'my bad.' I don't do disrespect, no matter how right you are." Tekena huffed, as though he was getting annoyed all over again narrating the story.

Itohan nodded. She could understand both sides, but he was the passenger and she was sure the hostess was trained to deal with difficult passengers. Osaro parked and Itohan turned around to face Tekena.

"Welcome again and it was very nice to meet you. I'll see you later," Itohan said.

"Likewise. I'll be here through the Thanksgiving holiday, so we'll definitely see each other."

"Great."

"I'm gonna walk her inside, then we can be on our way. Mac should be waiting on us by now." Osaro got out of the car, walked over to Itohan's side and opened the door. He helped her out and brushed his lips against hers briefly.

"I'll see you later?" he asked.

"Enjoy your time with your boys. I'll call you."

Itohan giggled at his frown. She rubbed her hand on his chest with her eyebrow raised, waiting on him to acknowledge her comment. Osaro nodded and grabbed her hand. He walked her to her door, kissed her on her forehead, and waited for her to enter.

The entire time she heard his footsteps fading away, Itohan felt like, after all this time, the peace that eluded her was now wrapping her in a cocoon. For the first time in years, she entertained the idea that God might've removed Aidenoje from her life for a reason. She contemplated that what she went through was just to bring her to her prince, her love, her protector and her shield.

Itohan walked towards her room and for the first time in years, lifted her head to the heavens and murmured, "Thank you, Father. Your will be done."

"Amen."

Itohan jumped then turned and found Keni apparently coming out of the shower.

"Ah Keni, what are you doing here? I thought you didn't come in until tomorrow." Itohan walked over and hugged her sister.

"I decided to help someone with her flight. Her father's sixtieth birthday was today, so I took her flight and she'll take mine tomorrow. I was trying to help her out, but I hated that flight." Keni walked to the guest room and Itohan followed.

"Why?"

"I don't even want to think about it. I met the rudest passenger ever. The cow thought because he was fine, I was his personal servant."

Itohan busted out laughing. It was a small world indeed and this Thanksgiving holiday was turning out to be an interesting one.

"It's not funny. I just need to sleep. Tomorrow should be better." Keni wrapped up her hair. "How are you *jare* and our bobo, Osaro?"

"Osa is good. Lemme go shower and we'll gist and call Joks."

Itohan walked to her room and smirked. She contemplated whether to tell her sister that they'd be having dinner with her rude passenger in a couple of days, or just let things play out by themselves.

22

"How much longer?"

Osaro aimed at the basket and took the shot making the three pointer he was famous for. "How what?" He bounced the ball, walking to the other end of the basketball court.

"Before you get down on bended knee."

It was Thanksgiving morning and he and the guys were at the nearby gym getting in a quick workout. He hadn't seen Itohan since he dropped her off two days ago. She meant what she said about giving him time with his boys. The couple texted and Facetimed each other, but his arms craved being wrapped around her. Since dinner was at his house, Auntie Lizzy had arrived the night before. Itohan and her sister should be arriving soon since they and Robin were helping his aunt prepare dinner.

Over the past couple of days, Tekena stayed on his case, teasing him about seeing a different side of him.

"You're forgetting the girl hasn't even said she loves me yet," Osaro said.

"I don't buy that. The girl loves you." Malcolm bent down to tie his shoes. He looked at Tekena. "You should see the way she dotes over him. Actions, man. They speak louder than words."

"That might be true, but I get where Ro is coming from. You do wanna hear the words," Tekena added.

Osaro and Malcolm looked at Tekena and started laughing. In his thirty years of life, they'd never known Tekena to have a serious relationship. They had no idea where his advice was coming from.

"And you would know this how? Don't tell me you've been holding out on us," Osaro said.

"I don't need to be in any relationship for me to know the basics. And nah, I can't deal with relationships. By the time I take these women out on more than a few dates, they're trying to change my profession. When they agreed to the date, they knew I raced cars. Why all of a sudden, after one lobster, they trying to tell me how dangerous it is? That's why I don't wine and dine. We order takeout, take care of our body needs and that's it," Tekena fussed.

Osaro and Malcolm looked at Tekena and he was legit upset. In that moment, Osaro felt kinda bad for his friend. It must be hard being at the top and having no one to share it with. As they continued playing the game, Osaro thought about his life without Itohan and his chest suddenly became tight.

"I'm still of the opinion you should give her time." Malcolm dribbled the ball.

"That's what I'm doing, but until she's fully mine, I won't be bending no knees," Osaro said with conviction.

"What do you mean by until she's fully yours? Ro, you into sharing women?" Tekena took a gulp from his water bottle.

"Shut up, fool. I mean emotionally. There's still a part of her that I can feel she has hidden and until she can come to me with it, we can't rise to the next level."

"Just keep praying for God to touch her heart. To release her from the past she's carrying. When she trusts you, she'll come to you," Malcolm offered.

"Here you go, always trying to preach unnecessarily," Tekena said. He was the only one among the three who wasn't saved.

"Ain't nothing unnecessary about taking things to God in prayer, Bro," Malcolm responded.

"Don't start, y'all." Osaro cautioned. It was always a serious debate between those two when Malcolm preached salvation.

"Ro, while I agree with you, I've seen your girl just once and I can tell she loves you. Like preacher man over there said, just be patient." Tekena paused. "Now, come on let me finish whooping you on this court, so I can go see what your fine auntie cooking,"

"I'm going to tell her you said that." Osaro chuckled.

"And I'm gonna deny you like Peter did Big J. How about that?"

Osaro grinned, dribbled the ball past him and dunked over his head. Tekena stood angry, while Osaro did the *Shoki* dance step. It was time to head home.

***

A freshly showered Osaro sat on the small bench inside his walk-in closet with his Bible in his hand. His towel was wrapped around his waist and hair in a bun atop his head. He and the guys had been back for a while. He loved that he had a full house. He could hear Auntie Lizzy talking to Eseosa, and Robin and Ehi passionately disagreeing on the pronunciation of tomatoes. Tekena occupied one of his guest rooms and should be freshening up as well.

He, however, needed some quiet time. **Lean not to your own understanding**. As the water had pounded his body and relaxed his muscles a few minutes earlier, Osaro heard the words repeatedly. In the recent weeks, he had spent many nights praying over Itohan. She attended church with him on a few occasions, but he often wondered whether he was doing enough to bring her closer to Jesus. He knew that he couldn't save her, neither could he force her to accept salvation, but he also knew that he couldn't be unequally yoked. She had attended church with him a few times and even Bible study, but she never took that step towards total commitment.

He flipped through his Bible and landed on Lamentations 3:22. *Because of the Lord's great love we are not consumed for His compassion never fails*. He meditated on the verse and his mouth began to move in prayer.

"She said she doesn't need me to save her and I know I can't. But I don't think I've been going about leading her to You the right way. I don't know, maybe I have, but she's just resistant. You know her better than I do. I know that she must come to You for herself. Lead her down that path, Lord. You deemed it fit to put her in my path for a purpose. I've never seen my niece happier, neither have I felt so happy. She helped me heal my pain. After You, she's everything to me, but I still see the hesitation and sadness behind her eyes. Help her to know, Lord, that in You alone is where her help can come from. I love her, Lord. Help me be what she wants and doesn't know that she needs. In Jesus' name. Amen."

Osaro sat for a few more minutes blessing the name of the Lord. He stood and pulled on a pair of blue, faded jeans and a crisp, white, polo t-shirt. He went into the bathroom to put his hair down, dabbed on some cologne and brushed his hair. Satisfied with his look, he opened his door and ran into Eseosa.

"Hey, Baby Cakes. What you got?" He looked at her hand.

"Uncle Tex gave me some gummy worms. When will Auntie Itohan get here?"

Osaro looked at the time. She should've been there at noon. "I don't know. Let me check."

His niece ran in the opposite direction and he made a mental note to give her next dental bill to Tekena. He'd been giving her all types of candy since he arrived. As Osaro approached the stairs, he dialed Itohan on Facetime. After two rings, the phone was answered but not by Itohan.

"*Oga* sir. What is it? We're on our way," Keni teased.

Osaro grinned and shook his head. He'd never seen a crazier human being, but she was cool people. As long as her crazy didn't rub off on Itohan, it was all good. He talked to her often because any time she was on the phone with his woman, she insisted they chat. He loved how protective she was over Itohan, but that also fueled his apprehension over her past.

"Calm down, Fighter. I just wanna make sure my woman is okay and on her way," Osaro said.

"Yes, baby we'll soon be there." Itohan yelled, although she didn't come into focus.

"All right, babe. See y'all soon." Osaro made his way downstairs and allowed his nostrils to guide him into the kitchen. He glanced over in the living room and saw Tekena with a pink, feather boa around his neck playing with Eseosa and her dolls. He chuckled at the sight, but his heart also swelled. It wasn't surprising, as he knew Malcolm and Tekena would do anything for his niece. They all loved Ivie – God bless her soul.

He smiled as he thought about his sister. Ever since Itohan came into his life, he no longer thought of her from a place of guilt, but of gratitude for having been her brother in this lifetime. He knew she was up there with his parents watching over them.

He entered the kitchen and walked over to his auntie who had her back turned to him, stirring something in the pot. He put his hand in the bowl of boiled gizzards and took one.

"Don't think I can't see you over there, Osaro. Take your hand out of my meat," Auntie Lizzy said, without turning around.

Osaro chewed the meat and walked over to kiss her cheeks.

"How many times do I have to tell you—"

"You got eyes in the back of your head. I know, my love. You've had them there since I was a kid." Osaro winked at her and opened the fridge.

"Where is my Princess?"

"Auntie stop calling her that." Osaro chuckled.

"In our land, it doesn't matter whether she's number two or number one million from the throne, there's royalty in her bloodline. Haven't I taught you anything about the Benin Kingdom?" Auntie Lizzy put her hand on her hip.

"You have, and I agree. She's just sensitive about it." He poured himself a glass of juice.

"You children of nowadays are always sensitive about something. No one can speak their mind freely about anything. Those that do speak their mind are forced to apologize the next day because people are sensitive."

Osaro wasn't up for listening to his aunt talk about the fabric of human beings lately. How everyone had turned away from the God on which this nation was built and people being sensitive and lacking compassion and downright hurtful. He walked back over to her and kissed her on her forehead.

"I'm going to miss you when you move back home," Osaro said.

"I'll miss you, too, my son, but now you have a reason to come home more often."

Osaro nodded. He knew he'd eventually expand his business, but he wanted to wait until Eseosa was done with elementary school and a lot depended on Itohan. Where she was, was home for him. They just had to figure out where that would be together. "Where is Ehi?"

"He and Robin went to buy ice."

Osaro sat on the barstool next to the island and pulled out his phone to check his email when the doorbell rang. He got up and walked to the living room, but Tekena was already at the door. Osaro held his fisted hand to his mouth to kill his laughter. He was sure his boy forgot the feather thing around his neck and now he had a princess crown on his head.

Osaro leaned against the couch, crossed his legs and folded his arms. He and Itohan had already discussed the probability that Keni was the hostess Tekena was talking about the day he arrived. The coincidence was uncanny. What were the odds that Keni would change her normal flight and end up in the same one Tekena was on? This should be interesting. Tekena opened the door.

"Jehovah is Lord. You! I knew you were crazy, but I wasn't prepared for this. You're confused on who you are, too?" Keni shouted, once the door opened fully.

Osaro laughed silently as Tekena hurriedly took off the boa and crown from his head. He stared at Keni with his mouth open. He had yet to move aside so the ladies could enter the house.

"Man, let my woman in the house." Osaro walked up to the door. The look on Itohan's face mirrored his as they stared at the pair.

"Oh no, sis." Tekena said to Itohan after he regained his composure. "Please tell me she's adopted. Or your parents dropped the ball. How come you have home training and she don't?"

Itohan giggled. Osaro missed that sound. He took the bag she was carrying and wrapped his other arm around her waist, drawing her to him for a deep kiss. Everyone's drama had to wait until he satisfied his need.

"Are you talking about me? Hold on, I'm coming." Keni said to Tekena. "Itoh, stop all that kissing. Where do I put this bag?"

"You gonna do something, Lil bit?" Tekena glared down at Keni.

Everyone watched them. Keni wasn't short, but Tekena was much taller. Seeing them square up against each other was nothing short of comical.

"Tex man, get the bag from her and come on," Osaro said.

"What I look like? Let her mouth carry it." Tekena waved him off and walked in the direction of Osaro's man cave.

"Big head," Keni murmured under her breath. "Who wants his help?"

Osaro took the bag from her and led Itohan into the kitchen. After they greeted his auntie, and he made the introductions, he left. He headed to his man cave to see what was up with his boy. He had never seen him so frazzled by a woman. As he was about to turn the corner, Malcolm walked in.

"Hey, what's up?" Mac said.

"Nothing, but you just missed World War III. Come on, let's go find Tex and see what's up with him."

"Whatchu mean?" Malcolm asked. Osaro gave him the rundown of events. Malcolm was just as surprised as he was. When they entered the man cave, Tekena was murmuring to himself and playing the video game. Osaro and Malcolm sat down.

"Look, don't even say it. Don't ask. Don't psychoanalyze me," Tekena said, without looking at them.

"Now you know we can't do that." Osaro said.

"Man, what's up?" Malcolm asked.

Tekena stopped the game and looked at him. "Mac, you weren't even there. How you come in trying to talk about it?"

"I ain't gotta be there. I know what I heard. In fact, I need to see this woman." Malcolm laughed.

Tekena turned to Osaro. "I don't wanna mess things up with you and sis. Keep Lil bit away from me, with her rude self. I'll toss her away if she comes at me again with the disrespect."

Osaro bent over laughing. "Me and my woman are good regardless of what y'all got going on. However, if you toss her sister, then she might hurt you and I ain't in it."

Tekena remained silent but waved him off.

"But for real though, this woman got you shook. You must be feeling her," Osaro said.

"Man, get out of here. She's not my type – got too much mouth and why is her hair golden like that?" Tekena shook his head.

"Yep, you feeling her. But check it, try and behave yourself." Osaro patted his friend on his back. He was going to get his woman. He needed some one-on-one time with her.

***

Itohan watched Keni grate the carrots with unnecessary force, occasionally murmuring to herself. She'd never seen Keni so worked up over a man. No matter who he was. This was more than anger; she was attracted to this man.

The young women all got to work helping the older woman prepare a feast. Soon after, Robin came to help, and then Eseosa – who was then tired of playing with Uncle Tex – joined in. Auntie Lizzy gave them PG advice on men and relationships. Itohan saw the sadness in her eyes when she talked of her late husband. She shared stories about raising Osaro and his siblings as her children and shared wisdom she had garnered on life over the years.

The one theme that seemed to linger was everything happens for a reason. There's always beauty for ashes in the end, but you can't do God's job for Him. Although there was chatter all around her, Itohan was lost in thought while she absently took the tails off the shrimp. All those topics gave Itohan a reason to pause and think about her own mom. Their relationship was better than it'd been in years, but it was now time for Itohan to go home and see her parents.

She felt a pair of hands snake around her waist. She smiled and turned her head upwards and Osaro placed a kiss on her lips.

"Come on, let me talk to you for a minute," he said.

"Make sure all you do is talk. All that kissing is getting on my nerves," Keni said.

Itohan laughed at her sister and walked to the sink to wash her hands.

"Mind your business, Sis, or I'll go get Tex," Osaro teased.

"Ugh," Keni grunted.

Osaro grabbed Itohan's hand and they headed out of the kitchen. Itohan could hear Keni threatening thunder and lightning if Tekena came close to her with what she referred to as his foolishness.

"Those two shouldn't be in the same room. Lord, help us get through this meal in peace," Itohan said.

They walked to the patio and Osaro leaned against the table pulling her close. "Enough about them. How are you? I missed you."

She wrapped her arms around his neck. "I missed you too, baby. I have some exciting news."

His eyes perked up. "Tell me."

"Remember that fiftieth birthday party where I was the photographer two weeks ago?"

"Yes."

"Apparently, one of the attendees is a corporate event planner. She reached out to me and said she had a corporate event and would like me to cover it," Itohan said, excitedly.

"Oh, baby, that's great! I'm so proud of you. When is it? Which company? And why didn't you call me immediately when you got the gig?" Osaro fired off.

Itohan couldn't help but thank God for bringing her a man like him. He was always genuinely happy for her. He encouraged her all the time, reminding her not to get so comfortable with teaching that she forgot her dreams. He listened patiently even when she knew he loved just the facts. He always told her that he wanted her right by him in this life and the next. He fed her mentally, and emotionally while adoring her physically. His light but possessive touches made her feel wanted and cherished. When she was about to lose her mind, he had enough self-control for them both. He often said why should he rush to claim what was already his.

Itohan watched his mouth move in pride and praise of her earning her first big corporate gig. Some of what he said, she heard;

some of it she didn't. Her heart raced as she felt her emotions bubbling up. She could no longer hold what she was felling for him.

"I love you," she blurted out.

It was as though time stood still. He looked at her, his lips slightly parted. His hands were still securely on her waist, but it was as though he feared to move in case the moment never repeated itself. Itohan decided it was her turn to reassure him as he always did her.

"I love you Osaro Ikimi AKA Ro, AKA Osa, AKA my man." She giggled at the face he made as she read all his aliases. Her humor was mixed with trepidation since he hadn't responded to her declaration. An awkward silence passed between them and she lowered her eyes.

"No baby, don't do that." He lifted her head with his index finger. "It's like I've waited for you to say those words for so long. I started to doubt…"

Itohan placed her finger across his lips to silence him. Her eyes watered and she cupped his face in her hands. "I might've been slow to recognize what you knew all along. Relationships haven't been easy for me. I needed time, but I love you, Osaro."

Itohan brought her face closer to his and nibbled on his lips. "I thank God for bringing you into my life. Thank you for being patient with me," she said softly.

"Love is patient." Osaro rested his forehead against hers. The minty freshness of his breath tickled her nostrils. She was tempted to kiss him but had to say her part of 1 Corinthians 13. It was something he taught her. They had formed the habit of never going to bed angry, so whenever they disagreed, Osaro would make sure they took turns reminding each other what real love was. It became something they did even when they weren't mad at each other.

"Love is kind," she responded.

Osaro lifted his head and stared deep in her eyes. Then he said, "Love protects and trusts."

Itohan felt a pang of guilt. *She had to tell him.* "It's not self-serving, nor easily angered."

"Love hopes, and it never fails." Osaro held her gaze. "I love you, baby. Thank you for trusting me with your heart. I promise to protect it always."

"Baby, I need to—"

Itohan was interrupted by approaching voices. The lovers looked behind them and saw Keni and Tekena arguing about something while trying to get out of the back door at the same time. Itohan and Osaro shook their heads at the pair.

"Tex, leave that woman alone," Malcolm said from behind them. He then focused on Osaro and Itohan. "What these two are trying to say is simply that dinner is served."

"Oh okay man, I appreciate it," Osaro said. He then turned to Itohan. "What were you saying, baby?"

Itohan suddenly lost the courage she had a moment ago. How do you say you were once married, but forgot to mention it in four months? "Nothing. Just that I love you."

The look Osaro gave her sent her heartbeat up. It was as though he knew she wasn't being truthful. After a few moments, he spoke again.

"And I love you." He brushed his lips against hers. Although his eyes told a different story, she was glad he didn't push it. Why ruin the festivities? She would tell him about Aidenoje later. She'd just professed her love.

Baby steps Itohan, Baby steps.

Osaro held her close as they both walked around Keni and Tekena still bickering about nothing important.

23

In less than twenty hours, they'd be ushering in the new year. Osaro walked outside the twenty-five hundred square foot house his aunt now called home in Benin City, Nigeria. The days between Thanksgiving and Christmas passed by like lightening. Right after Christmas, he and Ehi finalized his aunt's move to Nigeria. The whole family decided to make a trip of it. Itohan had left Florida a couple of days before Christmas. He missed his lady, but was glad she was taking this time to reconnect with her family.

While the house was being built, Osaro had made short trips home, so he had a working knowledge of what needed to be done for his aunt to feel at home. The small generator house at the back was one of those things that was a necessity. Now that his auntie was settled, he was eager to spend the rest of the time with the love of his life in the tranquility of their homeland before they headed back to the States and real life.

The day he dropped Itohan at the airport was the last time he set eyes on her, until last night. In his opinion, his visit to her family home went better than expected. After her parent's initial shock at how he wore his hair, conversation and dinner flowed nicely. Osaro smiled when Mrs. Adolo politely asked him if his locs weren't too heavy for him to carry on his head and Dr. Adolo frowned when Zogie said he might try locs. Keni just teased him as usual.

He loved the small family unit. He, of all people, knew the importance of family. He hadn't expected anything less than her father's questions, so he wasn't thrown off in any way. As a matter of fact, he thought he really won Dr. Adolo over with his short and long-term life goals.

The honking cars in the distance brought Osaro out of his thoughts. He glanced at his watch. He should be getting ready to meet up with Itohan in a few hours. They had plans to visit the

National Museum, something he was really looking forward to. After that, dinner and then, it would be time for Watch Night Service, which both families would attend together.

Osaro scrolled through his phone and smiled at the email from his project manager. Right after Thanksgiving, they received news they won the South Tran contract. Papers would be signed in January, but everything was a go. Resources and people were being put in place because at the turn of the new year, it was full steam ahead.

Osaro sat on the swing set on the porch and his mind drifted to the day Itohan said the three words that her actions had shown him all along. He stretched and took in a deep breath, inhaling the crisp Harmattan air. He buried his hands in the pockets of his sweatpants and his lips turned up in a grin as he reminisced over how she had him shook for a minute there.

Since Thanksgiving, they had been inseparable. He lived for their morning and evening chats and texts, laughter, petty arguments and sometimes big differences in opinions. Through it all, he was becoming more certain that Itohan was the one for him. The one he wanted to spend the rest of his life with, have kids and grow old with. For him, she brought a feeling that was indescribable. His woman still hadn't accepted Christ into her life, but she was closer to it than she was when he first met her. It was on one of those nights when they were sharing the Word that she gave him new insight on his guilt.

"Baby, you thinking that there was something else you could've done is arrogance. Like you can somehow change what God allowed to happen for a reason," she'd told him as they pondered 1 John 1:9. He was happy for the insight, but even happier that Itohan understood the Scripture. It gave him hope that she'd soon get saved.

The door creaked. Osaro tilted his head and saw his auntie appear. The smile on her face told him he had done his job.

She walked over to him and rubbed his shoulder. "*Omo meh.*" She sat next to him and admired her huge compound closed in by a brick wall and black-steel gate.

Osaro smiled inwardly at her calling him her child. Whenever she did that, his heart smiled. She was his family, but she didn't have to step up to the plate and raise him and his siblings and for that he'd forever be grateful.

"Auntie, you good?"

"Osa, you have no idea what you and your brother have done for me."

"Nothing compared to what you did for us. Selflessly, you took us in and raised us like your own. This is just the beginning."

"I miss my brother, your father. I loved him deeply and nothing could have made me turn my back on his kids." She folded her hands across her chest.

At the mention of his parents, Osaro sat straight. He stopped the swing from moving. A day didn't go by when he didn't think of what his life might have become. However, through the tragedy, all things had worked out for good.

"My Dwayne would have enjoyed this peace and tranquility."

"Would he have agreed to come down to live in Nigeria with you?"

"That is one thing people never understood about us. We were willing to do anything for each other. When we got married, Dwayne knew my dream of finally returning to my fatherland. And he supported me wholeheartedly." She paused. "As you know, we weren't rich, but our love made us wealthy. Through thick and thin, we survived. There were good times and don't let me get started on the bad times. But we were committed to making it work and making sure that the love of Christ was radiated in our union. Selfless love."

"Auntie, you make it sound so good, but not everyone gets to experience that."

"But you will." She turned to him. He raised his eyebrow at her. She smiled. "I see the way you look at Itohan. Even if you didn't open your mouth, anyone can tell you love that girl. I'm just happy she loves you back."

Osaro had nothing to add, so he remained silent. Everything his auntie said was true. Itohan was his baby, his love, his queen and other half. She completed him.

"Just remember that storms will come because neither of you is perfect. Hold on to your friendship. It's what will keep you when you can't stand each other. The enemy is serious about causing commotion in godly relationships. I'm assuming that eventually, this thing both of you are doing will lead to marriage. When you make it a three-chord bond with God in the middle, you can weather any storm."

Osaro thought about the words of wisdom his auntie gave him. He knew for certain he wanted Itohan for a wife. Did she want to get married? They talked about it in general terms and she didn't seem opposed to it, but when he actually proposed, would it be another mountain he'd have to climb? Her rejection would literally kill him. Not wanting to mess up the day's mood with the thought, he pushed it to the side. He'd live in the moment and once his launch was over, he would pop the question.

***

After the awkwardness of not seeing or being close to her family in three years passed, Itohan could say she was enjoying the relationship she had yearned for, forever. She'd been in Nigeria for about ten days and was truly enjoying herself. It was great relaxing at home and hanging out with her younger brother, Zogie, who still lived in Benin.

They visited all her old stomping grounds. Even though she visited those places with Aidenoje, having Osaro in her life helped her ignore the anger that sometimes threatened to overtake her when the nostalgic memories hit. When she walked down the street in the evenings, she could see the prior judgment in people's eyes was now replaced with curiosity. Unlike before, however, she wouldn't give people the satisfaction of making her feel uncomfortable.

Itohan stood in front of the full-length mirror in her room and looked at the white blouse and print midi skirt she had on. She had saved the most important tourist site for last. She was taking her man to the National Museum. She hadn't been since she was a kid and being that Osaro didn't grow up in Nigeria, she wanted him to experience the rich history of their people. Her door opened and in walked her brother.

"He must be coming." Zogie glanced over at Itohan and plopped down on her bed.

"Why are you here?" She glared over him as she opened her lip gloss.

"To make sure you're decently dressed. What else?" His eyebrows furrowed like he was well within his right.

Itohan turned to face him and placed her hands on her hips. Zogie, being about a foot taller than her, sometimes let his height mess with his brain, making him forget his place. "You must've forgotten I'm the older one."

"And, you're still my sister and I need to make sure we won't have any problems." Zogie looked at her like she was the one that was crazy. "He seemed all right yesterday but still…"

"Zogie, I'm with Osa in America by myself so if there was a problem, it would have happened by now."

"Well, I'm making sure it doesn't happen under my watch."

Itohan felt his eyes on her as he nodded in approval at her attire then he went back to scrolling through his phone.

After a few moments he spoke again. "I'm happy for you. I haven't seen you glow like this in a long time."

"I'm happy." She paused. "For a while, I was so scared to open up to him. I can't afford to be hurt again. I wouldn't be able to bear it."

"I know nothing about love. What I can say is that to know if a man is really checking for you. He'll chase you, sacrifice, take risks and call you every single day. He would want to be with you all the time. He'll let you know how important you are to him. There won't be any 'maybes' in your vocabulary." Zogie sat up against the head board.

Itohan walked over to the bed and sat on it. "That was the same way Aidenoje started out."

"No, it wasn't. I was there remember? That punk would go weeks without talking to you. Then when you were just about to move on, he would pop up. Remember that? Then when he saw you were serious about moving on after getting tired of him playing his games, he made it official. I wasn't in your relationship, so he might have loved you after a while. I just knew he was into games from the jump. A grown man has no time for that. That's why I won't get that special lady until I know I can be there for her mentally, physically and emotionally. I never want another woman to feel what you felt. And that would happen because I know I'm not ready."

Itohan turned to her brother with misty eyes. Zogie scooted from the bed and hugged her.

"I haven't told him about Aidenoje," she blurted out.

Zogie pulled back. "Why? I mean I get the punk is in your past, but that's vital info. You've been married. Even if it was not legally or in church, you were still married traditionally, that is."

"I don't know. When I met him, I still was so hurt and angry at God for allowing Aidenoje to do that to me." She sighed. "Then we got closer and I was in denial. Then so much time passed, and I was scared to."

"Sis, please tell him. If you're serious about this man, as I can see he is about you. Remember, he's from Benin, too. If you guys want to get married, his people will send someone to investigate you, according to tradition. You can't have them report that and have him completely blindsided."

"I know, I know. I didn't think we'd get this far and now that we're here, how do I tell him? 'Oh by the way, I was married for three years, then my husband asked for a refund, leaving my parents disgraced, me shamed and running to the US."

"It's not as bad as you're making it sound. Truthfully, I don't know how you should tell him. You guys have been dating for close to four months now?"

"We've known each other for four, but dated for three," she said softly.

"You have to find a way. He'll probably be mad, but not as mad as he would be if someone else tells him."

Zogie drew her back in his arms. Itohan was so blessed to be close to both her siblings.

"Isn't this what your friend should be telling you," he spoke over her head. "I'm disappointed in Ajoke. I know Keni's not all the way there, but Ajoke is always the voice of reason," Zogie joked.

"Don't let your sister hear you saying she's not all the way there," Itohan said.

"If she stays home there might be a chance. But she went to a party last night. I don't know if she is even back."

Zogie and Keni had a cat-and-mouse kind of relationship, but there was no love deeper than theirs. Itohan walked to the mirror and fixed her eye makeup. She thought about what her brother said. The thought had nagged her even before she came home. Every time she tried to tell Osaro about her previous marriage, her courage would fail. She needed to find the right time. Maybe tonight. She didn't want to carry that secret going into the New Year.

"Don't worry, Sis. Everything will work out. If he acts up too much, I'll kick his behind."

Itohan laughed and swatted Zogie on his shoulder. Just then her mother entered and looked back and forth between two of them.

"*Ivbi mwen,* my children. I miss seeing us all like this. This Christmas has been the best in a very long time and I thank God for healing our broken pieces," their mother said.

"Mommy, it was not that bad. Why are you talking like we were at war?" Zogie asked.

Itohan and her mother exchanged glances and laughed at him. Zogie was the peacemaker or hot head of the family, depending on the day. He hated when there was any kind of discord in the family and would go to war with anyone that talked about them on the outside. Sometimes without taking the consequences into consideration.

"Itohan, your man friend is here," her mother said, ignoring Zogie.

Itohan furrowed her brow. Osaro hadn't called to say he was on his way. She picked up her phone and saw that he had called, but she had the phone on silent. Glancing at herself in the mirror, the thought that he was with her father by himself crossed her mind and she made a dash for the door.

"Mommy, you left him alone with Daddy?" Itohan asked on her way out.

Mrs. Adolo waved her off. "Any man that can't stand up respectfully to your father and brother is not worth your time."

"Right," Zogie cosigned.

But Itohan had no time for him now. Osaro was very much worth her time and all the man she needed, but her father's mouth had the tendency to leak. Just her luck, he would say something about Aidenoje. And that couldn't happen. Not before she told him about it herself.

24

Hand in hand, Osaro and Itohan walked into the Benin National Museum located at King's Square. Osaro found out the area was called King's Square because the monarchy sat in the vicinity.

"Baby, I can't wait for you to go on this tour," Itohan said, excitedly.

"You gonna be my personal tour guide?"

"Stop being naughty and pay attention as the tour guide tells you about your history. Americanah."

Osaro chuckled. Itohan found it so funny when she teased him about not knowing as much as she did about their culture. "I'm going to remember that when you need me to tell you something about that same America you don't know."

She stuck her tongue out at him and he drew her close. His woman was looking exceptionally stunning. In fact, when she entered the living room when he was talking to her father earlier, his heart pounded. The scent of her perfume preceded her and invaded his nostrils, causing his hormones to go wild. Her chocolate skin shone in contrast to the white shirt she wore. Her hair was straightened with a part in the middle and her face had a little make up. She was beautiful, and she was all his.

"Did I tell you that you look beautiful, I love you and I'm glad you are mine?"

Itohan held her chin with her thumb and index finger in a contemplative stance. "Hmm, let's see. Beautiful, yes. Love me, I think so, but glad I'm yours, no."

He kissed her nose. "Okay, I just did smarty."

She was about to respond when the tour guide appeared. In their group was another couple, then a group of five people.

"Hello, good day and welcome to the Benin National Museum. My name is Uyi and I'll be your guide today. This is an hour-long tour and please, we do not allow pictures. Also set your phones on vibrate, so they don't disturb." He paused, then continued. "The restrooms are on our way in case you need to use them, but bear in mind that the tour would continue. Okay, before we start, let me give you a little history of the Benin," the guide said.

Osaro listened in awe and half annoyance as the guide told them of the originators of the land and its connection to the Yourubaland. He also told them that the previous name of the city was Ile-Binu but when the Portuguese came in the 1940's they changed the name to Benin, so they could pronounce it better.

What arrogance to go to another man's land, decide they couldn't pronounce it, so they changed it? Osaro was further angered when the guide shed some light on the Benin Expedition of 1876 in the hands of the British. They looted the precious artifacts and bronze and they were in a museum in Europe 'til this day.

After the brief lesson, they started the tour. Osaro held Itohan's hand as the guide took them through the museum. The museum housed three galleries. On the bottom floor was the Oba Akenzua Gallery. It contained artifacts from Benin City. Among the artifacts at the Oba Akenzua Gallery was a bronze casting of the head of Queen Idia.

"The history of the Benin Kingdom cannot be completely told without extensive mention of Queen Idia. But for her perseverance and encouragement, the Kingdom would probably not be in existence today," the guide said.

"Why?" Itohan asked.

"Legend has it that the Benin Kingdom, then under the reign of Oba Esegie, was faced with the threat of war from the neighboring tribe, the Ida's. Queen Idia was his mother and was a great warrior who assisted him by raising an army to defeat them," Uyi answered.

"Wow," another person said.

"It is even said that she helped him become king at that time. When Oba Esegie's father died, he had two sons and didn't lay out who would succeed him. Queen Idia made sure her son did," Uyi said.

Osaro remained silent and soaked up the rich history of his people. They moved on to the second floor, which was called the Unity Gallery because as the guide said, it contained artifacts from neighboring communities around the state and the country. When they got to the bronze casting of a dreadlocked king, Itohan looked at him and winked.

"There are those who trace the history and traditions of the Jamaicans to Nigeria. This is because of Oba Akego's dread locs. His locs were said to have mystical powers," Uyi said.

"Are you sure you're not his descendant?" Itohan whispered.

Osaro raised his brows and frowned at her in jest. "I'm positive, I'm not."

The rest of the tour went by quickly because there weren't any more questions.

As they walked out, Itohan grabbed her stomach. "I'm hungry. Let's get something to eat."

"You're the tour guide. Where are we headed?" Osaro opened the door to the rental car he'd been using since he arrived, and she got in. He walked to the other side and got in the back with her.

"Driver, *abeg* take us to Mama Osazee Paper Place," Itohan said to the driver. When Osaro arrived, Itohan got one of her father's drivers to drive him around.

"Okay, Madam. You remember their food is spicy. Can you cope?" the driver said.

"We both eat spicy food, even in America." Itohan laughed.

Osaro felt Itohan's hand cover his on his lap. He turned to her and drew her close, placing his hand over her shoulder.

"What's wrong? Why are you quiet? Didn't you enjoy the tour?" she asked.

Osaro shrugged. "It was great. I learned a lot, but I'm angered. It's like sometimes it's a crime for a people to be great."

"What do you mean?"

"The Europeans where drawn to Benin because of its art, bronze and ivory then proceeded to massacre and burn the city in retaliation for two men that were killed. For me, that's not okay. I mean, not that they died. But they massacred people, burnt down the city, then took the artifacts to their own land and distributed them to other museums around Europe?"

"Why do people do what they know isn't right?" She paused. "I don't know. I guess when you have power over another, you can do what you want."

"Things like this make me so glad that as Christians, we live by a different code. We're all one in the kingdom and that is how we should treat each other here on earth."

The remainder of the ride was in comfortable silence. Itohan laid her head on Osaro's shoulder with her eyes closed. The creases in her forehead told him she wasn't sleeping, but thinking. He wondered what about but decided not to ask. If it were a month or so ago, he would worry, but now, they told each other everything, so he wasn't worried. If anything was bothering her, he knew she'd tell him soon.

***

Later that evening, Itohan's family and Osaro entered the church for Watch Night service. The praise team was singing a medley of African praise songs. She and Osaro sat in the pew behind her family. She put down two books to hold spaces for Robin and Ehi, who were running late. Auntie Lizzy opted out of coming because she didn't want to keep Eseosa out late.

Osaro got down on his knees and started to pray. Itohan looked at him. This man was a godsend to her, but for a moment this afternoon, she didn't feel worthy of his love. She loved how patient, loving, and caring he was with her. She loved him so much it hurt, but she felt unworthy when he spoke about the love of Christ as they ate lunch. It was as though he offered all of him to her and she was still half-stepping. Not intentionally, but she was. The guilt of her secret and the potential blowback of her eventual confession weighed heavily on her all day.

After a few minutes, Itohan knelt beside him and he reached out and took her hand. Her lips didn't move, as she had no idea of what to pray about in that moment. Her relationship with God was better, but it wasn't where it used to be years ago. Not knowing what to say, Itohan tuned her mind and spirit and honed in on the song that was being sung. The song talked about God being the God of yesterday and the God of tomorrow; being the very present help in the time of need. As Itohan listened and felt Osaro squeeze her hand, she was overcome with emotion. She wasn't sure if God would even welcome her back.

Return to Me, and I will return to you. Itohan heard those words in her spirit.

"Help me, Holy Spirit," she mumbled.

Nothing can separate you from my love.

"I'm sorry God. I really am sorry. Help me to live again…free."

I have wiped out your transgressions like a thick cloud and your sins are like a heavy mist. Return to Me for I have redeemed you.

Itohan spent the remaining few minutes in reflection and releasing the anger and pain that had her shackled for the past four years. She asked God to help her truly move on and embrace the gift of love He had so graciously blessed her with. When her whimpers got a little louder, Osaro squeezed her hand a little harder, offering the comfort she needed. He handed her a tissue for her nose and eyes. She was shocked when he took the used tissue from her and stood up to dispose of it.

The music stopped just as Osaro reappeared. She mouthed "thank you" and handed him her hand sanitizer. Soon after, the service started with the pastor preaching about new beginnings.

"All the former things, disappointment, betrayals, struggles and impossibilities are left behind and now we will embrace the new. Thus says the LORD, I am doing a NEW thing. It will spring up. Do you perceive it?

The congregation shouted in the affirmative.

The pastor preached for a few more minutes about the danger of outwardly changing instead of a renewing of the mind. "Anybody can make a list of New Year resolutions, but how long do they last if your mindset doesn't shift?" He later blessed the congregation and returned to his seat.

"Praise the Lord, church," an elderly lady said.

The congregation responded with, "Alleluia."

"Thank you, Pastor, for that word. Brethren as we approach the New Year in about fifteen minutes, we want to invite you to give your life to Jesus and receive the gift of salvation. The floor is open as the praise dancers take us into the new year with "Open Heavens" by Glowreeyah."

Itohan looked around the church. The atmosphere was electric. People were praying and praising, while some worshipped in tears. The dancers were in the middle of the sanctuary and the pastor stood to the side with his arms outstretched. Itohan's mind and spirit fought against the other about going out before the whole congregation. Maybe she'd just let Osaro pray with her later. She looked over at him. He was in full worship mode. Overcome by a force she couldn't explain, Itohan rose and walked down the aisle into the arms of Jesus. She was the prodigal daughter but was glad that God still welcomed her home.

25

Osaro had "I'm Blessed" by Charlie Wilson featuring T. I. on repeat as he drove down the highway to his office. It was the third week in January and nobody could tell him he wasn't blessed. He had a family who he loved, a woman who was the most beautiful creature God created, who loved him, and a business that was doing well. He and Itohan had been floating on cloud nine, ten and eleven since the New Year. His lady was saved, and he didn't have to force, cajole, or give her any kind of ultimatums. He loved her as he should, and she made the decision on her own. God had answered his prayer and led her home.

He sang the lyrics to the song as he parked his car in his regular parking space. Minutes later, he was in his office. It was a big day. The South Tran project kicked off. He'd gotten in from Maryland late last night where he and Malcolm had gone to sign the contract. Signatures on those pieces of paper had made them instant millionaires. They signed the five-year, twenty million-dollar contract.

They had two months to put into reality the vision they had pitched in their proposal. The company wanted a late March launch date, so their plan was to give them a prototype by mid-February for testing and adjustments. Once approved, they'd hand over the app and web design. With this deal, RoMac would be the webmaster and oversee security. Osaro wanted to be a week early on delivery.

Osaro greeted Nancy as he headed to his office. He took off his jacket and hung it across the back of his seat. Setting his briefcase down, he looked through the small stack of mail that was on his desk. Nothing of relevance caught his eye, just promos and offers for credit. He shredded the envelopes and powered on his laptop. As he waited for it to start up, Nancy walked in with a cup of his favorite java.

"Thank you. Is Mac in yet?" he asked.

"No, he's not. He called and said he needed to make a stop first."

"Okay, thank you." Osaro sipped on the beverage and was scrolling through his emails when his cell phone buzzed. He pulled it from his jacket pocket and smiled at Itohan's message.

Baby, I missed you last night. I know today is a big day and I want to tell you how proud I am of you again. I love you baby and I have a special meal prepared for us tonight. xoxo

Itoh.

Osaro felt a pang of guilt rip through him. He'd been working so hard since they returned from Nigeria. He hardly saw her as much as he wanted in the last three weeks. They always Facetimed each other when they couldn't see each other. But the previous evening, they hadn't even talked for a good five minutes when he fell asleep.

With the hiring of a team to getting the team up to speed on the client requirement, he had a tight schedule. Normally he would be able to work with just a few hands, but the size of the project required additional help. Earlier this morning however, he promised himself that he had to get a handle on managing it and his personal life. Itohan accepted he'd be busy, but at the same time, he wasn't planning for his personal life to crumble under the weight of his job.

Osaro quickly typed his response apologizing for falling asleep on her and not talking to her before she went to her new studio. Hitting send, he waited a few minutes for her response, but he knew she might be busy. She had a pre-wedding shoot this morning.

He got into the activities of the day. A few of his smaller clients needed maintenance/refreshing and he could get to at least three of them before he and Malcolm had to go into their teleconference room to meet up with the South Tran IT team via Skype.

Several hours later, Osaro stood at the front of the room with the different people that would pull the project together. He had two back and front-end developers, a graphic designer, testers, a java script editor and a project manager that would coordinate everything. He, as a full developer, would be involved in all aspects of the design and development.

"Welcome, everyone. Tera, here will be our project manager. All of you come very highly recommended and I'm sure you can manage your part without much intervention from me. But Tera will keep all of us on schedule," Osaro said.

He folded his sleeves to the three-quarter mark and waited for any comments. Malcolm was at the other end of the conference table. He wasn't needed for this part, but they always tried to make an appearance in the other's area in case there was an emergency and one of them was absent. Osaro handed out the packets that had been prepared for each team member with their task and delivery date. Minutes later, they started brainstorming and Osaro stood in front of the white board taking down the ideas.

***

Later that evening, Osaro walked up to Itohan's door a half an hour late. They were running behind on the milestone he wanted to reach today. Then he had to go home to check on Eseosa, shower and rush back out. Granted, he should have left work earlier knowing she had dinner cooking, but the time got away from him. Hopefully, his charm and these flowers could get him a pass. He pressed the doorbell and waited. He tugged on the collar of his black polo t-shirt he wore over grey lounge pants. Minutes later, the door opened, and he could tell right there and then that he was in bigger trouble than he thought.

Itohan rolled her eyes at him and turned around, immediately heading to the kitchen. He hadn't seen his woman in about a week and even though he was late, and she had the right to be mad, the attitude had to go. He walked in, closed the door and headed to the kitchen. The aroma of the meal she'd prepared lingered in the air and he remembered he hadn't eaten since breakfast.

She was at the stove stirring something. He admired her shape all the way down to her legs, which were covered in black leggings that stopped at her calves. She had on an oversized, light orange t-shirt that stopped mid-thigh. Her hair was in a bun atop of her head. It wasn't neat, as several strands fell loosely by her face. The scowl she gave him when she turned confirmed for him that he had the sexist woman alive. Still giving him the silent treatment, she folded her arms across her chest and glared at him. Osaro finished putting the flowers in water and walked over to her.

"I'm sorry," he said.

"Osaro, you're thirty minutes late. You could've told me you wouldn't be able to make it. It would've been fine," she said, her voice low in disappointment.

Osaro cupped her face in both his hands. He attempted to kiss her, but she turned away. He frowned at her.

"I'm mad at you, Osaro." She walked away from him and opened the warmer at the bottom of the oven. She brought out his favorite meal, fried plantains and peppered snails. Her contoured face showed her annoyance. He knew he should've called her earlier and said he couldn't make it. It was a week night and she had gone out of her way to make dinner for him.

"Stop calling me Osaro and I said I was sorry," his voice held more irritation than he would have liked. It wasn't with her, but he was more frustrated with himself.

"Be glad I didn't call your middle name. Osaro Michael Ikimi." She rolled her eyes and her lips turned up in a faint smile.

"Come on, baby. I'm sorry time got away from me. It's not an excuse, but it's the truth. I miss my woman. Give your man some love." He attempted to kiss her again and this time she let him. He smothered her with kisses until he was satisfied. He stepped back and studied her face. The smile he was looking for appeared and the disappointment in her eyes was replaced by love.

"I'm sorry. I'm being selfish. I know today is a big day for you, but I've missed you so much." She snaked her arms around his waist.

He kissed her on her forehead. "No apologies necessary. I'll do better. I don't want you thinking work comes before you, because it doesn't."

She playfully pushed him away from her. "I'm not that insecure. Go wash up. Let's eat."

Minutes later, they were seated at a candle lit dinner. Osaro took some time to admire the setting. He hadn't thought she'd go to these lengths.

"How did it go today? You told me a little bit earlier, but I want details." Itohan picked up a peppered snail with her fork and bit into it.

"Nothing but brainstorming and coding. South Tran was specific about what they wanted. So we're aiming to exceed their expectations."

"And you will, baby. Is Maryland their headquarters?"

"Yeah, although they have some subsidiaries."

"So, you're going to be bogged down until you get it done." Itohan pouted.

Osaro leaned over to her and kissed her pouted lips. "Stop pouting. Yes, but like I said, I will make time for us." He knew he had spoiled her, but he wouldn't have it any other way.

"Don't mind me. I'm happy for you, baby. I really am."

"I know you are. That's just another reason I love you." He finished his food and took a sip of the Ariel Chardonnay she'd selected.

"And I love you more than you'll ever know. You saved me," she said softly.

"As much as I love you baby, I can't take credit for that. That's the Big Man upstairs." Osaro winked at her, stood and kissed her hair. He picked up his empty plate, grabbed hers and headed to the kitchen. "Baby, that was a great meal. Thank you."

A few moments later, Osaro had the sink filled with soapy water and was washing the dishes. He always did that after she cooked whether it was at his place or hers. His mind drifted to the events at the office. They had gotten behind and he prayed it wouldn't be a pattern, as he needed to go over and above for this. The planned expansion he had in a couple of years depended on it.

The feel of Itohan's arms wrapping around his waist jolted him back to the present. She hugged him, leaning her head on his back. He paused and allowed himself to get lost in her embrace. No matter what was going on, in her arms he found his peace, his comfort and his safety. She had to be his wife and he had the proposal all planned, but he wanted to wait until he could take her out of town next month.

He leaned his head back so his head touched hers. No words were spoken as they took in the emotionally charged moment. Their love had grown into something he sometimes found difficulty explaining. As such, with the way she clung to him, he felt that something was bothering her. She was touchy feely with him lately and he loved it, but this was different. He rinsed and dried his hands then turned around.

"What's wrong, baby?" Osaro wrapped his arms around her.

Itohan still had her head on his chest. She didn't let go. Osaro stepped back and lifted her chin with his index finger.

"You do know you can tell me anything. What's wrong?" he asked again.

She looked at him with misty eyes. "Promise me you won't ever leave me."

He was tempted to kiss her tears away, but he wanted to give her a chance to say what he knew she needed to say. Osaro walked her over to the dining table. He pulled out a chair and sat. He pulled her in his lap and she wrapped her arms around his neck.

"I'm better with you. You're better with me. My soul is tied to yours. Leaving you is like losing a part of me. In due time, I'm going to ask you to marry me. That's just for formality because you're my wife already."

Itohan giggled. "Supposing I say no?"

"Now, how you gonna ask me that, but just told me not to leave you? At some point I'm gonna wanna make love to you and that's not happening if we don't get married."

"At some point?" She furrowed her brows. "So you don't find me attractive now?"

"Truth be told, I wanted to take you in your classroom the day of that parent-teacher conference, but the Christ in me got my self-control tight. But even Jesus knows I can't hold out forever."

"Yeah, way to clean that up." She grinned.

Osaro chuckled. "You got me off topic, woman. What I was saying is that leaving you will never happen. Now you gonna tell me what's up? How is my big, bad, hardened baby in her feelings?"

Itohan shrugged. "You do that to me. I knew I should have run away from you."

"You wouldn't have gotten far. Stop stalling, tell me what's up," Osaro encouraged.

"I don't know. Sometimes I don't feel worthy of your love. I'm so scared that this will end. I don't think I can bear it."

"Have I ever given you a reason to doubt me? Even when you were mean and stubborn I was there, so that should never cross your mind. I'm the one that's not worthy. You royalty for goodness sake."

She laughed and he was relieved. "Stop that. And I wasn't mean. I was cautious."

"Yeah, whatever you say." He cupped her face. "I want to look you in the eye when I say this. I don't want you ever doubting me again. "I'm in love with you, not the idea of it, but in love with you. You, Itohan Stephanie Adolo, good or bad, moody or cheerful. The one that thinks gummy worms are the best thing God invented. The one with the attitude problem when she loses at Scrabble because I don't let her cheat and put a 'u' in color. The one that – for the love of me – I can't understand why she likes pineapples on pizza. The one that makes up words to the songs she doesn't know and swears she's the next Whitney Houston. The one whose passion for photography is so contagious that she finesses me into being her model. The one who loves me so much that she listens with rapt attention when I ramble about Ruby Rails coding program when all she wants to do is watch *Lion King* for the one-millionth time. You make sure I'm taken care of emotionally and mentally. Physically, we'll get to soon. But do you see? Hurting you is hurting me and why would I want to do that to myself? I love you and I'll never leave you. God willing, we'll grow old together."

Itohan had a few tears roll down her check when he was done.

"I love you so much and I'll never intentionally hurt you." He thumbed her tears.

"I know."

Osaro kissed her wet face and carried her to the couch.

"Lay down here. Let me finish up in the kitchen and make you some of that tea you act like you can't live without." Osaro smiled and ducked before the throw pillow she tossed at him could get to him.

"And I was going to give you best-boyfriend-ever award, but for that little *yab* you had to throw at me."

"I don't want that raggedy award. I'm aiming for husband-of-the-year award," he mushed her head and walked away as she fussed about him loosening her bun.

Moments later, he was done cleaning up. As he poured the boiling water over her Chamomile tea bag, Osaro pondered Itohan's rare emotional meltdown. He'd told her exactly how he felt, no filter. With her, he had none. He hoped he'd laid to bed whatever fear had her so vulnerable. He wouldn't be able to work if something was wrong. His business was important, but his woman was his priority.

26

"You're playing with fire."

Itohan turned and glanced at Ajoke, but remained silent as they went down the stairs of her apartment complex to her car. Itohan tugged on her white and black jumpsuit that she complimented with black heels. The attire had shifted under the weight of the lighting equipment they were carrying to her trunk.

"Itoh?" Ajoke called out when they got to the car.

"Don't you think I know that? Maybe he'll never find out. Maybe it won't be on my record. All Aidenoje did was pay bride price and take it back. We didn't really get married and we have no kids." Itohan started the car.

Ajoke stopped by St. Petersburg on her way back from South Carolina for a nurse's convention. Since she was here, Itohan gladly put her to work. Becky, the lady that helped her with lighting when she had big photography jobs, had taken ill. She did say she'd still try to make it since this was a big corporate job for Itohan. However, Itohan didn't want to take chances. She was going to hire someone else before Ajoke said she'd be stopping by this weekend. Being that both she and Keni had done lighting for her before, Itohan rented the equipment and told her to make herself useful.

"Even you don't believe that. We're *Naija* and you know it means something. But that's not the point. If Osaro finds out from anybody other than you, you're finished. He would think everything you guys have had going on has been a farce."

Itohan put the car in reverse and turned out of the complex onto the connecting side street. The Simisola CD she was absolutely in love with began to play. The current track was "Original Baby" where the songstress spoke about striving to being a better version of herself, but couldn't be someone else. Itohan felt the lyrics. Thanks to Osaro, she was indeed a better version of herself; but no matter what he or anyone said, once he knew her truth, he wouldn't want to be with her. Right now, she wasn't ready to give him up.

"Joks, you're right. I've tried so many times to tell him. I even tried earlier this week when he came over for dinner the other day. It was on the tip of my tongue, but I couldn't do it."

Ajoke grunted.

"I promise I'll tell him when we go out of town next weekend."

"You better. I won't allow you to cry on my shoulder if *yawa gas o*." Ajoke tugged on her ear to emphasize her warning. "I've said my own. Tell me about this client you have me working for."

"The woman that contracted my services described it as gala/launching-like event, but not too formal. I have no idea what that means, but she has my money in the bank and taking pictures is my thing…" Itohan shrugged.

Ajoke chuckled. "You're something else."

"No *for real sha*, I think the company is honoring some of its staff and they decided to do a dinner and invite some stakeholders. So, we're doing the black carpet and covering the evening."

"Cool. I'm so proud of you. Dele keeps saying he wants to take pictures like his godmother."

"My baby. I miss him. I need to come to Atlanta soon."

"Yes, you need to."

An hour later, Itohan and Ajoke set up the lights to get ready for the black carpet. The event was taking place at the Hilton in downtown Orlando. She and Ajoke packed overnight bags so they didn't have to deal with the almost two-hour journey back to St. Petersburg.

Itohan walked into the huge banquet hall to survey the angles. She liked to take note of key places she needed clear so she could get the perfect shots. The space was decorated in a blue and silver theme, from the tablecloths, to the chair covers, to the balloons that had Net Glow written on them. *Maybe that was the new technology they were launching.* Itohan shrugged and continued to walk the empty room. It could easily seat three hundred people and she wanted to capture the essence of the evening.

***

An hour and a half later, the event was in full swing. Itohan and Ajoke, who was a lifesaver, were working the room effortlessly. Itohan had since changed her pumps for something more comfortable. She hung her camera around her neck and walked over to the cash bar at the back of the room. She ordered a Coca Cola and glanced across the room. Everyone was being served the cake that had been cut. She was sure she'd captured almost everybody in her shots in different takes. The last part of the evening, she was told, was handing out awards to the members of staff.

Ajoke walked toward her and ordered a Sprite. They were engrossed in conversation when applause broke out in the room. Itohan and Ajoke turned as the microphone was being tapped. Itohan's heart stopped. It just stopped.

"Ladies and Gentlemen," the Master of Ceremony spoke. "We've been waiting for this moment. With a sick child involved, we doubted but hoped, and now, I'm pleased to announce the man of the hour. The one who keeps our company glued together. The brain behind Net Glow, Mr. AJ Kenneth and his lovely wife of five years, Priscilla Kenneth."

It can't be. No, it can't be.

Itohan watched in horror as the man she hated most in the world graced the stage, holding hands with a Caucasian woman who was living her life. When did the man she knew as Aidenoje Iyere become A.J Kenneth?

This is why I couldn't find him. He changed his name. The betrayer is using his father's middle English name and shortened his first name to A.J!

"Itoh, Itoh" Ajoke called out to her.

She was too stunned to answer; her body began to heat up and shake uncontrollably. She wobbled in place as a wave of nausea took over her body. This man stole seven years of her life and for five of them he'd been living happily ever after… with kids. Rage took over as her legs began to move forward. Her hands needed to be around his neck. Now that she had seen him, he didn't get to live happily, after what he had done to her.

"Itoh, come on now, babes. Don't do this here." Ajoke held on to her hand and tried to steer her in the opposite direction. "Please think about the name you've built for yourself. Think about Osaro; think about your parents. You don't want to go to jail for assaulting this man in America. *E jor*, please, let's just get out of here. Please, I'll call Patricia and tell her we have to leave."

Itohan heard her friend pleading with her, but rage blocked it out. How could God allow him to be happy after the humiliation he had dished out to her? Where was the payback? Where was her retribution?

"Itoh, answer me, please. Do you want me to call Osaro? Oh, shoot I can't because he doesn't even know this man exists," Ajoke said.

Itohan snatched her hand away and glared at her friend. She looked back at the stage and Aidenoje was holding the microphone, giving a pep talk to his employees. She trembled. Tears fell – not tears of sorrow, but of anger. They stung her cheeks. The pain over her lost years pierced her heart and cut deep. Thinking for a split second over Ajoke's words, she turned and left the room. In a corner of the lobby, she pulled her hair and paced. Memories of yester years came flooding through. All that time in emotional captivity and Aidenoje was just living his life.

"Jesus, why? This isn't right. I'm finally able to live my life and you display him before me. Is this a test? I'm telling you now, I'm failing it. I'm not strong enough. I need to confront him. I need to know why. Come on now, this is too much. How are You going to allow him to be happy after everything? It's not fair. It's not fair," Itohan raged.

She put her hand over her chest. It felt like a vice was being clamped down on it. She physically hurt from the anger that racked her body. Her breathing hitched as hot tears poured down her cheeks. She made her way to the bathroom. She had to pull it together. As broken as she felt right now, she would die if he came out and saw her.

Minutes later, her breathing had calmed. She'd used the restroom and was washing her hands when Ajoke entered. In silence, her friend wet a paper towel and helped her wipe the running mascara from her eyes.

"Itoh, I'm so sorry. I had to stay out there and take pictures of the punk to fulfill your contract. Apparently, he's the main attraction. He was so caught up in the admiration of his followers that I don't think he recognized me." She paused. Itohan had no response. "The pictures might not be good since I'm not you, but just in case. I also told Patricia you're not feeling well. She said they were almost done, so it was okay to leave."

Itohan's lips quivered as she tried to string together an audible response. Unable to, she nodded and Ajoke drew her into an embrace. Itohan's head pounded from the sudden tension. Her heart hurt, and the sobs flowed.

Ajoke rubbed her back and murmured, "God is the strength of your heart and your portion. See, He already turned your mourning into dancing with Osaro."

Itohan heard the words, but her mind couldn't make sense of them. All the emotions she had buried deep in her returned. The Lord hadn't avenged for her. She wanted her pound of flesh. She stepped back from her friend. She wiped her face, her expression blank. She looked in the mirror again. She was somewhat presentable. She could feel the heat of Ajoke's stare at her sudden mood change, but Itohan wasn't in the mood to assuage anybody's fears.

"The woman said I can go *abi*?" Itohan asked.

Ajoke nodded hesitantly.

"*Oya*, let's go."

"Itoh, I don't like the feeling I'm having. Please don't go out there and confront that man. Let's just go," Ajoke pleaded.

"Isn't that what I said? Let's go." Itohan walked to the door.

"Itohan, I know you're mad but please, let the past remain in the past."

Itohan didn't respond but walked out of the bathroom and Ajoke followed. Thankfully, her friend had packed up their equipment and left it at the front desk so they didn't have to go back into the hall. One of the bellhops helped them load it into her car and the ladies drove in silence. Itohan was now determined to make the journey back home, so Ajoke got behind the wheel and drove them back to St. Petersburg.

Itohan's mind wandered. Now that she had the name Aidenoje was going by, she could do some research on him and see what he'd been doing the for the last seven years.

Her phone buzzed and it was Osaro for the third time tonight. She didn't feel like talking, so allowed it to ring until her voicemail picked up. Seconds later Ajoke's phone rang. Itohan took it out of the cup holder and it was Osaro calling her.

"Joks, *abeg* answer him, but tell him I'm asleep or something."

"I see your crazy has started. You want to allow this nonsense man who cared nothing about you to ruin what you have going on," Ajoke scolded.

"*Abeg* just answer the phone. In my state, I don't want to talk. He'll know something is wrong and then what do I say?"

"And whose fault is that?"

The phone stopped ringing and then started up again. This time Ajoke answered the call.

"Hey Osaro…yes we're fine. Errn…your wife? She had a serious headache so I gave her pain killers and she dozed off. Okay, I'll tell her to call you." Ajoke hung up the phone with a frown on her face. "I don't like it that you have me out here lying. That man did nothing to you. Talk to him."

"I will," she said in a low voice.

"Again, please just let it be. Don't look for Aidenoje. Just let it be," Ajoke warned.

"It's not fair."

"Life is not fair, but God is a just God. Everything you go through, trust that God has some growth for you and it will be good. Look, you have Osaro."

"Stop saying that. My love for Osaro is not an antidote for the years of humiliation and pain. Not to talk of the money Aidenoje got from me. He didn't pay me back, but had the audacity to ask for his dowry back. And now he's here with his white wife and 2.5 kids living the American dream. *On top my head abi?* No, my dear. It's not right. It's just not right." Itohan's body began to shake again. "How do you know God didn't let me see him so I can help Him avenge?"

Ajoke frowned. "Now you know you're talking nonsense. And how do you know the man has 2.5 kids?"

Itohan shrugged. "His wife looks like the type to want two kids and a dog."

"Now you're reaching. You know nothing about them."

"Why do you think we're going back home tonight? My laptop is there. I'm about to have a Ph.D. in all things AJ Kenneth."

"Itoh please, I know you. You just accepted Christ barely a month ago. Lean on Him and don't let your feelings carry you down the road of no return."

"It's hard, Joks. I'm telling you now. I've lived to see him again for seven years – seven years – and you want me to pretend seeing him didn't do anything to me. The smugness of his face and how lovingly he looks at her."

"Is it his love you want?"

"No! I have my Edo man, Osa. But I want him to hurt. Just like I hurt. My life was at a standstill for all that time."

"You know we've been friends for over two decades and I'd be foolish not to tell you the truth. He hurt you, yes; humiliated you, yes; stole from you, yes. But you allowed your life to be at a standstill because you refused to live, holding on to pain. You refused to forgive and move on, shackling yourself to him. We don't have to wait for people to be sorry before we forgive. Do you know how many people would be waiting on Christ's forgiveness if that were the case? Keni and I have been telling you for years to let it go. See, he has school-aged kids and a wife and you're just meeting Osa. I'm not saying this wasn't the time for you to meet Osa, but you wouldn't be this angry if you had lived your life with a free mind instead of waiting to avenge something God has control over."

Itohan remained silent and leaned her chair against the headrest.

She reclined her chair and pondered Ajoke's words, her life, and her future. She even thought about her renewed faith. Tears ran down her cheeks.

"Give me your hand."

Itohan looked over at her friend as she navigated with one hand and stretched out another to her. Itohan placed her hands in hers.

"Father God, we come to you in the name of Jesus. The Bible promises us that You mend the heart of the broken hearted. We're also told to lean to You and not to our own understanding. Father, we don't know why Aidenoje did what he did or what Your purpose is in letting us see him now. What we do know is that You are our ever-present help in time of need. Father God, my friend is hurting. She needs You, Lord. Comfort her, God. Remind her that in You lies the peace for her troubled water. Wrap her in Your bosom Lord, and in the knowledge that You will do what is right and just. In Jesus' name."

"Amen. Thank you."

Itohan turned to her side and looked out of the window. The night was dark, but she prayed God's light shone through, because although she knew what her friend wanted her to do and what she should do, her mind was currently a battlefield and was winning the war over her soul.

27

Two weeks had passed and Itohan was madder than she thought was humanly possible. It was Monday morning and she had pictures to edit, invoices to send out, emails to answer and her social media business accounts needed updating – all which had taken a backseat during her pity break. The fact that she couldn't function, her boyfriend was mad at her and the reminder of Aidenoje's betrayal had since taken away the hurt. Now, she was raging.

The day after the event, Ajoke wanted to stay with her for another day, but Itohan just wanted to be alone, so told her she was fine. It took everything in her not to look Aidenoje up or whatever name he went by now, over the internet that night. She was so fed up with hearing "God knows." She knew she should lean on her new-found faith, but she didn't have the energy to. So instead of listening to Ajoke go on and on about it, she went right to bed.

The next day Itohan had called her sister. Between the both of them, they called her every day to make sure she didn't do anything stupid. She hadn't because she hadn't figured out just what to do yet.

Aidenoje was now a top shot. Net Glow was his brainchild and it was an app that allowed customers to schedule personalized pickups of their shipments and track them all the way to the destination. If she weren't so upset, she'd be proud. According to Google, they did, in fact, have two kids and a dog. Itohan gagged as she remembered the family portrait that came up. Married five years, which meant he was married a whole year before he remembered he had someone at home waiting—her. It was probably at their one-year anniversary that he said, "Oh yeah, I have a loose end back in Nigeria I need to tie up," then sent his family to humiliate her. He had to be humiliated, too. How? She didn't know, but he had to feel what she felt.

Itohan hummed to Vivian Green's "Emotional Rollacoaster." The song had been on repeat for two weeks. She loved Osaro. She knew that, but struggled to get off the emotional roller coaster that Aidenoje's reappearance had her on. She knew nothing good came out of their relationship. She'd been waiting on this opportunity for four years, so nothing else mattered. To see he was doing just fine made her disappointed in God. Every day she woke up and asked for God's help in not jeopardizing what the future held for the past. But then, like clockwork, she'd find out another tidbit that made her furious that he got to do her dirty and flourish.

Valentine's Day was last week, and she'd been in no mood to celebrate. Her head wouldn't stop pounding and she was in a funk. Osaro, being the loving man that he was, came over and nursed what he thought was a migraine. He cooked dinner and cuddled her until she fell asleep.

In the following days, she still hadn't felt any better. Unfortunately, Osaro paid the price. She ignored his calls most of the time. When she did answer, it was lackluster. It all came to a head the previous evening when Osaro barged into her house and basically told her that he was too grown to play her games, demanding to know what was wrong with her. She felt so bad because he had done nothing wrong. Hence her current mission was to get back on her man's good side. Despite his anger at her behavior, he called her every day to make sure she was okay. She'd been so selfish and hadn't even asked how his project was coming along.

Itohan pulled into the parking lot of the local coffee shop she always patronized. She needed all the energy she could muster up to get back to the grind and take her mind off everything. Going over the "why's" and "what if's" was exhausting, and she needed a mental break. Minutes later, she stood in line, scrolled through her phone and tried to answer as many emails as she could while she waited.

"Look at that. My wife shops there all the time. Let me call her to make sure she gets our bankcard canceled," the man in front of her said.

Itohan looked up and he was pointing to the small television that hung in the corner. She squinted her eyes to zoom in on the screen and saw there was a breaking story about the breach of customers' information at Kline Baffs, a popular online boutique for woman. Itohan didn't shop there. She preferred to feel and see what she was buying first, but Ajoke swore the store was a slice of heaven on earth.

She made a mental note to call her friend on the way to her studio. The man moved to the side to mix his coffee, and she moved up in the line. Itohan placed her order and waited.

"I don't know how well they protected their system," he told his friend." But I know another company going through a class action lawsuit right now, because they didn't do all they could cyber wise to protect their clients. One other larger company even paid the hacker not to release the info when they found out they were hacked."

"I mean that's a bad look, man." The man's friend said. "People that patronize your business shouldn't also have to worry about their information getting into the wrong hands." They picked up their beverages and walked away.

Itohan paid for her coffee and a warm cinnamon roll she knew she shouldn't have, and turned to leave. On her way to her car, she put in her headphones and dialed her friend.

"Joks, *how far now*?" Itohan asked once Ajoke picked up the phone.

"*I dey o. How your side?* Please tell me you're going to work today?"

"Yeah, I'm on my way."

"We thank God for Jesus. I thought you had closed shop for that man."

"I don't want to even go there with you. I needed time, something you and Osaro don't seem to understand," Itohan stressed.

"Well, I kinda understand, but still, as your friend, I can't let you go down." She paused. "Now as for your man, don't blame him. He has no knowledge of what's going on. All he knows is that his lovey-dovey girlfriend started ignoring him. Better go and make up with that man before another sister in the Lord snatches him up."

Itohan opened her car and rolled her eyes as if Ajoke could see her. "Whatever – that won't happen."

"Okay, *o*. Keep ignoring him and telling yourself that."

"When did this turn into my relationship conversation? I was calling to ask you if you saw the breach of Kline Baffs?"

"My dear, I saw it *o*. They sent their customers an email explaining the situation. I've gone to change all my info at the bank. Because of something like this, some CEOs are made to resign. It shows incompetence."

At the mention of the word resign, Itohan zoned out. To be forced out of your job because of something you had no direct control over – that had to be humiliating.

It took no time for Itohan to make it to her office. One could tell she hadn't been there in some time. Still on the phone with Ajoke, she set her purse down and proceeded to air the studio out. It was only after Itohan assured her friend she was going to make up with Osaro later in the day that she agreed to get off the phone.

Itohan powered on her laptop and opened her editing software. Sipping on her beverage, she immediately got to work. Tearing into her Cinnamon roll, she pondered Ajoke's words again. *Some CEOs are made to resign.* She pulled out her iPad and typed "Cyber Attacks" in the search box. She spent the next two hours absorbing all she needed to know.

28

Osaro sat behind his desk and his fingers absently circled the brim of his now lukewarm Mountain Dew. His stomach was in knots as he waited in his office for one of the developers to show him the redesign for the app. The last month had been stressful, but it all led up to this moment. He was anxious and excited.

Be anxious for nothing. He heard the verse in his spirit. He'd had to remind himself of that a lot in the past weeks. He untied his hair and let it fall down his shoulders. He rested his head on the headrest and took in a deep breath.

It wasn't only his job giving cause for concern, but Itohan as well. Over the last couple of weeks, she had been acting strange and he didn't like it one bit. The issue he had was she refused to share what was bothering her.

"Hey, man. We ready?" Malcolm interrupted his thoughts, walking into his office.

"No, not yet, Ace is still working on it. He'll show us something soon." Osaro sat up.

"Oh, ok cool. Man, I still can't believe this is now a reality, after courting those folks for a year."

"That's favor, man. Do you see all those other companies that were in the line-up? They've been in operation for years," Osaro said. Excitement took control of him any time he thought about the multi-year contract.

"God is awesome. While we're waiting on Ace, how did Sis take the surprise for Valentine Day?" Malcolm asked.

Osaro had planned to take Itohan to Alvin's Lounge for music and dinner, but when he showed up, she had a headache and wasn't feeling well.

"It didn't happen."

"Why? What happened?"

"I got there and she said she was ill." Osaro sighed.

"Why you say it like that? Wasn't she sick? What's up with you man? You talking in code. I thought y'all were straight."

"I thought we were too, but she moving kinda funny. I don't know if something happened or she was really sick. I mean her trust issues run so deep that it's hard sometimes, man." Osaro rubbed his chin. "I thought we were over that. I love that woman – I've shown her, but she makes me so crazy," Osaro vented. In silent prayer, he asked God to intervene, but this was the first time he'd put a voice to his frustration over her recent shift in behavior.

"Ro, man, I don't know what to tell you. Cupid's been minding his business and I've been minding mine. Just ride it out. Maybe she's going through something."

Osaro's next words were interrupted when Ace entered with his laptop.

"You ready, Boss?" Ace asked, standing at the door.

"Yep, come in. Let's do this." Osaro stood and walked around his desk. Ace sat next to Malcolm and Osaro stood behind them. For the next several minutes, Ace walked them through the app. He showed them the mobile and desktop versions. The design was dope and Osaro was impressed on how the group he hired took his design and upped it several notches. Ace showed them the log in and log out options, how multiple users in a family could share the account. It was easy navigation and he was confident of the security of the customers' information.

As they'd always done, Osaro and Malcolm went back and forth a couple of times during the demo. There were a couple of things Osaro wanted as enhancement while Malcolm countered, citing the budget with man hours, logistics and materials.

"Okay, man I get it. We can't get the software for fingerprint recognition. But it would be nice, because even I don't wanna be remembering my password. You know how many things we get passwords to nowadays?

"You better pick up a piece of paper and write them jokers down. We ain't getting that. Now if they up our money in the renewed contract, maybe," Malcolm said.

Ace laughed and Osaro joined it. There was a knock on the door and the trio turned. The vision of the beauty that was going to be his wife very soon stood in the doorway. Osaro took a minute to absorb the view. Itohan stood there with a smile on her face that he silently vowed to make his life's mission to keep there.

"Hey guys, hope I'm not interrupting, but I came to take my man to lunch." She sauntered toward him, not missing a beat. "You guys will be all right without him for a couple of hours, right?"

She stood in front of him not taking her eyes off him. Osaro stared back. She wore her hair curly, the way he liked it. Her light denim shirt was tucked into some dark green pants that hugged her hips like they were painted on. Her heels brought her up some, so he didn't have to bend his head to capture her lips.

Throats clearing caused them to come up for air. She giggled and used her thumb to wipe her gloss off his lips.

"Jeez man, I thought you'd never let her breathe," Malcolm said. "Hey Sis, what's happening?" He went over to her and kissed her cheek. Ace chuckled.

"Nothing much. Just living and surviving."

Ace packed up his laptop. "I'm Ace. I work for the big man here. It's nice to meet you."

Itohan smiled and returned his greeting.

"Boss man, I'll have those changes you need later today." Ace walked out of the office.

"Just rude. Can't even make the introductions before sucking Sis's face off," Malcolm scolded.

Osaro pulled Itohan to him and draped his arm over her shoulder. "Whatever man, have you seen my woman? Besides she doesn't need to know Ace anyway."

Itohan swatted Osaro's hand. "Be nice. Malcolm, how's your grandmum?"

"She's good. A'ight, lemme go so you can take this in love man to eat."

"Get off my man, Mac. I love him too. So, we in love together."

"That's right, baby. Stand up for your man," Osaro said.

Malcolm walked to the door and paused. "Oh, tell Keni, Tex said what's up."

Osaro laughed.

Itohan looked between the two of them. "Did he really say that?"

Osaro shook his head and went to his desk to pack up. He was going to spend the rest of the day with his woman. He planned to ask Ace to send him the changes by email and he'd check them out later.

"No, but he might as well. Always huffing and puffing any time her name is mentioned." Malcolm laughed and walked out of the office.

Osaro walked toward Itohan. "You must be feeling better."

She lowered her eyes briefly and raised them again. "Yes, I am. I'm sorry."

"You gotta stop trying to hold on to your burdens, baby." He paused. "Love is surrendering control. If something is bothering you, you gotta let me help you. I love how strong you are, but I'm your shoulder to lean on."

"I know. I love how you love me. I didn't mean to shut you out." She rubbed her hand on his chest.

Osaro smirked and put his hand over hers. "Stop that. I got just about that much control left." He demonstrated with his thumb and index finger. "My goal is to challenge and push you past your dysfunction." He winked at her. She pouted. "You know you got dysfunction. I have them too, but I let you help me fix mine. You keep holding on to yours."

"I'm sorry. Thank you. Sometimes I wonder why you still love me." She lowered her eyes.

"That's not how love works. You don't just shut it off. You drive me crazy, but never thank me for loving you."

She brushed her lips against his. "Let's go eat. Then you can tell me how far you've gotten with South Tran and we plan our makeup Valentine's Day vacation."

Osaro grabbed her hand and held his laptop bag in the other hand. He stopped in the conference room, gave Ace an update and soon after, they left the office and walked into the clear February day.

***

"I love this! It's beautiful." Itohan jumped up and down in front of Osaro.

"You're so silly. I know without a doubt, I have the most beautiful sight in front of me." Osaro brushed his lips against hers.

Friday afternoon, three weeks later, they were finally on their weekend getaway at the Bruslete Resorts in Key West. He chose somewhere close because South Tran decided to launch a week early. The completed prototype didn't need any adjustment or enhancement, so South Tran decided to offer their VIP customers a special rate for early enrollment. Malcolm was back in St. Petersburg, but Osaro needed to get away with his girl.

Itohan smiled up at him. "I know the launch is tomorrow and you needed to be there. Thank you for bringing me here."

Osaro kissed her forehead. "Everything in my power stops for you. I've been so busy, but you're always my priority. This weekend, I want to make up for the time we've missed."

"I've missed you, too. So, what are we doing first? O Lord, I have so many sites that come to mind for pictures."

They walked up to the reception area. The reservation Osaro had was for two king-sized rooms, one floor apart. After they checked in, Osaro walked Itohan to her room. Once he checked that everything was okay, he walked over to where she was and caressed her cheek.

"Okay baby, rest and let me know what we're doing. It's your world. You own me."

"I own you every day – not just here. But dress for the beach and meet me in the lobby in forty-five minutes." She waggled her eyebrows at him.

"Check you out – all bossy, and that mouth of yours."

"You like it though." She winked at him.

"Yes, I do. I like it very much." Osaro walked out of the door. "Put the deadbolt on." Once he heard it click, he left to go to his room.

***

Osaro climbed the upper deck with the bottle of wine and some glasses he had the yacht crew chill for him. This was their second night at the resort and he was so thankful they took the time away to reconnect on a much deeper level. The sight of Itohan so happy, arms spread, the breeze sending her hair in different directions, looking out into the open sea confirmed again for him what he knew all along. God had presented him with his rib and it was the perfect choice.

He set the tray down and picked up her camera. He snapped her a couple of times. He wanted these memories to be embedded in his heart and on film. After a few clicks, she caught on and started posing with her goofy self. His heart burned with passion and desire. He set the camera down.

"Come here, baby." Osaro motioned to her.

Itohan walked to him. "Why so serious?"

He patted his lap and she sat. "When I met you, I was broken. On the outside, I looked all put together, but on the inside, I carried the weight of a burden I thought was mine. I over extended in everything, from raising my niece to my job to caring for my aunt. Because I thought, how dare I relax when my perceived failure contributed to their circumstance, one way or the other, I knew that wasn't right in my head…" Osaro tapped his index finger on his temple. "I knew it, but there's something about your spirit knowing God and His mercy and the mind being the battlefield. You must fight every day. You brought sanity and calm into my life. You made me see in the flesh what I already know in the spirit." Osaro chuckled. "Funny thing is, you did it while you had forgotten about God yourself. Through our pain, we became strong. You're the ying to my proverbial yang, baby, and I love you."

"You knew before me. I had no idea and I fought you tooth and nail."

Osaro nodded real fast. Itohan giggled.

"You brought me close to God after so many years. In you, I'm safe. You're my rock, my Christ personified on earth. God gave me you and I still feel like after all the stuff I had in my heart when we met, I'm not worthy," Itohan said.

Osaro tapped her knee and she stood. He got down on one knee and she gasped. Her expression was not the one he imaged. Instead of surprise and excitement, her face held fear and panic. In the split second, his heart thumped against his chest. Was she going to reject him?

"Itohan Stephanie Adolo, there's no scenario in this life that I can imagine myself without you. Will you marry me?"

She remained silent, trembling and shaking her head. Osaro slowly stood. She was sobbing. He gave her some tissue from the tray and they sat on the bench.

"Talk to me," his voice was low because now he didn't trust it. He was so sure they wanted the same things.

"I have…something…to …tell you." Itohan sobbed.

Osaro remained silent, his heart beat rapidly against his chest.

"I was once married," Itohan confessed.

Osaro moved away from her. "What did you just say?"

If she'd played him, he begged Jesus to let him loose because he was sure going to destroy something.

29

Osaro stared at her and Itohan felt his gaze go from warm and loving to cold and hating. Itohan rubbed the back of her neck. She should have listened to her friends and brother when they told her. In retrospect, she would have been able to deal with a mad Osaro better than the one that now looked at her with disgust and anger.

"I asked you a question." His voice was void of emotion.

"I said I was once married. But baby it was a long time ago. Let me explain," she said.

"Talk." He didn't look at her. It was as if it hurt too much. He placed his elbows on his knees and bent his head. For the next several minutes, Itohan rushed through her story. She told him how she and Aidenoje met, to the wedding, to her years seeking revenge. She spilled everything; everything short of the fact that she had seen him recently and had a plan for revenge in place. With the way Osaro was looking at her, that would just have to die with her. He didn't know Aidenoje. They had no affiliation. Aidenoje lived in New Jersey and Osaro lived in Florida.

"I thought you trusted me," he asked. His tone held no warmth.

"I do. I was just scared. I tried to tell you so many times. But I couldn't lose you," she said hurriedly. "You don't understand what that did to me. I hated myself for being played. Then I hated him, then I hated men. You changed all that for me, but you're right, I didn't trust you at first to tell you. As time went on, I knew you would never hurt me. I trusted you, but I was scared, baby. I'm sorry."

Itohan prayed inwardly that he didn't ask her whether she had seen him. She'd hate to lie to him because fear simply wouldn't let her say it. She stood in front of him. As time passed and Osaro hadn't said anything, her heart rate accelerated.

"Baby, I want to marry you and I'm sorry for not telling you…so sorry—" Itohan pleaded.

"If we don't have trust and open communication, we don't have anything, no matter how much we love each other. When I asked you to marry me, I accepted your strengths and agreed to live with your weakness." His voice was eerily calm. When he finally looked up at her, his gaze was loving. "You gotta trust me, baby. Understood?"

Itohan nodded her head rapidly and rubbed the back of her neck.

"I'm still mad at you, but that doesn't mean I don't want you to be my wife. Do I have to kneel again?"

Itohan smiled. "No, baby, you don't." She jumped up and down.

Osaro stood and slipped the 2.5ct emerald-cut diamond in 14K white gold ring on her finger. He pulled her towards him and she gladly obliged, admiring her ring and wrapping her arms around his neck. After they'd, disconnected she felt a nudging in her spirit.

Nothing is covered up that won't be revealed.

"I don't want a long engagement. My auntie is on standby. Once I give the word, she'll take some of my distant uncles to your family home, to get the first introduction and investigation out the way." He lifted his hand and brushed her hair from her face. "I already asked your dad."

"You did?" Itohan's eyebrows rose.

"Yes, I knew you'd be my wife, but I wanted you to be sure I'd be your husband."

"I know, I know." Itohan looked down on her ring again. She couldn't wait to tell her sister and Ajoke. She didn't want a long engagement either.

"So, this ex of yours that did me a favor, did you ever find out where he is? Has anyone in your family heard from him?"

Why did he just ask me that? Itohan was stuck just as she was home free. She looked at her ring and knew this was the end because she'd have to tell the whole truth.

"Well, I—"

Osaro's phone rang. He'd had it with him all day because the soft launch for the VIP clients was today. "Hold on, baby, I gotta get this. It's Malcolm." Placing his index finger over one ear, he held the phone up to the other. "Hey man, what's up?"

Itohan watched panic take over his body.

"You got to be kidding me. Dang it...but I was sure we did it right. Okay, let me see if I can get a flight."

Osaro cursed under his breath and Itohan had never seen him so mad and frustrated.

"Baby, please tell me what's going on."

"We need to head back. The app I built, Net Glow for South Tran just crashed. Mac says it's some kind of malware, but I need to get back to fix it before I'm sued for millions." Osaro made his way to the lower deck to tell the crew to turn the boat around.

Itohan plopped down on the bench. *Did he say Net Glow? Jesus, please let it be another Net Glow. It must be another Net Glow because Aidenoje's company was Transzits Corp.*

If it was the same, she had just sunk her future, holding on to her past.

***

"I'm finished!" Itohan placed her hand on her head and paced her bedroom. Osaro had dropped her off about thirty minutes ago after he confirmed her worst nightmare.

"Itoh, whatever it is, can be fixed. Do you know what time it is here in *Naija*?" Keni asked.

"Sis, I know. I know it's the wee hours of the morning and I'm sorry, but I need you and Joks right now," Itohan spoke into the phone that was on speaker three-way.

"Itoh, what's going on?" Ajoke asked. "I thought you and Osaro were in the Keys?"

"Yes, we were *o*. We had a wonderful time. He proposed, and I said yes and then his phone rang. I'm finished *o*. I'm finished. I should have listened," Itohan cried.

"Hold up, pause, back up. Did you just ramble over the fact that you're now engaged?" Keni, who was now wide awake, screamed.

"Itoh, please, please tell me you didn't go through with it," Ajoke asked calmly.

"Go through with what? Are you withholding info from me? Okay *I dey vex*," Keni said.

"Itoh?" Ajoke called to her again.

Itohan sobbed because she did go through with it.

"Itohan, stop all that crying and tell us what's going on. Do we need to sneak you out of the US?" Keni asked. "Did you commit a crime?"

"So, you know we saw Aidenoje or AJ Kenneth, whatever he calls himself now. Well when we met him, he was doing this app launch for the company he runs, Transzits Corp. So…so…" Itohan sniffed.

"So, after being angry for a couple of days, she had the bright idea to hire someone on Craigslist to find network vulnerabilities in the server so it could be infected, and he would be humiliated," Ajoke supplied.

"*Ehen*? So, what's the problem? We all know what that man put her through," Keni said.

"So? She has Osaro who is so much better for her. Why couldn't she leave well enough alone?" Ajoke said.

Her sister and Ajoke went back and forth arguing while Itohan continued to cry.

"Okay Itohan, what's the issue? Did they catch you?" Keni asked.

"No, directly I didn't do it, but indirectly I did. However, the app…the same app is the app that Osaro had been working on for months. This is the deal he had been working on for a year." Itohan sobbed.

"What?!" Keni and Ajoke exclaimed in unison.

"I didn't know," Itohan pleaded.

"And that makes it better? I warned you that this would come and bite you," Ajoke scolded. "You've allowed your past to cost you your future, your fiancé's reputation and possible money."

"But wait *o*. I know Osaro likes sucking your face. Every time I turn around you two are kissing. Don't you talk? How did you not know? I could care less about Aidenoje," Keni said.

"We do. Because of something in his early days of business, he doesn't talk about his clients. So, I don't push unless he offers. But for this one, he always said app and he kept calling the company South Tran." She sniffed. "Even when I went for the event, I didn't know it was an app launch. By the time I knew, I was already in a funk and we just didn't talk about it. South Tran is just the parent company. He was developing the app for one of its subsidiaries, Transzits, which happens to be the company Aidenoje was hired to manage. The company is based in New Jersey. The Orlando thing was just a reward retreat for the employees." Itohan sobbed. "I didn't know…"

"Ha! Seriously you're finished," Keni concluded.

"Keni, don't say that. I'm so mad right now but Itohan, that man loves you. You have to tell him," Ajoke said.

"Love *o bu onye e be*? What does love to have to do with it? She lied, was deceitful and cost the man money. I love you, Sis, but you know I'll tell you as I see it. You have two choices. Option one, take it to the grave. Option two, revert to option one," Keni said.

Itohan sat on the floor and drew her knees to her chest. She hugged them and cried. In the background, she heard the debate on what she should do. She wondered what Osaro was doing now.

On the way home, there was little or no conversation as he was on the phone talking to different people. Her heart broke as he kept blaming himself for not paying attention, knowing this was a top client. The guilt of letting others down was back and she hated herself for it. Although she could just play dumb, and be the supportive fiancée, she loved him too much to let him hurt thinking it was something he did or didn't do. She knew it would hurt like crazy when he broke up with her, but she'd rather hurt than let him think he was incompetent at what he did.

"I'm going to tell him."

"Are you sure?" Keni asked.

"Yes, I am. I can't let him blame himself." Itohan said. "I'm broken. Now that I think of it, I might just be beyond saving. Osaro did everything for me, but the sight of Aidenoje took me back. I couldn't resist. Maybe I wasn't really saved. I couldn't resist the temptation. What does that say about me? I've hurt the man I love deeply," Itohan said.

"God is a God of second chances. Do you know how much David messed up? And he was a man after God's heart. You have to repent then confess, but then you have to be ready for the consequences," Ajoke said.

"You're right. I'll call you tomorrow." Itohan hung up the phone and for the rest of the night, she cried out to the Lord for strength and help. Sleep eluded her, and she read Psalm 51 and listened to Lauren Daigle's "How Could It Be" repeatedly. In a moment of anger, she thought she was hurting Aidenoje. It felt good at the time. She was now faced with the reality that she'd just killed her hope of true love.

***

"You what?" Osaro roared.

Itohan was still delirious from no sleep or food from the previous day, but when Osaro called and said he was coming over for a minute, Itohan quickly showered. This was her opportunity to come clean and let the chips fall where they may. Osaro and his team worked all night taking down the app and assessing the damage. From his end, it didn't seem as catastrophic but at a minimum, it would require recoding. He told her he had another meeting with the client in a few days.

Apparently, her Craigslist hire wasn't as good as the money he charged her. Itohan didn't know it was possible to be so overjoyed that she was ripped off. But she was so happy. However, she still had to come clean. And she just had.

"I'm so sorry. I didn't know it would affect you," Itohan begged.

"And that makes it better?" Osaro paced the width of the space of her living room. Itohan could see him visibly shake in anger. The energy in the room had her terrified. Suddenly, she heard a loud thud. He had flipped over her coffee table.

"Baby…"

"Don't. You don't get to call me that. You do not get to bat your eyes and play victim. I've been patient. I thought that maybe if I loved harder or showed you that I'd never do you like your ex did you, that you'd give your whole heart to me. Here I am pledging my all and the woman I thought I could spend the rest of my life with isn't even all the way mine."

"Baby…Osa…Osaro. You do have my heart. People tell me to let it go, but that man humiliated me. Everyone is so quick to speak, but they don't know what that man took from me."

"It's been seven years!"

"It's been four!"

"Are we seriously debating how long it's been? He hurt your pride, but whatever you think he took, you allowed it. I hope the emotional and financial pain you caused was worth it."

Itohan remained silent.

Osaro ran his hand over his hair and turned from her. "Argh…" he roared. "I'm pissed that I've potentially lost a multimillion-dollar contract. But you know what?" He sneered. "I'm more pissed that the love of my life loves another, and I just wasted close to six months fighting a ghost I didn't know existed."

"I'm sorry."

"Sorry doesn't fix this. I can't trust you. First, you keep the fact that you were married to this man. Then you see him and decide to commit a cybercrime with the intent of getting back at him? Were you really mine?"

"Osaro, I love you, baby. I do." Itohan sobbed. "I'm so sorry. Believe me. If I had known it would affect you, I wouldn't have done it."

"That right there is the problem. Even if it didn't affect me, the fact that you could do that baffles me. It means you still have feelings for him," Osaro stressed.

Itohan walked over to him and stood in his face. "Osa, listen to me. That's ridiculous. I don't have any feelings for him. I know this isn't the right thing to say, but I hate him."

He chuckled and shook his head. With disgust in his eyes, he roamed the length of her body. She now wished she had stayed on the other side of the room.

"You see, that's where people get it wrong. The opposite of love isn't hate. The opposite of love is indifference. The fact that he ruled your life for all these years means you still care for him. In a negative way, but you still care. But the joke is on you, because while you halted your life and jeopardized our future, he was busy living his."

Itohan grabbed his hand. "Osa…"

He jerked away from her. She made a second attempt to hold him. He pushed away from her.

"I really hope it was worth it. You can pawn the ring." With that, Osaro walked out of her house and life.

The gap he left was bigger than the one he'd attempted to fill.

30

"Dear Jesus, I have nothing left. I don't know what will happen today, but I know I'm so tired of all the pain and my heart hurts so bad. You said we should come to You. I'm here. I don't even think I'm worthy enough to ask You for anything, but I do know You love me more than I even love myself. If I loved myself, I wouldn't have jeopardized the one thing that made me happy. With a contrite heart, I ask for Your forgiveness. Soften Osaro's heart toward me and even Aidenoje's. In Jesus' name. Amen."

Itohan looked in the visor of her rental to check her face one last time. It had been so puffy from crying nonstop for the last three days. She purged, self-reflected, cried out to God for forgiveness and proceeded to forgive herself. She had called and sent Osaro several texts apologizing and asking for forgiveness. Her calls went unanswered and she saw he read all her texts but provided no response.

In the early hours of the morning, Itohan boarded the first flight out of Florida to make the two-hour journey to New Jersey. Now she was here at Tranzits to see the man she'd hoped to see for seven years. She got out of her rental car and walked the short distance to the office complex. She walked up to the receptionist and asked to speak to Mr. Kenneth.

"Do you have an appointment?"

"No, I don't, but tell him Itohan Adolo is here." Itohan hoped her effort paid off because if she left here, she didn't think she'd have the strength to come back.

Minutes later, she was being ushered into his office. He stood behind his desk and gave her a shocked, pitiful stare. Itohan didn't want his pity. She had enough of that for herself. She needed to come clean but before that, she had to ask the question that had been burning in her soul for the past four years.

"Why?"

"Itohan, what a surprise. I—"

"No, please. Let's not do that. All I want to know is why?"

"Can you at least sit down?" he urged.

Itohan pulled out a chair in front of the desk. Aidenoje came around and pulled out the next one.

I'm such a fool. The man I stopped my life over is so close to me and I feel absolutely nothing. I threw Osa away because of this.

"The least you owe me is honesty. Tell me the truth. Why? Why would you humiliate me, then not have the decency to give me closure? You just disappeared."

Aidenoje took in a breath, then exhaled. "When I got here, I had every intention of sticking to our marriage. But as I reached the end of my program, my papers were about to expire. I didn't want to come back home. There was no way I could stay without marrying an American."

"Are you kidding me? I'm American. I asked you if I could come over," Itohan said.

"Yes, but I couldn't have people at home think I was living off you. Priscilla and I started dating. It was going to be a marriage of convenience. But along the line, I genuinely fell in love with her. When she had our child, I knew I would never leave her," Aidenoje explained.

As Itohan listened to him, she berated herself more. God had shut that door, but she couldn't keep it closed. He never loved her. If he had, it wouldn't have been so easy for him to do her that way. However, instead of her thanking God for helping her escape a bitter end, she was so stuck on the gloom that she failed to see the rainbow. She got her "why" and it did nothing for her. It was time to do what she came for and move on with what was left of her life.

Itohan confessed what she had done. "My boyfriend...well ex-fiancé, is the developer of your app. The crash wasn't his fault. I inadvertently sabotaged him to get back at you."

"You know Osaro Ikimi?"

The mention of his name ached her heart. She missed him so much.

"Yes. He's a good man. If you want to report me, then do that. But please let him keep his contract."

"His contract is not up to me as he got that from our parent company. I don't think it's in jeopardy because there was no real damage from the malware you sent," he smiled at her and paused.

She didn't return the gesture.

"It was caught on time before any real damage was done. He had a very good team watching. The minute we had a problem, they went into action."

Itohan smiled inwardly. At this point, she didn't care what happened to her as long as Osaro was okay.

"As for you, after all I have done and cost you, what happened was nothing. It's fixed and over. I do want to say I'm sorry," Aidenoje said.

"Thank you." Itohan stood and walked out of his office. With that simple gesture, she left all her emotional baggage behind.

Itohan's heart stopped as Osaro approached. He had on reflective shades, so she couldn't see his eyes, but felt the intensity of his glare.

"What are you doing here?" he asked.

"Please can you take those off, so I can see you?" she asked

"Why? I've been showing you who I am and you refused to see me then. Why now?"

"Stop being mean. That's not you at all." A beat of silence passed between them. "What I did had nothing to do with you. I didn't set out to hurt you. I'm not saying my actions didn't. It just wasn't my intention."

"What are you doing here?" he asked again, ignoring all she had said.

"I came to see Aidenoje—"

"You what?" He took off his glasses and almost knocked her

over with the look he gave her.

"It's not even like that. I came to confess, apologize and ask why. You, my sister, and my friend don't understand, but I needed closure."

"Hmmm."

"Osaro, I'm sorry. I don't know how else to say it. I've been calling you for days. I sent you text and voice mails – none of which you responded to. I know we can't get back what we had, but I at least want to be your friend."

"You sacrifice for what you love. You were so focused on revenge that you were willing to sacrifice our love for it. That means you love winning more than you love us. Suppose you ended up in jail? I would've lost my mind, but you didn't think about that. I can't be your friend, baby. I wasn't built to be your friend. I love you, but I'm not ready to forgive you. I'm still so angry at you," Osaro said.

"How can you say that, when you taught me about forgiveness?"

"Well, I guess like you, things are not as they seem." With that he walked away, crushing her heart with each step.

***

Saturday evening, a month later, Osaro passed Ehi a bottle of Maltex as two of them sat in his living room. Eseosa and Robin were in the kitchen baking cookies.

"Why are you being so stubborn about this?" Ehi asked after a few seconds. Osaro didn't want to talk about Itohan and she seemed to be everyone's favorite topic of discussion.

He last saw her that day at the parking lot in New Jersey. He'd heard from Eseosa that she had subbed for her class a couple more times. It was Spring break, so he wasn't sure what she was up to now. Why couldn't she just have been honest with him? How did she go from someone he couldn't live without to someone who made anger flash through his body? He hated what they had become and asked God to help him get his heart back from her or give him a sign he should take her back.

"Can you please leave it alone? Not tonight," Osaro pleaded.

"No, I won't. This is a woman you loved enough to want to marry. You don't marry just because. You marry because you can't stand the thought of being without them. What's blocking you is pride. Push that aside, Bro. I'm telling you. Can you honestly stand to see her with someone else?" Ehi sipped his drink.

"You can pretend you'd be able to avoid her, but God can be funny like that. He'll put her new man in front of you every day."

Osaro clenched his jaw. The thought disturbed him.

"Go to the grocery store, they're there. They might start attending our church, appearing and disappearing everywhere like Casper. Do you want Cupid and Casper haunting you at the same time?" Ehi laughed. "I'm not saying don't be mad, but you better be mad and still hold on to her. Don't be so busy trying to teach her a long lesson, she'll get bored and exit the classroom. She apologized, and you still got your contract. Now practice what Jesus taught us and forgive her."

"You done?"

"Yep."

Osaro opened his mouth to speak when Eseosa entered the room with the baked cookies.

"Uncle Ro, see my cookies," she said.

Osaro smiled at her and took one. "Nice, Baby Cakes."

"Uncle Ehi, you want one?"

"Hit me up, Baby Cakes."

Eseosa handed one to Ehi. "I wish I could give Ms. Adolo one." Her face was solemn.

"I'm sure Auntie Robin will help you bake more when school starts. You can give it to her then," Osaro said.

"She's not coming for a long time."

Osaro sat up. "What do you mean?"

"She told us she's not coming back for a while because she's going home." Eseosa skipped to the kitchen.

"I regret to inform you, Bro, she has left the classroom." Ehi said. "Let's just pray that Cupid hasn't shot her another arrow."

The realization that Ehi could be right shot Osaro to his feet. Itohan was the love of his life, no doubt, but as the days passed by, he wasn't even sure how to fix them. He needed a plan, but this piece of news just blew that need to smithereens. He didn't care what Cupid had in mind. Itohan was his and nobody touched her but him.

31

Itohan walked around the local market and bought tomatoes, snails, pepper and some other assorted meat. She was going to prepare her famous stew. Her father requested it specifically. She had told her parents what she'd done and about Osaro. Surprisingly, they didn't have much of an opinion. She saw their disappointment, but she guessed they were done with telling her about her choices. Her father did tell her Osaro's family came for introduction and the investigation was concluded. She told him not to expect them back since Osaro had called off the engagement.

She hadn't expected to feel this hollow. She didn't remember it being this bad when Aidenoje left. The emptiness she felt hurt, but after a couple of weeks she gave up and spent time working on herself. She spent a few days with Ajoke in Atlanta. Back in Florida, she got a call from Eseosa's school that they needed her again, but that only lasted a couple of days. After that was over, she decided to head home to Benin. This was her restart after Osaro. She was seriously contemplating moving back permanently. If it wasn't for Aidenoje, she wouldn't have run away in the first place. Granted her whole heart belonged in the US, but the person she wanted to give it to no longer wanted it.

"Itohan?"

Itohan turned and saw Auntie Lizzy. She walked to the woman and greeted her.

"Ah my daughter, how are you?"

"I'm well, Auntie. How are you?"

"I'm fine. When did you get in?"

"A couple of days ago. How is Eseosa?"

Auntie Lizzy smiled. "She's fine. You won't ask about your

husband?"

"Ah Auntie, Osa and I are no longer, but how is he?"

"He's fine. I heard that, but don't worry. He will come around."

Itohan wouldn't hold her breath, but she needed to go before she broke down in tears, so she agreed with the woman by nodding.

"Come by the house tomorrow."

"I have to go to Spring Road, but I'll stop by briefly," Itohan said.

The women said their goodbyes and headed in opposite directions.

The next day, Itohan walked into Auntie Lizzy's compound with her Beats on her ears. She hummed to "Fight Song" by Rachel Platten as she walked up the windy driveway. By the time she approached the stairs and looked up, she saw the person she wasn't expecting to see. She gave him a faint smile. Her eyes took him in.

His expression went from longing to regret and for a split second, relief. He had his hair loose and hanging down. Dressed casually, Osaro was still the sexist man she knew. She took in a deep breath.

"Hey." She took off her earphones.

"Hey, yourself. How are you?" His hands remained buried in his pockets as he surveyed her.

She scrunched her eyebrows. "I'm okay and you?"

"You left."

"I didn't know you wanted me to stay."

"I was angry," he said.

"I know."

"But I still love you."

"I know."

"Love is patient."

"Love is kind."

"Love keeps no records of wrongs."

"Love protects and trusts. It hopes and never fails," she said.

"You still kept the ring?" he asked.

"Yes. It's close to my heart where it belongs." She showed him the ring on her necklace.

Osaro stepped down a couple of steps, never taking his eyes off her. He reached Itohan and pulled her close. He took off her necklace and removed the ring.

"Do I have to kneel again?" He smiled, and her heart swelled.

She beamed at him and shook her head.

He slid the ring on her finger. "Thank you for agreeing to spend the rest of your life with me."

"Thank you for trusting me with your heart again, baby. Nothing would make me happier." Itohan stood on the tips of her toes and they sealed their reunion with a kiss.

THE END

Epilogue

Two months later, Itohan sunk her feet into the warm grains of sand as she and her new husband strolled along the Andilana Beach in Nosy Be, Madagascar. She held on to Osaro's arm draped around her neck and wrapped her other arm around his waist. When he told her, this was where they'd come for their honeymoon, she was elated.

That day on the steps of Auntie Lizzy's house led to a whirlwind of activities. They didn't return to Florida until Osaro and his family had completed all the traditional rights, which took a couple of weeks. Osaro understood her need for the actual traditional wedding to be low-key. That same weekend, the couple wed legally at the Benin Magistrate Court. The church wedding, however, was where Auntie Lizzy and her mother weren't compromising. Their firstborns were getting married and they wanted to celebrate in style.

"Oh, I'm already getting marital privileges, so knock yourselves out," Osaro had told them.

The couple remained in Florida while the older women planned the event. Just last week, the couple returned to Benin for the big ceremony. After that, they boarded a plane for the island.

"What are you thinking about Mrs. Ikimi?" Osaro asked, bringing her out of her thoughts.

"Nothing. Everything. Us. Life."

Osaro stopped walking. He lifted her shades from her eyes. "Don't think too hard. We're three chords strong. We already got battle scars, so I know we can do this."

Her tears had a mind of their own and fell from her eyes. "I love you so much."

"I love you, too," his voice sent shivers down her spine. He cupped her face and captured her lips in a passionate exchange.

This was full circle for her. A little over a year ago, it was at this same beach she first laid eyes on her hot hoodlum. Who knew then that the man she snubbed would be the one God sent to heal her pain and teach her how to live again.

Other Books by Unoma Nwankwor

Stand Alone Novels
    An Unexpected Blessing (Feranmi & Alex) 2013
    When You Let Go (Amara & Ejike) May 2014
    He Changed My Name (Ayanti & Mensah) February 2016

Sons of Ishmael Series
    A Scoop of Love (Rasheed & Ibiso) Jan 2015
    Anchored by Love (Jabir & Damisi) Nov 2015
    Mended With Love (Kamal & Ebele) October 2017

The Ultimatum Series
    The Christmas Ultimatum (Olanma & Abayomi) Dec 2013
    The Final Ultimatum (The sequel) Oct 2016

Non-Fiction
    In The Dark: Confident Expectations for Today & Tomorrow (April 2017)
    Light Pearls in the Dark Prayer Journal (2017)

Made in the USA
Columbia, SC
13 March 2018